# TOTSAKAN

### the Demon King and the
### Hermit's Riddle

## TAMLIN BEA

# TOTSAKAN

## The Demon King and
## the Hermit's Riddle

### Tamlin Bea

Paperback ISBN 978-1-915490-02-5

This edition published in 2022 by BLKDOG Publishing.

A catalogue record for this book is available from the British Library.

Cover art by Andy Johnson.

www.blkdogpublishing.com

# CHAPTER ONE

A storm had been threatening Bangkok for an hour. Dark clouds were visible above the city's tall buildings as a school bus slowly weaved its way towards the city centre, from one long traffic light to the next. Inside, Rawin and his classmates were messing around, their 14-year-old minds not focused on their destination – the Temple of the Emerald Buddha in the Grand Palace. Then the rain came, bringing flash floods to the streets and relief from the scorching heat.

At the coach park near the palace, Cattaleeya – known to all her friends as Catt – waited eagerly. She was looking forward to seeing Rawin, her best friend who was now in school in Lopburi, more than a hundred miles to the north. Catt's T-shirt said it all: *I might be wrong but it's very unlikely*. That revealed more about her than her black leggings, white trainers and multi-coloured stripy socks.

After what seemed like forever as the rain clouds lifted and the streets began to steam dry, Catt saw the bus draw up. She knew it was the right one because it said Lopburi Express on the side. She and Rawin had exchanged texts on their mothers' *Line* apps – something they weren't allowed to do often – so that they knew where to meet up.

Catt watched as the children started cascading off the bus. Rawin was almost the last, in his PE kit and trainers.

When he saw Catt, he smiled. He wasn't a very

demonstrative boy – a bit shy sometimes, though not timid or lacking in courage. When they were at primary school together, Catt noticed how he stood up to bullies if they picked on the smaller children. Somehow he knew exactly what to say that had more effect than a punch. At times she wished she could fight with words like that, but she preferred to use the *taekwondo* skills she had learned from her earliest years. When she did that she was in her element, like a fish in water or a bird in the sky. Her body always seemed to know what to do. Her friends and family remarked on how quickly she progressed from the white belt to the brown. Soon she would be a black belt. Sometimes she thought she was born to fight.

Rawin's teacher called the children together to walk in double-file to the entrance of the Grand Palace, past the statues of giant demons that stood guard there. Catt's mother had arranged with Rawin's teacher to let her join the visit because it would be the only chance she would have to spend time with him. The teacher reminded Catt's mother that they wouldn't be allowed to talk very much while they were in the temple viewing the magnificent murals of the Ramakien epic. No, no, that's fine, her mother had said to the teacher. They would just have to enjoy looking at the murals together and find time to talk during the lunch break.

The children were clutching exercise books, pens and pencils. They had been told to make notes of the paintings so that they could answer questions when they were back in class the next day. They were also told to sketch the paintings they liked the most which they could show their art teacher.

In the Temple of the Emerald Buddha, the children followed their teacher to the first of the paintings that lined all four walls of the marble-floored complex, the world's longest mural. Though most Thai children know about the Ramakien story, they don't really know it very well. The plot is intricate and complex. Everyone knows of Prince Ram, the hero and incarnation of the supreme god Lord Narai in his battles with the evil demon Totsakan. Even better known is the wily monkey-soldier Hanuman. Catt was sorry that she did not know the story better because she would have been able to interpret the paintings for herself. The teacher didn't

'Just step closer.'

Rawin saw a gap between two of the barriers that separated viewers from the mural. He pushed them apart. It was almost as if he couldn't stop himself. An arm shot out from the painting, grabbed him around his waist and pulled him towards the mural. Then he disappeared.

'Oh my God,' said Catt. 'Oh my God.'

explain things very well. Rawin, on the other hand, understood much of it and occasionally whispered explanations to her as they went.

After they rounded the corner to see another expanse of striking paintings stretch out along the walls ahead of them, Catt grabbed Rawin's arm. 'Look!' She turned him back to the painting they had just passed. Rawin's first reaction was to feel a little embarrassed but he allowed her to steer his attention to the picture as they stopped and let the children behind them overtake and go on around the corner. Now they were alone.

'What?' asked Rawin quietly.

'That monkey in the picture. He's holding a phone.'

Rawin frowned with disbelief. Catt was not the sort of person to play practical jokes, but this did seem a little wacky. Until he saw it himself. The monkey was ... wait ... really? Talking on a phone.

'Some vandal must have drawn it on the painting,' Rawin said. 'That's terrible. This is a national treasure.'

Just then a phone rang in Rawin's backpack.

'I didn't know you had a phone with you,' said Catt accusingly.

Rawin swung his backpack off his shoulder and started rustling around inside trying to get hold of the ringing phone. 'It's not mine,' he said, irritated that he couldn't find it. He needed to switch it off before the teacher heard it. The children weren't supposed to have phones with them. 'My uncle lent it to me. He was worried that something might happen to me in Bangkok – he doesn't trust the big city.' At last he fished it out. He looked at the screen: 'Unknown caller.' He pressed the answer icon and lifted the phone to his ear.

'Rawin,' said a voice, 'Step closer to the painting.' He looked aghast at Catt.

'Why are you looking like that?'

'Someone's telling me to step closer to the painting.'

'What?'

'Someone's telling me to step closer to the painting,' he repeated, looking around to see if anyone was playing a trick on them. Hesitantly he asked, 'Who is this?'

'The sages.'

'Sages?'

'Those who knew you were destined.'

'Destined?'

'You and Rawin. Both of you.'

'Destined to do what?'

'To help us in the long war against the Spectre, the Demon King.'

Rawin stood up. He stroked the back of his head and shifted one foot in a sort of half-circle shape in front of him. 'Catt, I know this probably sounds crazy, but I think we're inside the Ramakien story.'

'It's not a story,' the monkey corrected him. 'It's a war. And we need your help.'

'Oh, come on,' said Catt almost scornfully. 'If Rawin is right and this is the Ramakien, you know what happens. The good guys win in the end. You don't need help.'

'The sages told us you were brave and intelligent,' said the monkey. 'But they did not say you could look into the future. How can you say what happens in the end?'

'Because that's the story. We were all told it when we were little children. And it ends that way.'

'I told you,' said the monkey, 'this is not a story. Perhaps when you read the story you're talking about, it feels like the end had already been written even when you are in the middle. But we are alive, living, not in a book. If good is to win in the end, we have to make it happen. We cannot just hope or believe story-tellers and think our fate has already been decided. Is that what you do in your world?'

Just then there was a terrifying scream from the darkest part of the forest. Charging them at horrendous speed was a hideous demon swinging a sword above its head. It had a huge bulbous nose, ogling eyes and a wide, curved mouth with fangs protruding from each side. Catt and Rawin recognised it at once – it was one of the demons from the Ramakien story, like the guards at the entrances to public buildings back home. But this one was very much alive and clearly intended to kill. In the single moment they had to think before what seemed like certain death, they realised that what the monkey had said was true: no story-teller could save them now. They had to do it themselves.

The monkey sprang sideways to block the demon's path and took hold his sword in a flash. They flew up into the air, swinging their swords at each other, howling and cursing as they scrambled and crashed across the treetops in savage combat. Catt and Rawin watched horrified at the spectacle above them. Eventually the two battling creatures crashed to the ground just a few yards away. Both were stunned from the fall and exhaustion. Catt felt a surge of courage well up inside her, something that felt like a command from somewhere inside her: 'Fight.' She began to spin, her arms and legs rotating like a propeller as she pummelled the demon with one blow after another. Dazed and staggering, the demon screeched and disappeared into the forest.

The monkey struggled to his feet. 'Thank you,' he stammered. 'Thank you.' He went back to the rock where he had sat before and slumped down. 'I didn't think we would need you so soon.'

Rawin stood transfixed by what he had just seen. Not just the elaborate dance of near death that had taken place across the treetops, but the extraordinary power and control of his friend in dispatching the demon. Eventually he managed to say something: 'Catt, you OK?'

'I'm OK,' she replied without emotion. Her composure surprised even her, but it felt right, like a perfectly fitting garment. Secretly she was feeling pride bursting inside her, but she knew she could not show it or she would seem arrogant. All her life she had to struggle with two forces – one that made her feel confident and keen to express herself boldly, the other that told her not to be too assertive (her aunt called it 'bossy'). She found that as much as she tried not to be, she usually did feel confident and keen to say what she thought. When she overstepped the mark, she always knew she had done so, and if her dad was present, she would look at him and see that he had already dropped just one eyebrow in disapproval. He was very good at speaking without words like that. But most of the time she got it right and he managed to lift the corner of his mouth about a millimetre to form a smile of approval that only she was able to see. She suspected that her mother's silence at times like that reflected her own inner battle between wanting her daughter to be a nice modest Thai girl while at the same time wanting her to feel good about herself.

It was the monkey who spoke next: 'You can see why you had to come here. If you had not intervened, that thing would have killed me,' he said sombrely. 'This will not be the last time you are needed.'

'So that is the Spectre you told us about?' Catt asked.

'No, the Spectre is this one's master,' replied the monkey.

'Totsakan?' said Rawin. It wasn't so much a question as a statement.

'That's right,' replied the monkey.

Catt looked puzzled but was confident that Rawin knew what he was talking about.

'So who are you, then?' asked Rawin.

'My name is Sukreep.'

# CHAPTER THREE

C att was all mixed up inside. She felt strong after driving the demon off, but at the same time she was uneasy. She had a vague sense that they were 'inside the Ramakien story', as Rawin had expressed it, but she didn't know the story well. Her strongest feeling right then was that she wanted to go home.

'Rawin,' she said with a note of pleading in her voice, 'can we talk?' She cast an eye at Sukreep, who could tell she was distressed.

'You two go ahead,' said Sukreep. 'This must be very confusing for you.' He turned away towards the forest, as if he was keeping a lookout for danger.

Catt approached Rawin and looked him straight in the eye, a little desperately. 'I need to know what's going on here and it seems you understand, at least more than I do.'

'Not really. But what I can tell you is that if this monkey is Sukreep, as he says he is, then we don't need to fear him.'

'Well, that's a relief,' replied Catt with a hint of sarcasm. 'OK, he sounds kind enough, but what he did to us does sort of make me feel some fear. One minute we are on a school outing in Bangkok and the next we are nearly killed by a hideous creature. And all because of this Sukreep person...

monkey… whatever. Who is he?'

'Well, in the Ramakien story, you remember Prince Ram, right? He is the hero, sort of. His wife Sida is stolen from him by the Demon King Totsakan and he goes on a long quest to find her. Well, Sukreep helps him. Basically Sukreep is on the side of good. And he says he needs us to help him.'

'Are we going to do that?' she asked in a doubtful voice.

'I'm not sure we have a choice,' shrugged Rawin.

'We aren't even being given the choice of deciding who we think is good and who is bad here,' said Catt resentfully. 'If, as Sukreep says, what is happening now is not the story we read – or that was read to us – then maybe he is not one of the good guys and we are being used. How would we know?'

'True,' said Rawin thoughtfully. 'But I have a feeling, almost like this is *my* story too. It's not just what Sukreep said about us having to trust him, about how we will understand it all in the end. I feel in a way that I understand already. I feel this is something we *have* to do.'

'Rawin,' said Catt tenderly, 'you have a single mother who must be sick with worry right now since no one will be able to tell her where you are. You need to find a way to get out of here. We both do.'

Rawin stayed silent, looking away from Catt. He pressed his lips together and screwed up his eyes. She could see he wasn't agreeing with her.

'What's the *matter* with you?' she snapped, her mood changing. 'Why is this so difficult for you to see? Your mother needs you. You should want to go home. And I certainly want to go home. For all we know we could die here. Seriously. We nearly died ten minutes ago.'

At last Rawin sighed and said: 'OK, let's talk to Sukreep.'

The children walked over to where Sukreep was sitting on the rock. The monkey turned his head slowly towards them and raised his bushy eyebrows as a way of inviting them to talk.

'We want to go home,' said Catt firmly.

'Me too,' replied Sukreep. The children greeted this remark with a puzzled silence. Then Rawin turned to Catt and said quietly: 'I've just remembered. He is in exile from his kingdom. His brother banished him after a quarrel and he has had to live in this forest ever since.'

'Oh God,' said Catt. 'This gets worse every time you open your mouth. Are we supposed to help him return to his kingdom? Kill his brother, perhaps?' She instantly regretted saying this. She had never spoken to Rawin like that before. In fact they met when they were still not even old enough to walk. Rawin's mother worked as a housekeeper. Catt's mum was a lecturer in economics and her dad was a professor of architecture. Catt went to a modest private school near their home in the southern suburbs of Bangkok. Rawin's mother had just managed to save enough money to send him there too. When she and Rawin were old enough to attend nursery class, they walked down the street together holding hands, one of Rawin's parents ushering them safely into the gates during the morning school run.

Much had happened since those days. A year earlier, Rawin's mother had moved back to her family's village near Lopburi after her sister died. She needed to take care of her two nieces and small nephew. As she couldn't afford to bring them to Bangkok, she took Rawin with her and they started a new life, he in a rural secondary school, she as a chambermaid at a hotel in Lopburi. They had very little money and Rawin had to help look after his cousins while continuing with his schooling. But he and Catt had remained in touch and had never argued before. She felt awful now.

She breathed deeply, composed herself and turned to Sukreep. 'Mister Sukreep, please, we do not belong here. We want to go home. Please let us go.'

'I am sorry,' replied Sukreep gently. 'I understand how you feel, but I do not know how you can get home.'

'What?' cried Catt, angry now. 'You brought us here. You must know how we can get home.'

'I don't. I'm truly sorry.'

'Then how did you get us here?'

'Telepathy.'

Catt hesitated for a second. 'You mean telephone?'

'Telepathy,' he repeated. 'This weapon.' He held up the phone that he had used to make the call to Rawin. 'It was given to me by the only one who can tell you how to get home.'

'Do we have to communicate with this being via telepathy as well? Or will a telephone do?' said Catt, exasperated.

Rawin felt he had to intervene because he could see the tension rising. 'We would like to talk to this person,' he said politely. 'Can you tell us how to do that?'

Sukreep breathed in long and hard. It seemed he was reluctant to speak the words that were about to come out of his mouth. 'He is a *rishi*, a wise hermit, but to find him you have to travel a long and dangerous path. I can show you the way.'

Catt buried her head in her hands. But Rawin remained calm. 'Well, so be it,' he said. 'Show us the way.' He began to rummage around in his bag. 'My phone,' he said.

'It'll never work here,' said Catt. 'Telepathy, remember.' She was surprised at her own sarcasm.

'There, done,' announced Rawin with a satisfied smile holding the phone up. 'Four bars.'

'Seriously?' Catt asked.

'5G,' nodded Rawin. 'Better signal than Lopburi.'

'Crazy,' scoffed Catt. 'Now I feel safe.'

It took an hour trekking through the forest in silence before the three arrived at a clearing where the woods ended. Before them in the distance loomed a huge mountain, reaching forbiddingly above swirling white clouds against a deep blue sky. The mountain was bathed in a pink glow from the late afternoon sun. But it was not the mountain that held the children's gaze. For just ahead of them they saw a gaping gorge with sheer cliffs falling away from the ground they stood on. They could not see the bottom as it seemed to go on forever, scarred by craggy rock faces and trees reaching up from below and out from the sides of the cliffs. A wind howled through the valley and burst upward, shaking the branches. A rickety bridge of rope and wooden slats stretched from their side of the gorge to the other, probably a hundred yards wide. It swung with each gust of wind that roared up from below.

'You must cross here,' said Sukreep gloomily. 'On the

other side you will see a footpath bordered by toadstools. It will lead you to the rishi. You will easily see it.'

Then he stopped and drew a breath. 'However, I fear you will not make it to the other side.'

# CHAPTER FOUR

Rawin turned to Catt and watched her shoulders hunch forward dejectedly, hands on her thighs, as she almost slumped to the ground. But she quickly shifted into a squatting position and raised her head defiantly, gathering her strength. Her voice rose as she declared: 'I am *not* going to die here. I will do this. I will find that rishi and demand to be allowed to go home. I did not ask for this, but I can see we have no choice now. Rawin, I am scared. Terrified. But I will not give up. I refuse to give in. Let's go.'

She stood up straight and began to walk towards the swaying bridge.

'I will wait here for you,' said Sukreep glumly.

'Yeah?' Catt snarled, only half turning her head back. 'Forever?'

Rawin was already walking beside her. A gust of wind swept up from below as though the elements were mocking them even before they had begun the journey. Catt broke into a jog, heading for the bridge. Rawin sped up to stay beside her. They slowed slightly before stepping onto the wooden slats, grabbing the ropes at waist-height on either side. The bridge jerked and swung with their weight.

'Come on,' shouted Catt, not because Rawin wasn't with her, but as a rallying cry for both of them.

They managed to lurch their way across twenty yards of the bridge, making good progress. Then they noticed a wide gap where several slats had disappeared. They stopped together, almost as if they were in step as part of a dance routine. Neither spoke as they looked down at the gap.

Rawin fumbled in his backpack for his phone and, still swaying precariously, tapped something into Google.

'Five point nine four metres. World record long jump for a 14-year-old.' He had to shout over the noise of the wind gusts.

Catt hung on to the ropes and smiled, despite the danger that lurked ahead. Rawin, dear Rawin, she thought. You always have an answer.

Rawin continued: 'The gap looks to me like about four metres. We can do this. I'll go first.' He tucked his phone back into his bag.

Stunned into silence, Catt watched as Rawin went back about ten yards and steadied himself with the ropes. His face stiffened with concentration and then he began to run, stumbling from the constant swaying of the bridge, but just managing to build up some speed. 'Aaaaah!' he cried out as he took off, pedalling his legs as if he was on a bike. He hung in the air for what seemed like minutes, willing his body forward, until at last he crashed waist first on to the other side of the gap, clutching madly to the part of the bridge that was still intact. 'Yessss!' he shouted, 'Yesssss!' as he pulled himself up and turned to look at Catt across the gap.

She said nothing, but instead staggered back to the same spot on the bridge where Rawin had begun his run. She took several calming breaths, adopting the stance in taekwondo that enhances concentration. And then she set off. About a metre before she was about to take off, a strong gust of wind lifted the bridge and she lost her footing and crashed screaming through the gap, her arms flailing. With her left hand she managed to grab a length of rope that was dangling from where the bridge had been damaged and held on as her body swung in a circular motion. Rawin's throat closed up. He wished he could shout something encouraging, but nothing would come out. He felt tears well up in his eyes as helplessly he watched Catt hang on to the rope and her life. Astonished, he watched her jerk through a series of swinging motions that brought her within reach of the side of the bridge where he had landed.

'Your hand,' she shouted above the sound of the wailing winds. 'Give me your hand.'

Rawin lay face down and hooked his right foot around the bottom rope that held the slats together and then flung his right arm down through the gap as far he could, opening his hand. Catt swung and twisted, shifting her body weight so that she could get nearer his hand. She brushed past it once, just missing. Then again. But she only managed to slap against Rawin's fingers as she swung many hundreds, perhaps thousands, of feet above the foot of the gorge. Rawin found his voice again: 'You can do it, Catt,' he shouted. 'No one is as strong as you. You're the best. Come on, girl. One more time.'

Neither could remember how they managed it, but a minute later they were kneeling on the bridge holding each other so tightly they thought they would burst. 'We did it,' they said almost in chorus. 'Oh my God,' said Catt, 'I'm not dead. Come on, let's get moving before this whole thing collapses.'

They scrambled back on to their feet and staggered further across the swaying bridge. They were well past half way when Catt, who was just ahead of Rawin, halted and swung her hand firmly behind her.

'Demons,' she said. 'On the other side. They're watching us.'

'Done,' said Catt, squaring her body for the fight. 'What then?'

'Hand it to me. I'm going to cut the ropes – all of them. We will have to grab hold of the ones under the bridge on their side and hold on tight.'

'Are you crazy?' she shouted into the sky without looking back.

'Trust me,' he replied. 'There's a rocky outcrop below. There are trees with branches sticking out of them like outstretched arms. We can grab on to them to stop us falling when the bridge swings down that way.'

'I hope you did the maths,' she called back. And then a few seconds later: 'Of course you did.'

The first demon was almost upon them. The bridge lurched unevenly with its weight. In an instant Catt swung her right leg in an arch, passing in front of the crouching demon's grotesque snout. The demon pulled its head back, unbalancing itself and turning away. At that moment Catt's body pirouetted in mid-air and her left leg connected firmly with the side of the demon's head, causing it to lash out with its sword. But it missed. Catt's leg had already returned to the floor of the bridge to provide her with the support she needed to drive her other foot into the demon's stomach. The demon tried to protect its body against further blows. In a flash Catt snatched the sword from its grasp. 'Goddit,' she cried, spinning around and expertly tossing it like a spear to Rawin, who managed to grab it firmly by the hilt as it sailed through the air.

The other two demons were now closing in as the first one tried to rebalance itself.

'Quick,' shouted Rawin. 'Back here. We've got about ten seconds to do this.' He slashed at the top ropes, first one and then the other. This left the bridge swaying, the wooden slats held in place by the bottom two ropes only. The demons, having nothing to steady themselves, shuffled awkwardly, arms outstretched as they tried to keep their balance.

'Now, grab the bottom rope on the left,' shouted Rawin. Catt clasped the rope with both hands as Rawin cut through the one on the right. The bridge swung sharply down 90 degrees as it lost the support of one side. She slipped and lost her grip, sliding down towards the gaping gorge below. But just as she began to fall she managed to clutch the wooden slats that remained. Rawin hung on to the rope itself and the demons scrambled in panic to hold on to the slats. Rawin struggled to turn his body, because now he needed to slash through the rope behind him. He twisted and gasped with exertion, striking with the sword. But the rope remained intact. He wrenched his body the other way until he could swing the sword one more time. It sliced straight through, splitting the bridge in two, each side now plunging down into the abyss, each still secured to the cliff face above. Catt held on to the wooden slats and Rawin clutched the rope as the side they were on swung downwards, spilling all three demons into the darkness of the gorge below, their arms and legs thrashing in a futile attempt to halt the fall to their certain death.

The children now had only seconds to save themselves from a similar fate. As the bridge swung towards the cliffside, they fixed their eyes on the trees that extended from the rocky outcrops. They both saw what they were looking for in the same split-second – a cluster of branches and thick foliage looming about fifty feet below them as they plummeted towards the cliff face.

'Now!' shouted Rawin, and they both let go and hurtled downward until they crashed into the thick leaf covering they had spotted. Branches snapped, leaves showered in every direction and birds burst out of their nests in panic. The children let out yells of agony and fear as their bodies twisted and tumbled further into the thicket of branches until they finally came to a halt. Catt was below Rawin, who waited for a few seconds to work out if any of the many pains he felt all over his body were serious. So far so good, he thought. And then he called out: 'Catt. You OK?'

'Not sure yet,' she called back. And then, 'I reckon so. Sore. Really sore. But nothing broken as far as I can tell.'

The trees that held them swayed and shook in the wind, but they had plenty of branches to hold on to. Rawin soon spotted a gully in the cliff that ran up at a sharp angle. Carefully and with increasing confidence they worked their way back up until they got to the ridge. They sat down heavily on the safe firm ground and brushed off the twigs and leaves from their clothing.

After a few minutes recovering, they looked around them and saw a path leading up the slope of the mountain, flanked on both sides by pretty red and white toadstools. The scene was almost enchanting.

'Time to find our way home,' said Catt, scampering to her feet. 'Let's go.'

# CHAPTER SIX

S ukreep had been helplessly watching every frightening
moment of the children's attempt to cross the gorge.
When they managed to get over the gap halfway across
the bridge, he had felt some relief. But when he saw them
plunge downward after Rawin sliced through the last rope, he
turned away with a heavy sadness. Why had he given in to
their demands when they said they wanted to go home? Why
had he told them where to find Rishi? How stupid of him. He
had allowed his compassion to override his better judgement.
In short, he had been weak when he really should have been
strong. The reason the children had been summoned into this
world was of much greater importance. Sometimes in life, he
thought, bigger things have to come first; we cannot always
give in to our feelings.

And now it was all hopeless. The war against Totsakan
might be lost. And certainly the children were now lost. It was
the worst outcome he could have imagined. He didn't know
how he would explain it to those who had assigned him the
role of bringing the children to fulfil their destiny. His tail
sagged as he lifted his body wearily and slouched down the
path away from the cliffside, not even sure where he was
going. Away, just away. He didn't even begin to think about
trying to find the children's bodies and perhaps to give them a
decent burial. His thoughts were clouded in a darkness that
he felt he might never escape.

fell as the demons managed one final swing of their swords, but most were able to gather on the slope and back off more cautiously up towards the woods, awaiting further orders from Hanuman. The demons halted where they were as they tried to work out what their next move should be.

Hanuman, Chompoopan and Sukreep dashed up the slope to join the gathering monkey-soldiers, many of whom were carrying their injured comrades or supporting the walking wounded. 'Find water, catch your breath,' shouted Hanuman, with one eye on the demons. He knew it was just a matter of time before they would come for them, sensing victory.

Hanuman turned to Sukreep. 'What happened?'

'It was my fault,' replied Sukreep.

'How so?'

Sukreep took a while to gather himself and find the right words. 'The children were horribly surprised at what happened when I summoned them. The girl in particular didn't believe or trust me. She demanded to be allowed to go home.'

'Did you explain?'

'I did, but she insisted on knowing how it had happened and how they would get home. So – I'm sorry, this was my mistake – I told them how to go to Rishi so that he could explain.'

'And?'

'They were attacked by demons on the bridge. I saw them fall.'

Hanuman and Chompoopan slipped into a mournful silence. Sukreep hung his head and closed his eyes.

After a long interval, Hanuman breathed in and uttered the words they all feared were inevitable: 'The demons are regrouping. They are stronger and more confident and we are weak. They will come for us. We will fight, of course, but prepare to die.'

# CHAPTER SEVEN

Catt and Rawin had recovered from their ordeal on the bridge and regained their energy and purpose. They half-ran much of the time, encouraging each other as they made good progress up the gentle foothills of the pink-tinged mountain. They were out of the forest by now and the sky was clear, providing a powder-blue backdrop to the majestic scene that lay before them. They had no directions to go by other than to stick to the path, but there was something welcoming about its meandering course and the pretty toadstools that flanked it. Any fears of encountering more deadly demons had gone by now and the two children pressed on confidently.

After a long silence, Catt said: 'Thank you, by the way.'

'For what?'

'Everything back there.'

'I could say the same to you. It was a team effort, I reckon.'

'A team of two,' replied Catt. 'The destined two. Harry and Hermione, Thai style.' She laughed cynically.

Rawin remained silent, as if concentrating too hard on their brisk walking to answer.

'Maybe you believe in that destined thing,' prodded Catt.

Silence.

'Well, do you?' she tried again.

Rawin breathed in deeply. 'I don't know what to think,' he said. And then: 'But there is something about all this that feels strangely familiar.'

'You mean you feel like you've been here before?'

'No, no,' he replied. 'Not like that. Not physical. Something more, sort of, I don't know, spiritual.'

'I thought you weren't the spiritual type,' Catt said.

'I mean sort of dreamlike. Not religious. More another world.'

'Well,' Catt laughed, 'that's true.' She scoffed. 'We're not in *our* world. So I guess you're right.'

'Yes,' said Rawin, and then he hesitated. 'But I feel strangely as if I am meant to be here.'

'*Meant* to be?' Catt frowned. 'What does that mean?'

'I don't know,' Rawin said calmly. 'It's just a vague feeling.'

'Is that why you hesitated when I said we needed to find out how to get home? You seemed not to be so eager.'

'Well, Catt, it doesn't make any more sense to me than it does to you, but I feel a sort of power we have to obey, even though we don't understand it.'

'That sounds scary,' Catt said. 'I'm not sure I like that idea.'

'Yes, I know,' Rawin said, 'but I think it is good scary. Not bad scary. You know what I mean?'

'I don't like any kind of scary.'

Just then they noticed ahead of them, set back in the base of the mountain, a modest wooden building with a traditional steep palm leaf thatched roof. There were no walls, just sturdy round pillars at the four corners and a smooth shiny wooden platform floor.

'Feels a bit like home,' Catt quipped. 'Maybe that's why you said it felt familiar.'

Rawin laughed.

They approached slowly and stopped in front of the building, looking around to see if anyone appeared.

Just then a child walked from the surrounding fern bushes and sat down cross-legged on the floor. His hair was bound in a knot above his head and he wore red baggy pants and an embroidered waistcoat. Beautiful gold bracelets covered his arms and round his neck was a stunning necklace of huge pearls. The boy seemed aloof, aware of Catt and Rawin but not bothering to greet them or even acknowledge their presence. He looked capable of mischief.

Rawin and Catt looked at each other, bewildered. They both knew they had seen a child like this many times in people's homes and in temples. But those were dolls or lucky charms, not a live person.

'Kumon Thong?' whispered Catt to Rawin.

'Looks like him, but what's he doing here?'

There sounded a deep gong and a cloud of orange smoke billowed out from the far end of the building. The child jumped up and stepped aside, pressing his hands together in front of his face to show respect, head bowed. As the smoke cleared, a slightly stooping old man with white hair and a flowing beard reaching down to the middle of his chest shuffled forward. He held a tall wooden staff in his right hand. He looked at the children.

'Gandalf,' whispered Catt and tried not to giggle.

'Dumbledore,' Rawin whispered back.

And then they both held their breath to suppress their giggles. It was not a good idea to be seen to be laughing now.

Catt's hands were over her mouth as she tried to hide her chortle. She then very deftly pressed her hands together elegantly in a traditional greeting, supported by a graceful curtsey. Rawin quickly made the same respectful greeting and bowed.

'Children,' began the old man, 'I am Rishi. I have been looking forward to meeting you. Come closer.'

With heads slightly bowed in respect, the children stepped forward until they were near enough for Rishi to be able to place a hand on Rawin's shoulder.

'You have come in the hour of greatest need. The evil Spectre has begun to overwhelm our world and we fear he and his forces will soon turn it into moral darkness. You should waste no time. Even now I am aware of a huge battle being waged that is wiping out the forces of good. Without your help many more will perish.'

'Er, your majesty, er, your honour, good Sir, Mr Rishi,' began Catt, 'Rawin here, and me, we, we… do not know why

'It depends on how you use it,' Rishi said. 'Rawin will know.'

Just as expertly as Catt had handled the sword, Rawin twisted the object into the shape of a snake. 'It's a Rubik's Twist, also sometimes known as a Rubik's Snake. It consists of twenty-four wedges that are actually isosceles triangular prisms, a polyhedron with rectangular sides. It's plastic and you operate it like a Rubik's Cube, but it allows you to turn it into any shape you like. It's not a puzzle. The creator Erno Rubik, who also created the Cube, said the test was to see how many shapes you could twist it into. He reckoned it would take a lifetime to exhaust all the possibilities, something like four to the power of twenty-three, which is seventy trillion.'

'Isosceles what?' said Catt with a chuckle, still several sentences behind Rawin.

Rawin put the snake shape he had made down on the floor. To his alarm there was a sudden puff of smoke and it turned into a real snake, arching its body and shooting its forked tongue out as it eyed the children menacingly. Catt jumped back and spun her sword expertly in her hand, ready to cut it down.

'JaoJuk!' Rishi said, turning and looking at the child. 'Are you being naughty again? Stop it.'

The child pursed his lips in a suppressed smile as if to say, 'I know nothing,' and immediately the snake turned back into a harmless plastic shape.

'Right,' said Rishi, 'it is time to go. You have everything you need. JaoJuk will accompany you from now on.'

JaoJuk performed an elegant bow and, without saying anything, beckoned for them to follow.

The three bounded down the slope, JaoJuk leading the way.

'Rawin,' said Catt after a while, 'I've been thinking. Rishi said we will not defeat the evil one *unless* we go home, but we cannot go home *until* we have defeated him. Did you understand that?'

'I have been thinking the same thing,' Rawin replied. 'I have to confess it doesn't make sense. But I was so relieved when he said we would definitely be going home that I kind of forgot the rest of it.'

'Me too.'

'Do not question Rishi,' JaoJuk interrupted. 'He speaks the truth and if you don't understand it, you must be patient until you do.'

It wasn't long before they reached the gorge.

'Ugh, do we have to go back to the other side?' asked Rawin. 'How are we going to do that?'

Catt looked across the gorge, wondering if they might see Sukreep, but there was no sign of him. He said he would wait. Perhaps he was resting in the forest, she thought.

'So now what?' she said to no one in particular.

JaoJuk turned to Rawin and waved his hand to ask him to come closer.

'The Rubik thing,' said JaoJuk.

Rawin got it out of his pocket and held it on a flat hand in front of them both. 'Can a snake help us to cross the gorge?' he asked doubtfully.

All three stood puzzling. But after a few minutes, Rawin began making counting noises quietly as he looked back and forth across the gorge as though he was estimating something. He took the Rubik Twist in both hands, and twisted it wedge-by-wedge into a gentle curve, like a bow. Then he looked across the gorge again before at one end carefully turning the wedges until he had made a small cluster below each end of the curve. Then he said, 'Done.'

'A suitcase handle!' Catt scoffed. 'And how precisely is that going to help us?'

Rawin looked confident. He turned to JaoJuk. 'Right JaoJuk, your turn.'

JaoJuk put his hands on his hips and looked impishly at the Rubik Twist in front of him. There was a bang and a cloud of smoke filled the air around them. Catt fell to the ground and rolled over as she gripped her sword in a defensive position. Rawin crossed his arms over his face and stood his ground. JaoJuk could not be seen.

When the smoke cleared they looked around them.

'My God!' cried Catt, 'What? How?'

Catt and Rawin stared in stunned amazement as a curved suspension bridge stretched from their side to the other side of the gorge.

'Not a suitcase handle,' laughed JaoJuk. 'Come on.' And he started running on to the bridge, followed by Rawin and Catt, whose mouth was still wide open in surprise.

They soon reached the other side. Then the bridge disappeared in a flash and Rawin was holding the Rubik's Twist in his hand, back in its original shape.

'Wow!' he and Catt said simultaneously. They followed JaoJuk, who was already running into the woods.

'Go. We will stand aside and let you walk away.'

Just then a voice as deep and loud as rumbling thunder could be heard from amid the ranks of the demon army: 'Do not listen to him.' It came from the mightiest of the demons, clearly much taller than those around him. 'This is a trick,' he bellowed. 'I, Channarong, will fight that girl, one to one, and show you who is the victor in this battle.'

The murmuring rose among the demons. Catt had sheathed her sword and she could be seen clearly, her fists defiantly on her hips.

Just then one of the demons cried out: 'Let Channarong fight her.'

Slowly a chant began to arise from the demon army, 'Channarong, Channarong, Channarong…'

'No,' shouted Hanuman. 'You are not in a position to bargain. Take your weapons and go.'

'Channarong, Channarong, Channarong…'

'I accept the challenge!' It was Catt. 'I am not afraid of him!' She raised her chin an inch as she looked disdainfully at the snorting demon who was already rocking with aggression.

'No, no,' said Sukreep to Hanuman. 'Don't let her do it. That monster is three times her size.'

'We cannot interfere,' replied Hanuman. 'If she believes this is what she must do, so be it.'

Kumphakan nodded to Channarong and the demon army started to drift apart to allow a path to Catt. The chanting began again. Catt watched unmoved.

Further up the slope, Rawin and JaoJuk sat on their haunches watching. 'I don't like this,' said Rawin. 'That demon looks indestructible.'

JaoJuk watched but said nothing.

As Channarong emerged from the ranks of the demon army, he began to run, his sword swinging in one hand and his grotesque mouth forming into a maniacal laugh. The long fangs in each corner of his filthy mouth looked menacing and his bulbous nose snorted like a steam engine. Slowly and calmly Catt unsheathed her sword again, taking it in both hands and pointing it at the approaching demon. She shifted one foot behind the other in a defensive stance, with her legs slightly bent. She waited. Both armies stood and watched, fixated in silence. When Channarong was just a few yards from her, Catt spun her sword in one hand and grabbed the blade end with the other, turning it so that the sun caught it full-on, reflecting its light into the eyes of the demon. He cried out and began to stumble as he tried to shield his eyes with both hands, almost dropping his sword. Catt pirouetted and rained two quick blows across Channarong's shoulders as he stumbled in confusion. He was still partly blinded by the sun's reflection. He was grunting and snorting in anger, but managed to regain his footing, bringing himself to a firm halt in front of Catt.

'Prepare to die, girl,' he barked. 'I am Channarong. You cannot beat me.' He swung his sword over his head.

'Nice to meet you, Mr Channarong,' said Catt in mock politeness. Then she spun on one foot and landed a powerful blow with the other in the demon's stomach.

The monkey-soldiers began to cheer.

'That didn't hurt,' lied the demon as he gasped for breath.

'Oh, then how about this?' Catt replied as she sheathed her sword and almost in the same motion did a backward somersault and caught the demon on the nose with both feet before landing back in front of him on two hands and cartwheeling away. Channarong let out a grunt of pain and felt his bleeding nose with one hand as he clung to his sword with the other.

'Had enough?' said Catt, in pretend sympathy. 'Surrender and I will let you go free with the others.'

Driven by anger and pain, however, the demon began to lumber unsteadily toward the girl, swinging his sword and bellowing curses. Hundreds of monkeys all breathed in deeply at the same time. Catt unsheathed her sword again and trained the sunlight on the floundering demon's face. The demon army fidgeted in discomfort, muttering in disbelief that their mightiest warrior was seconds away from death at the hands of a girl.

At that moment an elephant appeared on a high embankment behind the demon army. Astride its neck sat a tall imperious-looking demon with an emerald green face. He was dressed in the finest embroidered tunic with wing-shaped red and gold shoulder epaulettes and a sarong of exquisite patterns. His head was crowned with a high coronet and his wrists and ankles were adorned with glittering gold bracelets. He looked effortlessly regal, like a statue commemorating a conquering hero. The two armies fell silent immediately. Catt held her sword in the position that continued to blind Channarong, but she lifted her eyes for a second to watch the demon across the other side of the plain. He effortlessly unfurled a gigantic umbrella which blocked out the sun. Channarong's full sight was restored and he immediately regained his composure, swinging a backhand blow across Catt's face, knocking her off her feet. She fell to the ground, struggling to get up as Channarong closed in.

Watching on the slope above them, Rawin turned to JaoJuk. 'No, no, no. We have to stop this,' he said. JaoJuk's face was contorted with worry.

Catt crawled away as Channarong prepared for the kill. She managed to roll quickly to one side onto her knees and tried to stand, but Channarong swiped her with a powerful hand, knocking her on to her back. The monkey army began to murmur with despondency while the demon army began to chant 'Channarong, Channarong…' as they sensed certain victory.

Rawin pulled out the Rubik's Twist from his pocket, working it into a rectangular shape, his hands moving faster than they had ever done. 'Quick,' he turned to JaoJuk. 'Quick.'

Channarong stood mercilessly over Catt, his sword held aloft. He paused and laughed raucously. 'You stupid girl,' he shouted, and turned to acknowledge the cheers of the demon army. 'No one can beat Channarong,' he called out, raising his other arm as he swirled his sword above his head. 'I am the greatest.'

As he turned to deliver the death blow, he was forced to stagger back as a drone swept in between him and Catt, hovering beside her. She quickly dragged herself off the ground and clung on to it. 'Rawin, JaoJuk, thank you,' she said to herself. 'You guys are the best.' She stood up as the drone swept out of reach of Channarong and rose until it hung in the air above the two armies. Silence descended on the plain. The demon on the elephant watched defiantly. Rawin gave JaoJuk a fist-bump. Hanuman and Sukreep looked at each other and shook their heads in disbelief. 'The destined ones,' said Sukreep.

By now Catt had regained her composure and was standing on the front edge of the drone in her familiar pose, legs astride, hands on hips, head raised. She spoke so that everyone could hear, from the furthest ranks of the monkey army on the hill, across the plain to the demon hordes and beyond to the imperial-looking demon seated on the neck of his elephant high on the embankment.

'You do not know who I am,' she began, addressing him, 'but I know who you are.' She paused. 'Your name is Totsakan.' She paused again. 'People fear you. But I don't. I am Catt and I know about your evil, and it doesn't frighten me. I can see that your evil inspires your army, but they have never known the inspiration of virtue. I can see that they love your authority. But there can be no true loyalty in those who have never known freedom. You have ruled this domain with fear and lies, but courage and truth will defeat you in the end. When you threaten, we won't cower. When you take what isn't yours, we will win it back. And if you try to hide, we will hunt you down.'

# CHAPTER TEN

C hannarong had been standing below the drone, swinging his head clumsily back and forth in puzzled anguish as Catt hovered above him. Now he turned and ran back in panic to his comrades. This sparked alarm among them and they began to stampede in disarray along the plain. Catt had already hopped off the drone and it disappeared as mysteriously as it had taken shape in the first place. What no one else saw, apart from JaoJuk, was Rawin straightening the wedges of his Rubik Twist so that it regained its original shape and returning it to the side pocket of his backpack.

Totsakan and his elephant were no longer visible as clouds of dust rose from the plain as his troops scattered in chaos. Rawin shielded his eyes with one hand and felt around with his other, trying to catch hold of JaoJuk. But instead of feeling JaoJuk's small hand as he had expected, Rawin brushed against a huge arm that immediately lifted him. In seconds he was being borne away at speed to the sound of loud, thundering elephant feet.

JaoJuk ran frantically in the other direction, not sure what had happened, but aware that Rawin had been snatched from right next to him. Afraid that he might be taken too, his legs spun beneath him as he dashed in fear to where he thought Catt would be.

Rawin tried to see what was happening, but Totsakan

clutched his small body tightly while guiding his elephant at high speed on narrow paths across hillsides, through forests and over rivers. Eventually the Demon King pulled the animal up and dismounted, still clutching Rawin in one arm. He strode ahead and entered a cave, flinging Rawin down on the rocky ground. A burning torch hung on one wall. Totsakan grabbed it casually and crossed the cave to light a second torch. Then he took both, one in each hand, and lit two more until dozens of brightly burning torches lit up the cave. He turned and looked at Rawin, who had lifted himself up with one arm but whose legs remained outstretched where he had been thrown. He slipped his backpack off and pushed it to one side.

He watched as Totsakan paced the cave, occasionally swinging around and glaring at him. Just when Rawin was beginning to get used to seeing the demon in its full frightening form, Totsakan let out a loud roar as he was transformed into a tall, dashing man, his beautifully embroidered tunic and sarong now closely hugging his human shape as if they had been fitted by the finest tailor on Sukhumvit Road. He turned and looked at Rawin. There was something magnanimous, even charitable, about the look in his eyes. He had a strong but kind face and a soft smile beneath a sculptured moustache that made him look like a famous actor. Rawin gulped quietly and raised his eyebrows quizzically, waiting for Totsakan to speak. When he did, it was with a gentle, deep warmth.

'Are you frightened? There's no reason to be.'

After a minute or two of silence, Totsakan went over to one of the walls and lifted a tin mug from a gap in the stonework. He held it beneath a small stream of water trickling out of the rockface. When it was full, he brought it over to Rawin and handed it to him. 'You must be thirsty.'

Rawin took the mug but didn't drink.

'You can drink it,' said Totsakan, and then he let out a half-chuckle. 'I'm not going to poison you. Why would I do that? Even if I were the evil being that they say I am, what good would it do me to kill you now? A truly evil being would torture you first.'

Rawin felt his stomach turn. He sat holding the mug.

'Go on, drink.'

Having thought for a minute about what Totsakan had said, he decided it was very unlikely that the demon would poison him – at least not now – so he drank. It was the most refreshing water he had ever tasted. He finished it off.

Then Totsakan chucked him a stick of sugar cane.

'You probably need something to eat as well. That isn't poisoned either,' he smiled.

Rawin peeled away the cane's thick green skin and bit into the sweet juicy fibre. He hadn't eaten anything since being snatched from Bangkok by Sukreep. He felt almost dizzy as the sugar pulsed through his digestive system and into his brain. 'Thank you,' he said instinctively.

'What's your name?' asked Totsakan.

'Rawin,' replied the boy, but the word stuck in his throat and barely came out. 'Rawin,' he said more loudly and clearly a second time, as if being challenged by a teacher who had told him to speak up. 'I'm Rawin.'

'And who are you, Rawin?' Totsakan asked mildly.

'Uh, I'm from Lopburi.' He didn't know what else to say.

'And what are you doing here?'

Rawin couldn't answer that. For one thing, he didn't really know what he was doing 'here'. He remembered that he had told Catt that he felt they were meant to be here. But he couldn't very well tell Totsakan that he had somehow been 'destined' to help defeat him, the Spectre. He wondered whether Totsakan knew.

'Is that girl also from Lopburi?' ask Totsakan.

'No, she's from Bangkok,' said Rawin quickly, eager to have something he could say that did not incriminate himself.

'She said her name is Catt. Is she your friend?'

'Yes.'

'And do you know what she is doing here?'

Rawin hesitated again. It was clear that Catt had declared herself an enemy of Totsakan. Those things she had said standing on the drone were clearly very hostile towards him. She had also said 'we will hunt you down.' If he was a friend of hers, Totsakan must conclude that he is included in the 'we'. He stayed silent but slowly lifted himself off the ground and sat on a rock, head down.

'She seemed to think she knows me,' said Totsakan. 'I wonder how.'

He waited a little while but Rawin did not speak.

'She must have been hanging around with my enemies. Do you know who she has been hanging around with?'

Rawin decided he could not avoid taking part in this conversation any longer. It would be better for him to try to steer it in a direction that would give him some control over what Totsakan concluded, he thought. If he stayed silent, Totsakan was bound to conclude that he was allied with Catt. And then maybe he would indeed poison him – or something worse.

Rawin decided to get straight to the point rather than dodge Totsakan's questions and end up looking like a coward – or even a liar.

'If you steal another man's wife, you are bound to have enemies,' he blurted.

Totsakan didn't look taken aback at Rawin's sudden forthrightness after being so reticent until now. He rocked his head to one side and then looked into Rawin's eyes and chuckled lightly. 'You believe this?'

Rawin held his tongue. By now, after talking to Sukreep and Rishi, he knew he could no longer simply say it's in the Ramakien story. That was already sounding ridiculous to him. This was no story, not to those they had met, nor even to himself now. So he decided to be cautious: 'Well, that's what they say.'

'They?'

'I don't think you know them.'

'You mean the monkeys?'

'Not just the monkeys.'

'So you've been talking to lots of people?'

'Not lots.'

'But they all seem to know everything about me.'

'They know you have stolen Sida, that's all I know.'

'You know a lot,' he said in a gently sarcastic tone.

Rawin waited. He didn't know what to say. He let Totsakan speak next.

'But you are too young to know about love.'

Ugh, thought Rawin. Love.

'People kill and die for love,' said Totsakan, settling back on a comfortable smooth rock and looking a little dreamily into the distance. 'The great poets say that in love and war, everything is fair.'

'You are right,' said Rawin quickly, 'I don't know anything about love.'

'Yet the girl thinks I am evil. And you presumably agree with her.'

Rawin remained silent.

'You don't know anything about evil either, Rawin,' said Totsakan in the tone of an uncle who is keen to guide a child. 'Evil starts out small, and it moves very slowly, and it fills a heart just a little bit at a time.'

Rawin began to hang on Totsakan's words, for they sounded like the gentle teachings of a monk, not the proclamations of a devil.

'Evil does not feel like evil to those who practise it. It feels normal. Evil is what other people do.'

Rawin said nervously: 'You are right. I do not know anything about evil either.'

'But I do,' said Totsakan. He stood up and walked across the cave floor. Rawin's eyes followed him. 'You see, Rawin, I suffered evil for ten thousand years.'

'Ten thousand years?'

'I did not know the word 'evil' at first. I was not of high birth among those who served Lord Isuan, God of the whole Universe. My name was Nontok. I studied every moment I could and became the finest student of the teachings of the gods that there had ever been. There was only 'good', no evil in those sacred texts. But my duty was to wash the feet of the minor gods whenever they came for an audience with Lord Isuan. They did not know about my learning and my studiousness. They only saw me as inferior to them, a lower being who made them feel big.'

Totsakan breathed in and paused as though a pain had passed across his chest. Rawin sat silently, listening.

'That's how it works, Rawin. You can only really feel big if you put yourself above someone else. Big people, good people, cannot be big or good unless there are small people, bad people, so they point at some people and call them small and bad. And the more they do that, the bigger they feel and the more goodness fills their false proud chests. So these lesser gods, as I washed their feet, slapped me over the head and laughed at me. Sometimes they lifted my chin and looked me in the eye and then slapped me across the face. And they laughed and laughed and took turns to slap me and belittle me.

He looked up to the ceiling as if to find comfort or understanding there, anywhere. 'Ten thousand years,' he said.

'That must have been terrible,' Rawin said, before realising that what he had said was totally inadequate. The truth is there could be no words to describe what suffering that must have involved. So he quickly followed up: 'Did you escape? What happened?'

'I went to Lord Isuan and said, Lord, I have served you loyally for ten thousand years without complaint. I implore you to give me power to regain my dignity. And the Lord Isuan did so. And I made those who had humiliated me pay for their evil ways.'

Rawin became fascinated by the idea of powers given by the god of all gods. 'What was the power?'

'A diamond-tipped finger,' replied Totsakan.

'Wow,' said Rawin. 'That's amazing. What did you do with it?'

'I killed them all.'

# CHAPTER
# ELEVEN

JaoJuk didn't stop running until he reached Catt lower down the hill. The noise and dust from the fleeing demon army still hung in the air. Catt was preparing to join Hanuman and the monkey army when JaoJuk arrived.

'Where's Rawin?' she asked with some concern.

'He's gone,' replied JaoJuk flatly.

'Gone where?'

'Totsakan took him.'

'Totsakan took him! What do you mean?'

'He came on his elephant and picked him up and now he's gone.'

'Where did he take him?'

'Don't know.'

Catt felt a surge of irritation at JaoJuk's matter-of-fact manner. Couldn't the child show some emotion, some alarm at what had happened? Couldn't he at least say which direction they went, something, anything more than simply, 'he's gone'?

'Come on,' she barked, 'we have to find him.' She began to run towards the monkey army. JaoJuk ran as fast as he could to keep up.

Hanuman was looking triumphant as he stood beside

Sukreep and Chompoopan watching the demons retreating. They turned to Catt as she approached. 'Magnificent!' said Hanuman, 'you were magnificent. Look at them run.' He then opened his arms wide and said: 'Welcome, Catt, welcome. I am glad it didn't rain when you did that clever trick with your sword. I am Hanuman, by the way.'

'Mr Hanuman, I am pleased to meet you, but there is no time for pleasantries right now. Totsakan has kidnapped Rawin. We must rescue him.'

Everyone started talking at once. 'Kidnapped?' 'How?' 'Do we know where he took him?' 'Did someone see him?'

'JaoJuk was with him,' Catt said. 'He saw Totsakan take Rawin, but he doesn't know where.'

'JaoJuk?' said Hanuman. He looked at the small child standing next to Catt. 'Are you JaoJuk?'

'The Rishi sent him with us,' Catt said quickly. 'He has been extremely helpful.' JaoJuk looked down but showed no emotion.

'Can you help us find Rawin?' asked Hanuman.

'Don't know,' replied JaoJuk. Catt cast her eyes up to the sky in controlled despair.

'He can,' interrupted Sukreep. 'He gave me the telepathy.'

'He gave you telepathy?' repeated Hanuman disbelievingly. 'Is that true?' He looked hopefully at Chompoopan who simply shrugged his shoulders.

'I think he means telephone,' said Catt helpfully. 'Now I understand. Rishi got JaoJuk to give Sukreep the phone. Show them, Sukreep.'

Sukreep pulled the phone from under his armour and held it up for everyone to see. Again, Hanuman and Chompoopan looked puzzled. 'This thing can do telepathy?' asked Hanuman, intrigued.

'It's almost as good,' said Catt. Then quickly: 'Wait, I've got an idea. Give it to me,' she said. He passed it over. Catt tapped away at the screen then held the phone up to her ear as everyone watched in bewilderment.

'Damn,' she said after a minute, 'The number you have called is not available. Please try again later,' she repeated the words she heard on the phone. 'We will have to find another way.'

'We need to go to Prince Ram and Prince Lak,' said Sukreep. 'They will know what to do. There is no time to waste. Come. Please, Chompoopan, stay with our soldiers. Let them rest.'

Sukreep led the way, followed by Hanuman and Catt. JaoJuk stood still, not knowing what he should do. 'JaoJuk, come on,' said Catt. 'We might need you.' JaoJuk pouted and waddled reluctantly a few paces behind her.

'We need to travel fast,' Sukreep said, beginning to scamper with accelerating speed. Hanuman, of course, had no trouble keeping up as the two monkeys began alternating between their four-legged run at high speed and occasionally swinging up into the lower branches of trees. In what felt like no time they were far ahead of Catt and JaoJuk.

'Come on,' Catt said, striding back to JaoJuk. She stooped and lifted the child on to her back. 'Hold tight.' She began to sprint, lifting off the ground to clear fallen trees and thick undergrowth, gracefully darting through the forest. JaoJuk hung on to her shoulders and kept his eyes closed. They were soon alongside the speeding monkeys.

They travelled like this for more than an hour before Sukreep and Hanuman halted in a clearing beyond which the indistinct outline of a chalet could be detected through the trees. Hanuman let out a low chattering sound that rose in pitch and volume, ending in two short, sharp barks.

They waited. After a minute, he repeated the sound. The small group stood in silence waiting. Out of the blue an arrow whistled through the air and lodged itself with a loud thud firmly in a tree, quivering like a plucked violin string. A friendly laugh followed as a hearty, tall, athletic-looking man appeared from the wood and walked towards them. 'Just checking,' he chuckled. 'Friend or foe?'

'Foe,' said Hanuman. Then after a brief pause: 'Foe of the Spectre.' Then he too laughed. 'Greetings, Prince Ram. We are friends.'

Catt tried not to, but she couldn't stop herself from staring at the man who stood before them. Whenever he had been spoken of it was in such revered tones. In the stories she remembered throughout her childhood, this was the ultimate good person: brave, kind, loyal to his beloved wife, enemy of evil. A god, in fact. So why did he just look like an ordinary man? He wore a simple olive green silk tunic with a kaftan style collar that reflected the light. The garment was open down to the top of his chest, partly revealing a muscular torso. His lower body was covered by a brick-red sheet of cloth knotted at the waist like a Burmese-style *longyi*. And the longer she watched him, the less ordinary he appeared.

From where she stood, his eyes appeared both kind and intense at the same time, almost as if he had the power to look into your soul. His lips were thin, but they turned up at the ends in what seemed like a permanently relaxed, friendly smile.

Hanuman was still talking. 'Good Prince Ram, we are friends indeed, as the saying goes, but right now friends in need.'

'What is it you need?' Ram said, opening his hands out in front of him. 'I am at your service since you have always been at mine.'

'My good lord,' said Sukreep, 'perhaps I can explain.' He stepped towards Catt and placed his arm around her shoulders. 'May I introduce Catt.'

'Delighted to meet you, Catt,' said Ram, stepping forward and executing a flamboyant bow.

'Lord, Catt is here with her friend,' Sukreep explained. 'His name is Rawin. The wise hermit Rishi summoned them to be at our service in the quest to defeat the Spectre and restore the honour of your loyal and beloved wife. Rishi called them the "Destined Ones".'

'Ah, Destined Ones,' replied Ram slightly condescendingly. 'It is comforting to know that those who are destined, as you called it, are with us and not against us. But they are just children.'

Catt felt herself overcome by a mixture of, on the one hand, deference to this formidable figure, this god-man, and on the other hand the need for haste. There was no time to waste if they were to rescue Rawin. 'Sir,' she said with more confidence than she had expected, 'if you will permit me to speak, I must urge you to help us. Rawin – who Mr Sukreep has just told you about and who is my friend – has been kidnapped by Totsakan. We need to save him.'

Ram turned his head slightly and straightened his shoulders as he breathed in deeply. 'Is there no limit to this demon's evil? Kidnapping a child.' He turned and called in the direction of the chalet. 'Brother Lak, quickly, bring the horses and your weapons.' Then he looked at the group who stood before him. 'We should begin at the point where the boy was snatched. We can track them from there.' Then he looked paternally at JaoJuk. 'And you, little one, you can tell me who you are later, but I think you better hide here where it is safe.'

'No, Sir,' said Catt a bit more assertively than she intended. 'Sorry,' she hurriedly apologised. 'Sir, this is JaoJuk. We need him to come with us.'

'Well, little JaoJuk,' said Ram warmly, 'Catt says you have to come, and I don't think I can argue with Catt.' He smiled affectionately at the girl. She hurriedly smiled back, not quite sure how to respond, but feeling reassured by his easy manner.

Just then, a man who looked a little like Ram but younger appeared through the trees leading two horses.

'Ah, Brother Lak, thank you. This is Catt and JaoJuk. I will explain as we go – Catt's friend Rawin has been kidnapped by Totsakan. We need to find them.'

Lak greeted the group with hands pressed together and then mounted his horse, his sword at his side. He trotted up to Ram and passed him the reins of the other horse.

Ram turned to Catt and JaoJuk. 'You two had better come with me and my brother,' he said as he slipped his bow across his back. 'We need to travel fast.'

'I can keep up,' said Catt.

'OK, if you're sure,' Ram replied. 'You are indeed a confident one.' Then he turned to JaoJuk: 'Come little one,' he said kindly, and lent down from his saddle, lifting the child up with one strong arm. 'You come with me.' He placed JaoJuk on the front of the saddle and took the child's hands and folded them around the pommel. 'Hold on to that very tightly.'

They set off at a fierce pace, covering ground rapidly. Hanuman led the way since he knew the country better than anyone. Catt kept up with the fast moving monkeys as she had done earlier. She was aware that Ram occasionally glanced at her approvingly, as if he might have doubted that she would be OK, but pleasantly surprised that in fact she was as fast as any of them. JaoJuk held firmly to the saddle horn and kept his eyes tightly shut throughout the ride.

It was a long way, but eventually they reached the slope where Rawin had been taken. The rain had washed away the elephant's footprints.

'Damn,' complained Ram, 'We may have to split up and search in different directions. This is not going to be easy.'

Just then a phone rang. Everyone turned and looked puzzled in the direction of the sound. Sukreep began feeling around under his armour and pulled it out. Carefully and uncertainly, he held it in front of him in one hand and gently touched the screen and lifted the phone to his ear. Everyone watched in astonishment. 'Hello,' he said. He turned to JaoJuk. 'It's for you.'

# CHAPTER
# TWELVE

Half an hour had passed since Totsakan told Rawin
about his life. Then he had become pensive and did
not talk to Rawin again. It seemed to Rawin that by
telling him about his humiliation Totsakan had reawakened
painful memories and wanted to let them subside. Rawin
thought it best not to ask any further questions or say
anything about it.

After a while Totsakan walked slowly deeper into the
cave. The boy could see what looked like a chamber reaching
into the side of the rock wall. He watched as Totsakan
approached a small cavity. It contained what appeared to be
an urn, similar to one that contained the ashes of his
grandfather after his cremation. Totsakan lifted it and held it
in both hands as if it must have contained something fragile
or precious. He groaned as if he was in terrible pain. Then he
placed the urn back in the cavity and stepped over to a
wooden bench covered in some colourful cotton throws that
might have been used as a bed.

Totsakan sat on the bench and flung his legs round so
that he was half lying down, resting on his left arm. He ran
his fingers through his hair and closed his eyes, pushing back
his head as if in discomfort, remaining still for what seemed

like many minutes. Rawin tried not to stare. He felt he was intruding on someone's private sadness.

After a while Totsakan slowly opened his eyes and called out: 'Do not try to run away. You won't get far.'

Rawin didn't reply. But he felt uneasy about the fact that he had indeed been thinking of running away. Was it that obvious?

The silence that now filled the cave was gradually broken by the rising sound of heavy rain outside. There was an occasional rumbling of thunder as a storm swept across the mountains. The torches that circled the cave fluttered as gusts of wind swept in and sparks scattered in smaller flurries inside the cavern, swirling around Rawin.

Soon he managed to focus on the task before him. He worked out that he was far enough away from Totsakan to move without attracting attention, but too far from the cave entrance to run away without Totsakan seeing him. So, without getting up from the rock he was sitting on, he stretched out a foot, hooking it around the strap of his backpack, dragging it carefully closer. Moving very slowly, he reached into the side pocket of the bag and pulled out the Rubik Twist. If Totsakan saw him, he could just say he was passing the time by playing his favourite game. But without a moment's hesitation he began to twist and shape the plastic form in his hands. This way, that way, no, back, up, across, no, further across, now twist again. Slowly but surely he saw with relief that he had been able to shape just the thing he needed.

He put it down on the cave floor and reached back into the backpack. Carefully, he felt around until he was able to find his phone, glancing every now and then to where Totsakan was still lying on the bench. He touched the screen and saw the phone come to life. He turned the screen away from Totsakan so that the artificial light would not catch his eye. He touched the phone app and noticed that the most recent call that it listed was from 'Unknown caller'. He knew that this was the one he received from Sukreep when he was still innocently viewing the paintings in the Temple of the Emerald Buddha. His mind shot back to that moment, which now felt like a dream. What was a dream? That life or this one? Was he now living his actual life? If you are in a dream, you cannot die, but in real life you can. And right now he felt that it was quite possible that he could die. And that meant this was his real life and he needed to save it.

He glanced once more at Totsakan, and, satisfied he hadn't noticed anything, touched the phone icon next to the 'Unknown caller' and saw the screen switch to the 'Calling' icon. A signal. Yessssss. He clutched the phone between his hands and against his cheek to try to smother the distant sound of the ringing that came from it. A crash of thunder and the heavy rain filled the silence. Thank you, Heavens, for that, he thought.

'Hello,' came a voice from the phone. Rawin wanted to say 'Shhh, shush, shush,' but it seemed ridiculous. So he whispered, 'I need to speak to JaoJuk, quickly.' The voice on the other side said hesitantly, 'OK.'

Rawin's heart began pounding. If Totsakan caught him now, he might kill him. He felt that somehow the demon might have begun to trust him and this would be seen as certain betrayal. He had, after all, shared his most intimate feelings about how he had been humiliated. People do that – when they tell someone a secret or something very personal, they often assume that the person they've told will feel closer to them, that they could be trusted in future. Perhaps that was true in this case. Rawin's mind was racing now. While he waited the few seconds for JaoJuk to come on the call, he kept thinking, Do I need to escape? What is he planning to do with me? Is he trying to separate me from Catt, to 'divide and rule' us, as the saying goes, since she had declared herself Totsakan's eternal enemy? Catt will never understand if I do nothing now. I've got to get back to her and tell her everything.

'Hello.' It was JaoJuk's voice, hesitant.

'JaoJuk, listen quickly,' he whispered. 'A motorbike. I've made a motorbike with my Rubik Twist. Help me.'

'I have to know where it is.'

'Pass the phone to Catt.'

'Rawin, Rawin.' It was Catt's voice, a mixture of relief and near panic. 'I will come for you. Tell me where you are.'

'I've shared my location via text message.' He could

hear the ping from the phone Catt was holding.

'Goddit,' she said.

'I have to go,' whispered Rawin, touching the red 'End call' button. As he did so, the phone was snatched from his hand. He felt his stomach go into freefall.

'And what is this?' asked Totsakan.

Rawin reached down deep into his well of courage and composure. Keep your head. Stay cool, he told himself.

'It's a toy,' he said as calmly as he could.

'You still play with toys?'

'Everyone my age does. Older people too.'

'What does it do?'

Rawin took some comfort from Totsakan's question. What it meant was that he didn't understand the idea of a phone call, that he wouldn't know that I might be communicating with someone outside the cave, he thought. So he decided to become enthusiastic, which wasn't difficult, given that a 14-year-old boy does indeed enjoy a smart phone. 'Oh, you can do so much with it,' he said. 'Games, videos, music.'

'Show me.' Totsakan handed it back to Rawin.

Rawin touched the Games icon on the screen and then Candy Crush Saga. The screen filled with colourful candy icons to cheerful background music. He turned the screen towards Totsakan. 'See.'

'You like this?' said Totsakan. 'It looks silly.'

'It is, but it is good for when you are bored,' replied Rawin, now feeling more relaxed because he and Totsakan were engaging in conversation again. In fact he felt in charge of this conversation. He hastily added: 'There are other games that involve using your brain.' He smiled warmly.

'And what is the game you play when you talk to this thing?' asked Totsakan suspiciously.

'What do you mean?'

'You know what I mean, Rawin,' said Totsakan sternly. 'You were talking.'

Rawin felt his stomach turn again. Quickly he thought of a response. 'Oh that. Yes,' he said confidently, 'that's Siri.'

'Siri.' Totsakan wasn't asking a question. He simply repeated the word flatly because he wanted Rawin to know that he thought whatever he was saying now was a lie.

'Yes, watch,' said Rawin quickly. He held the phone up to his mouth and said, 'Hey Siri, play 'Don't know what to do'.' In a few seconds, Blackpink's hit began to sing out from the small device held in Rawin's hand. 'See.'

Totsakan looked unmoved by the music. He looked around, as if bored. But Rawin sensed menace.

'And this?' said Totsakan, leaning down to pick up the little plastic motorbike that Rawin had left on the floor of the cave.

'Erm, that's another toy,' said Rawin quickly. 'Careful. Don't touch it.'

Totsakan turned to the boy, suspicion written all over his face. 'Rawin, you are up to something.'

Before Rawin could come up with an answer, there was a flash of light as the Rubik Twist magically grew into a full-size motorbike, knocking Totsakan over.

Rawin knew what he had to do and that he had just seconds in which to do it. He grabbed his bag, slung it over his back, jumped on the bike, pressed the starter button and kicked the roaring engine into first gear. The bike reared up on its back wheel as he steered it toward the cave entrance, opening the engine's throttle to its fullest.

Totsakan recovered himself and stood up, but it was too late. Rawin was yards away already. The demon emitted a terrible, booming roar, like the sound of a giant elephant in distress, and as he did so, his body became contorted, unwinding itself back into its giant demon shape. He ran to the mouth of the cave as Rawin's bike roared into the forest, gaining distance at lightning speed.

He stood still and bellowed with rage: 'Rawin, you are like everyone else. You lie, you deceive, you betray. You are the evil ones.'

# CHAPTER
# THIRTEEN

Catt used Sukreep's phone to look up the location Rawin had sent. She opened Google Maps and copied and pasted in the coordinates. Immediately Google Maps responded: *Google Maps can't find 13.751416, 100.492564*

'Oh, no,' she said out loud. 'Google Maps can't find Rawin's location.'

Ram, Sukreep and Hanuman looked at each other and shrugged. They had no idea what she was talking about.

'I've tried five times,' complained Catt desperately.

JaoJuk hopped off Ram's horse and trudged grumpily over to Catt and held out a hand.

'Oh, JaoJuk, can you help?' said Catt despairingly. She handed the phone to the child.

JaoJuk took it, pressed the home button and said calmly, 'Siri. This is JaoJuk.'

'How can I help you, JaoJuk?'

'Where is Rawin?'

'Thirteen degrees, forty-five minutes and five point one seconds North and one hundred degrees, twenty-nine minutes and thirty-three point two seconds East,' replied Siri. 'Is there anything else I can help you with?'

Everyone watched in silent fascination. Catt was spinning her hand in a motion that suggested 'Come on, hurry up.'

'How do I get there from here?' asked JaoJuk.

'I'm sorry, you can't,' replied Siri. 'That location is in another Universe.'

'Show me where it is anyway,' said JaoJuk.

The Google Maps location opened and after a few seconds, zeroed in on the Grand Palace and placed a red marker icon on the Temple of the Emerald Buddha.

'Good,' said JaoJuk. 'Now change Universe.'

'Changing Universe,' replied Siri.

Another few seconds passed and the map turned to a muddy green colour with light and dark patches but no other clear landmarks. The red marker icon appeared in the middle of the green and black mess.

JaoJuk touched the screen on the 'Directions' icon. The map opened a line that said, 'Choose starting point or select current location'. He touched 'Current location'. A wiggly dotted blue line formed on the map and opened a box that showed a stickman and read '24 min 1.9km'.

JaoJuk handed the phone back to Catt without further comment.

'How did you know?' she asked.

'The same way I helped him when he called.'

'And...?' Catt demanded impatiently.

'Telepathy.'

The girl stared at the phone in her hand and then looked back at JaoJuk who was looking pleased with himself. She breathed in deeply and opened her mouth as if to start speaking. But she closed it again, slipped the phone in to her pocket and took off like a startled bat, quickly disappearing into the thick of the woods. Everyone else just stood there, watching her vanish.

'She will find him, of that you can be sure,' said Sukreep. 'We should return to the chalet and wait for further word from them.'

Catt bounded at breathtaking speed, pausing for a few seconds now and again to make sure she was following the dotted blue line toward the red location marker. Soon she saw a slight change in the environment. Rocky crags began to appear more frequently as the woods gave way to wide open spaces interspersed with high rock faces and a cliff face. She slowed down, beginning to sense she was getting close. She touched her sword for reassurance and felt the fighting spirit rise within her. If Rawin was in danger, she would stop at nothing to save him, she thought. In fact she didn't think it. She just knew it. And she knew she knew it. She felt like she was someone else outside her body watching her as the courage rose like an ocean wave, ready to crash unstoppably on the shore. Fear was unequivocally alien to her now.

A darkness began to take shape in the cliff face as she approached. One more quick look at the phone. The dotted blue line was now no more than a hundred yards from the red location marker. She pocketed the phone and began to edge forward, knees bent, crouching. She could see now that the dark shape was in fact the entrance to a cave. She hurtled to one side until she reached the rock face, pressing her back against it as she shifted quickly sideways and got to the opening. Seconds later she spun into the entrance, unsheathing her sword and darting to the left and then the right and raising and lowering her body like a cat. Then she heard a voice, which made her spin round, ready to face whatever danger was there.

'Your destination is on the right,' said the voice.

Catt quickly realised that it was Google Maps speaking. She fumbled in her pocket and brought out the phone, poking at the X on the application with her finger. She stood dead still, listening to see whether anyone else had heard the phone. Nothing. She turned her head slowly to the left, scanning the semi-darkness. There was a smell of smoke from a torch – or maybe many torches – that she thought must have been recently extinguished. All she could see were eerie shadows of the irregular rock formations. Then she moved her head very slowly to the right to scan that side of the cave. Again, no sign of any presence. She took two more steps to the right. Then: 'Your destination is on the right.'

'Oh, no,' Catt hissed as she groped for the phone again. This time she would close the application altogether, she thought. But before she could do so, she noticed a shaft of light from the top of the rock ceiling shining like a spotlight on the floor. She was drawn toward it like a moth and stood in its full glow, gradually lifting her eyes. The light was pouring in through a hole above her, causing her to shield her eyes from the glare. Once she had got used to it, she looked intensely at the shapes that were beginning to reveal themselves on the other side of the hole in the roof of the cave.

Catt gasped like a child.

'You have reached your destination,' said the phone.

# CHAPTER FOURTEEN

Rawin felt the roar of the motorcycle beneath him. He had only ridden one a few times before. Now the thrill of controlling a two-wheeled machine was completely eclipsed by the fear that gripped him – would Totsakan be able to catch up with him?

He followed a narrow footpath that wound through the forest, rising and falling up and down low banks and mounds, twisting and turning, the engine screeching. The adrenaline that rushed through him concentrated his mind and body so that he controlled the bike with the skill of a much more experienced rider. Down, up, round, down again, round again.

Just yards ahead of him he saw a fallen tree trunk across the path. It was too close for him to stop in time. He pulled sharply at both brake levers and turned the bike to the left, leaning over and dragging his left foot to help slow himself and aid his balance. But it was nowhere nearly enough. The bike smashed into the hefty obstacle, hitting it square-on, catapulting him out of the saddle and over the tree trunk. He hit the ground on the other side, tumbling down a slope until he came to a halt in a clump of ferns. He groaned as he felt the pain in his arms and legs, but was relieved to feel that he seemed to be OK and his backpack not damaged in any way, just covered in clumps of foliage. He sat up and waited for a minute or two while he checked his condition. Not badly hurt. Then he stood up slowly and walked gingerly back up to the track.

The sound of the motorcycle engine had died the instant the collision had happened. Rawin looked nervously at where it had struck the tree trunk. No bike. Instead, there, on the ground, lay his **Rubik Twist**, not in the rough shape of a motorcycle, but a mangled mishmash of wedges as if someone who didn't know how it works had been messing around with it. He snapped it up quickly and pushed it into his backpack. There was nothing he could do with it now. He knew that he had to rely entirely on his own resources to complete his escape. There was no way he would be able to contact JaoJuk to get him to use his magic again.

As that thought came to him, so he remembered his phone. Perhaps he could reach Sukreep and ask him what to do next. He called the same number he had used before. In a matter of seconds he heard Catt's voice. 'Rawin, Rawin, are you OK?'

'Yes, I think so,' he replied. 'And you?'

'What do you mean you think so?'

'No, nothing. Forget I said that. I'm OK.'

'Are you still with him, Totsakan?' she asked hesitantly.

'No, no. I got away.'

'Where are you now?'

'In the forest.'

'Where?'

'I'm not sure. Actually, I have no idea. Where are you?'

'I'm at the location you sent us by phone.'

'Oh, God. Really? In the cave? Who is with you?'

'I'm alone.'

'Are you sure? Totsakan was still there when I escaped.'

'Well...' said Catt, pausing, and then: 'He's not here now.'

'Catt, I've just thought of something. If you go straight out the front of the cave you'll see a path right ahead leading into the forest. You should be able to see the motorcycle tracks.'

'Motorcycle tracks?'

'JaoJuk helped me. We turned my Rubik Twist into a motorbike.'

'Ah, right. Now I know why you asked to speak to him first. OK, I'm on my way.'

The phone went silent. Rawin wondered what had happened to Totsakan. Had he come after him or gone elsewhere? If he had followed, he would surely have caught up with him by now. But the forest was quiet, apart from the occasional eerie caw of a crow. So Rawin sat down on the fallen tree trunk and waited. Talking to Catt had a strange effect on him. He felt greatly relieved – even comforted – hearing her voice. No matter how genial Sukreep had been and how very useful JaoJuk had proven, he felt no real affinity with anyone other than Catt. After all, they had been plucked from their own world, one familiar to them both, and ended up in this inhospitable, alien place and it was almost as if they had scarcely had time to talk about it before they were fighting or falling or running away, their lives in danger. And yet he wasn't sure whether they were on the same wavelength anymore. He felt uneasy that Catt appeared to have quickly embraced her role as a fighter and her identity as the arch-enemy of the Spectre. What she had said when she was standing on the drone still echoed in his head. He had found it very moving, in fact very inspiring. He remembered feeling a cold shiver run down his spine when she stood there fearlessly promising to hunt down the most frightening creature in the Universe. But the thing that kept spinning around in his head now but which he hadn't tamed into a coherent thought was, Totsakan had been kind to him. He hadn't felt like an arch-enemy. How would he tell Catt all this?

His thoughts were interrupted by the sound of trees being shaken and feet pounding nearby. He slipped behind a tree and looked anxiously back up the path. Was it Totsakan, raging at what he saw as his betrayal? Or Catt? In a strange way he feared both. But when he saw Catt leaping her way through the forest, his fear dissolved and he stepped out into her path. She slid to a halt in front of him, her face shining with anxiety, her body rigid. She placed her hands on her hips and her head forward like a disapproving teacher and looked at Rawin who stood in a sort of surrender.

'Oh, Rawin,' she said, loosening up and opening her arms, 'you're OK.'

Rawin stepped forward, opening his arms too, but as they moved closer to hug they shifted the same way and ended up in an awkward collision of arms and knocking heads.

'Um, sorry, sorry,' Rawin said hastily, stepping back. 'Wow, am I glad to see you.'

Catt unwound herself gracefully and clasped his cheeks between both hands. 'Me too.' And then she stepped back and looked around, surveying the forest. 'We need to find our way back to the others. Come on.'

'Who are 'the others'?' asked Rawin.

'Oh, that's right, you haven't met any of them. Only Sukreep. And JaoJuk, of course. Well, there's Sukreep's nephew, Hanuman, and Chompoopan, one of his commanders. And Prince Ram and his brother Lak.'

'You've met Prince Ram?'

'Yes, we went to him for help when we heard you had been taken by Totsakan.'

They walked at a steady pace through the forest, Catt ahead, alert. Every now and then she stopped and looked in every direction before moving on. Rawin wondered if she knew where they were going. Neither of them had been here before and one forest path looked much like any other. They walked for quite some time.

Catt broke the silence: 'Bloody hell, Rawin, I nearly died with worry about you.'

'Thanks.' After he said that, he wondered if 'thanks' was the right thing to say. Do you thank people for worrying about you? He thought what he must really have meant was, 'Thank you for caring so much about me.' That made sense. He knew he felt the same about her. Which is why he was still feeling uneasy about telling her what happened in the cave.

Just then Catt raised a hand. She turned to look at him and pressed a finger to her lips. They both listened in silence. There was a distant sound of voices and activity much like a busy street in Bangkok but without the traffic. Catt signalled for Rawin to follow as she scrambled up a bank to the side of the footpath where there was a break in the trees. She kept low as they emerged from the forest at the crest of the bank. Rawin followed. As they reached the top, they saw the land slope steeply away. They gasped as they saw less than a few hundred yards away from them a city surrounded by high white walls with hundreds of buildings – temples, pavilions, houses on stilts, golden domed pagodas, bustling markets, elephants. And demons. Hundreds of them, walking around, sitting, eating, laughing, grunting. The city itself was circled by a wide moat filled with ink-blue water.

'Langka,' whispered Rawin.

'Remind me,' said Catt, now a bit more relaxed because she could tell the city was too far away for anyone to hear them.

'Totsakan's capital.'

They watched in silence for a few minutes. Then Rawin pointed to a walled garden on the edge of the city. They could just make out that it consisted of emerald green lawns dotted with ponds bursting with pink and white lilies and cherry blossom trees around the edges. Pretty Japanese style bridges crossed the ponds and classical marble sculptures graced the entire space. In the middle of the garden was a delicately styled small summer house and in the middle of that was an ornately shaped traditional seat. They could just see that sitting in the chair was a woman and another nearby sitting working at a table.

'Catt,' Rawin said. 'You know who that is, right?'

'Sida,' said Catt. 'It's Sida. Come on.' She got up and started heading down the slope toward the plain.

'Catt, wait,' Rawin called out in a loud whisper. 'Where are you going?'

'To rescue her, of course.' She bent low and moved towards a thin line of trees to one side of the slope to stay out of site from the city.

'Catt, are you crazy? How would you get across the moat? And there are demons everywhere. We wouldn't get near her,' said Rawin, hurrying to catch up with her.

'Watch me,' Catt said. 'That's why we're here.'

Rawin was overcome with a powerful mixture of fear

and anger. He ran at full speed and rugby-tackled Catt, pulling her down. 'Stop, stop, we can't do this.'

'Let me go,' complained Catt. 'What do you think you're doing?' She pulled herself free and bounced up.

Rawin got up and faced her. 'You can't do this. You'll get us both killed.'

They were like two kids fighting on the school playground.

'What's the *matter* with you?' said Catt angrily.

'What's the matter with *you*?' Rawin shot back. His eyes welled up.

They stood eyeing each other. Catt broke the silence: 'We know why we have been brought here,' she said. 'It isn't just an accident that we've found this place. It is meant to be.'

'You're talking like a mad monk. Nothing is *meant* to be. We choose to do things or not do things. There is no invisible force driving us. What do you think this is, Star Wars?'

'Rawin, it was you, right at the beginning of this, who thought we were meant to be here. Don't you remember, you said you thought we had no choice, that this is something we have to do? Seriously. And now you are criticising me for coming round to the same view.'

'I don't think that any more,' said Rawin, disappointed with his own change of mind, but feeling he had to be honest with himself. And with her.

She was still passionate: 'Rawin, if we turn back now, we are not listening.'

'Listening? Listening to what? You're the one who isn't listening.'

'What am I not hearing, then? Come on, tell me. What are you hearing that I'm not?'

'You're not listening to *me*,' Rawin said a little more calmly.

'Oh, so you're the one who knows what the hell is going on here. OK, OK. I'm listening, Mr Smart One.'

'We've got to think about this. All of this. Are we even sure we know who the evil one is?'

'What?' Catt cried. 'You don't know who the evil one is? How about starting with the one who kidnapped Sida and then you. If it wasn't for your Rubik thingy and JaoJuk's magic, he would probably have killed you.'

The two were no longer standing nose to nose. Catt had her hands on her hips as she always did. Rawin had folded his arms; it was defensive, not hostile.

'It didn't feel like that.'

'What, you didn't think he was going to kill you?'

'No. In fact he was…. kind.'

'Kind?' she repeated. 'That monster was kind?'

'Actually, he wasn't a monster. In the cave he turned into a man. As I said, actually quite a thoughtful man with feelings.'

'What are you trying to tell me?'

'I'm just trying to tell you what happened. We don't know the truth about what has been going on here. We only have what other people have told us. Sukreep told us who the evil Spectre is and that we were the destined ones, but he also told us that not everything here is the same as it is in the book. And we know that's true now. So, we have to decide for ourselves what is right and what is wrong and who is good and who is bad, based on our own experience.'

'Why is everything so complicated with you?' Catt said. 'Nothing is simple. You always have to think about this and think about that and decide what the right thing is to do. Can't you see that some things are either black or white?'

'That's because few things *are* one or the other.'

'And so you are telling me that after a few hours in a cave with Totsakan, you think he's a good guy.'

'How long have you spent with Prince Ram?' Rawin responded. 'Do you know anything about him?'

'Oh, Rawin, Rawin. I don't know what to say. Do you want to give up?'

'It's not giving up.'

Catt was silent for a minute. Then she said sharply: 'Do you want to go home?'

Rawin breathed in deeply and then sighed. 'I do, but of course we don't know how to do that.'

'I do,' said Catt. 'I know exactly how to do that. We can go right now.'

# CHAPTER FIFTEEN

A gentle breeze drifted across the immaculately cultivated garden just outside the palace compound in the city of Langka. The cherry blossoms fluttered as busy warblers flitted from branch to branch and a larger plumed, red-cheeked songbird perched like an alert sentinel in the furthest reaches of the tallest tree. Their spirited chirping blended into a perfect minor symphony.

Sida sat gracefully on a bench, her back straight, reading an exquisitely bound volume of poems. She wore a light silk blouse the colour of a lotus flower – midway between cherry pink and royal purple. One arm was bare up to the shoulder, the other draped in the garment. A delicate gold breast chain crossed her front. Her lower body was swathed in an elegant sarong of the same lotus flower colour as the top, just a degree darker, with a thin gold thread inlay that reflected the light. Her hair hung loosely just below her shoulders, framing a face so beautiful it might have been sculpted in the finest marble.

She looked up and let her gaze drift across the hedges and up towards the woods that crested the slopes. A young woman sat at an ornate garden table nearby, hand embroidering a delicate silk garment. On a smaller table beside her stood a traditionally decorated porcelain jug and some glasses.

'Would you like a glass of chilled lime juice, my lady?' she asked.

'Sweet Benjakai, you are my kindest companion,' replied Sida. 'Thank you.'

While Benjakai poured two tall glasses of juice she said in a matter-of-fact way: 'Well, you know that your contentment is my contentment.'

'And do you feel content now, Benjakai?' asked Sida.

'If you do.'

'What do you think? Am I content?'

Benjakai remained silent for a minute, then smiled. 'Honestly, I cannot tell. I would so love to know that you are, perhaps even happy.'

'Aha, if I say I am happy, then will you be?'

'Are you?' asked Benjakai, handing the glass of juice to Sida.

Sida chuckled. 'If you hear me say it, you would surely not disbelieve me, would you?'

'I would never do that.'

'Then, dear Benjakai, consider yourself happy.'

Benjakai smiled, but said no more.

A gate at the far end of the garden opened with a clang. Closing it behind him, a slightly stooped man, bald except for a fringe of scraggy hair, took hesitant steps into the garden and looked over towards where the two women sat. He was dressed in a full-length sandy beige gown and around his neck was a long maroon scarf, flecked with refined gold-coloured needlework.

'It's my father,' said Benjakai cheerfully. 'Pipek.'

'How nice for you,' Sida said, 'to be able to spend time with someone you love.'

'Yes, I do love him so,' said Benjakai. 'you will too. Father,' she called out, 'come and say hello to Sida.'

Pipek walked over to the two women and nodded politely, clasping his hands together in front of him. He was in fact younger than his appearance suggested. 'Miss Sida,' he said with quiet authority, 'it is an honour to meet you at last. Your presence is much talked about and I have been eager to make your acquaintance.'

'Mr Pipek,' Sida said in a gracious tone, 'it is an honour for me too. Your daughter has been my faithful consort and I cannot be more delighted than I am to meet you, her father, whom she loves so fervently.'

Pipek smiled warmly and looked intently at them in turn. He nodded and shifted his arms behind his back, stooping slightly as he stood like someone awaiting instructions from a superior.

Sida filled the silence before it became awkward. 'And to what do we owe the pleasure of your company, Mr Pipek?'

'A matter of considerable importance, good lady,' Pipek replied. 'Something I am hoping you might be able to assist me with.'

'Daddy is a wise astrologer,' said Benjakai proudly. 'He is the younger brother of Master Totsakan.'

Sida stiffened, but quickly she pulled herself together and said: 'Then for both of those reasons you can tell me what is to become of me, Sir.'

'That is beyond my knowledge or power, dear lady,' Pipek replied.

'Surely you have some influence over your brother,' said Sida.

'Not directly, my dear lady.'

'Then perhaps you could indirectly tell him to free me,' said Sida curtly.

'These things are never simple,' Pipek answered. 'I can assure you that you have my sympathy. But that alone cannot be of any assistance in your circumstances. I need further information if I am going to be able to do anything to alleviate your plight.'

'Further information? From me?'

'I have been consulting the stars and hearing the dreams of many among us, and I have a strong feeling that something terrible is going to happen. There is a force that appears to have been awakened since your arrival in Langka, because of your presence here.'

'If you don't understand it, how can I? I am not a clairvoyant,' said Sida.

'But you might have heard or seen something that might

throw some light on this matter,' Pipek said, unaggrieved by Sida's bluntness.

Pipek moved closer, speaking in a low voice and occasionally looking around and behind him. 'As my daughter has told you, I am an astrologer. This force to which I refer is, I believe, strong enough to overcome us, even, strong enough to defeat Totsakan.' He looked around again. 'That is why I have come to speak to you. My great fear, dear lady, is that your presence here will be the cause of the annihilation of this city and all who live in it. But we could still avoid it if you can help me.'

It took a long time for Sida to process what she had just heard. But eventually she got to the point where she focused on that last statement – we can still avoid it. 'How can I help?' she said weakly.

'When you were, um, when you accompanied Totsakan to Langka…'

'You mean when Totsakan kidnapped me. Abducted me. Did I what?'

'Did you hear anything, see anything out of the ordinary?'

Sida softened slightly and appeared to be thinking back to what happened. 'Mr Pipek, all I can recall is this hermit, this seemingly wise man, coming up to me and urging me to go and become the wife of the King of Langka because he was more powerful than Prince Ram. Of course, I refused to do that. And then I discovered the hermit was Totsakan himself because he changed back to Totsakan and brought me back here.'

'And you don't remember anything else?'

'No, nothing. I can't even remember why there was no one there to stop Totsakan taking me.'

'Sida, good lady, it seems I must reluctantly inform you of what occurred that day in the hope that it will allow you to assist me now. I am sorry to have to tell you that you were tricked,' said Pipek in a whisper, briefly looking behind him. 'Mareet turned himself into a beautiful deer in the forest and you saw that beautiful deer and you asked Prince Ram to go and catch it for you because it was the most beautiful creature you had ever seen.'

'Mareet?' inquired Sida.

'Totsakan's goon,' Benjakai scoffed. 'He will do anything for his master.'

'Yes, I remember the deer. Prince Ram went to catch it for me and left me with his brother Prince Lak.'

'His brother?'

'Yes. And then we heard Prince Ram calling out in pain and Prince Lak went to help him.'

'But it wasn't Prince Ram,' explained Pipek.

'Wasn't it? But I heard his voice.'

'It was Mareet, imitating your husband's voice. He did it to deceive Prince Lak into leaving you alone and coming to rescue Prince Ram. But when he got to Ram, of course, Ram was fine,' Pipek went on. 'That gave Totsakan enough time to approach you as the hermit. And you know what happened next.'

Sida threw her hands up to cover her face. 'My poor husband. Cruelly deceived.' Then after a minute, she let her hands slide down until she pressed them together in front of her mouth. 'But that means he is OK. I feared he might be dead.'

'No, he is alive,' said Pipek, looking around behind him, 'and he is looking for you. And this force that I detect – it is with him. Langka is in mortal danger because of you.'

Sida let out a suppressed scream and shut her eyes.

# CHAPTER SIXTEEN

Rawin struggled to keep up with Catt, whose agility far exceeded his. He wondered where she was taking him, how she could possibly know the way home. 'You seem to know your way around these woods pretty well,' he remarked, trying to get her to say something about where they were headed. 'How do you know where to go?'

'Motorcycle tracks,' she answered bluntly.

'Ah, right,' he said, noticing that she was re-tracing the route he had taken when he rode away from Totsakan's cave. 'Good thing it hasn't rained again.' He didn't say so, but he felt Catt was walking ahead of him faster than was necessary because she probably didn't want to have to talk to him.

It wasn't long before it became clear that Catt was heading for the cave. As they approached it she crouched and slowed down, touching the sword at her side. Rawin also lowered his body slightly, following her. 'What are we doing here?' he asked in a low voice.

'You'll see,' Catt said, holding up a hand. She whispered, 'Come on,' and shot off to the left of the rockface. She inched sideways toward the entrance. Rawin did the same.

'No sign of Totsakan's elephant,' he whispered.

As they reached the entrance, Catt slipped her sword out of its scabbard and gripped it with both hands in front of her. She took one careful step after another until she was inside. Rawin followed.

'All clear.'

'Now what?'

'This way,' said Catt, moving discreetly to the right of the cave, looking up. Rawin looked over to the left of the cave where Totsakan's bench stood unoccupied. He felt a shiver as he recalled the unsettling time he spent in there, not knowing what was to become of him. He followed Catt slowly, looking around as he went. He couldn't see much as the torches had long ago been extinguished.

'That's odd,' said Catt, looking up at the roof.

'What?'

'It was here, I'm certain.'

'What was?'

Catt looked back at where they had just come from and remembered the route she had followed when Google Maps said, *Your destination is on the right*, and then *You have reached your destination*.

'It was here,' she said emphatically. 'Up there.'

Rawin looked up, but saw only a narrow dark crevice in the roof. 'There?' he asked, pointing at the crevice.

'Yes,' Catt said. 'Something's not right.' She looked around, but sure she was in the same place she had been earlier she looked up again.

'Catt, what did you see?'

'OK, this is weird,' she said, now looking at Rawin, her impatience with him now supplanted by frustration. 'Up there. There was a gap going right up that crevice. A sort of funnel with light shining down.'

Rawin searched her face for something more.

'I know I saw it. I know. I wasn't imagining it. It was definitely there,' she complained.

'What?' asked Rawin earnestly.

'Bangkok.'

'Huh?'

'Bangkok.'

'You saw Bangkok?'

'Well, not all of Bangkok, obviously,' said Catt irritably. 'The Temple of the Emerald Buddha.'

'Are you sure?'

'Yes, absolutely certain.'

Rawin stayed silent. He didn't want to state the obvious, that there was nothing to see here now. Just the cave ceiling. He waited for Catt to wrestle with the puzzle.

'I can't explain it,' she said eventually. 'I know it was here and I know I saw it. When I was following Google Maps to find you, it brought me right here. And there was light coming down from up there. And when I looked up I saw it. I know I saw it. It was definitely the temple.'

'And you thought we might be able to return home through there?' asked Rawin.

'Yes, I did, though I didn't think we were going to do so before we had done what we were brought here to do.'

Rawin swallowed. He said nothing.

'Well,' Catt said after a pause, 'you're not going to be able to return now. Not until we figure out why it was open then and why it is closed now. Sorry. You'll have to stay.' She sounded a bit school teacher-ish.

'No problem,' he said rather lamely. 'I wasn't sure I wanted to go anyway. At least we know where to come, even if we don't have the key right now. Maybe JaoJuk can help.'

'Maybe. Let's go back and find him and the others. We have lots to tell them. Come on.' She led the way back to the entrance of the cave, taking a few seconds to look around before going out into the daylight again.

They did not speak as they walked. But both replayed their conversations over and over in their heads, each searching for some sort of reassurance that they hadn't been unreasonable, something that might make them feel their anger had been justified. Rawin felt only a dull ache of sadness.

Catt's thoughts were more about how she would manage if Rawin left. She had already accepted that he did not feel as she did about what they were doing here. But could she fight without him at her side? Not because he was a great fighter – he wasn't – but because he almost always seemed to have a plan.

As her mind meandered through these thoughts a shocking scream shattered the forest. Her body jolted into action, her right hand reaching instantly for her sword. In another moment she held it at the ready in front of her, eyes darting in search of the unnerving sound. She swung round and saw a hulking demon, swinging its sword above its head, moving at lightning speed out of the thicket toward Rawin who stood dazed by the sound and the suddenness of the attack.

'Down,' she screamed. 'Rawin, down.'

The boy dived to the ground where he stood, just in time to avoid the blade of the demon's sword decapitating him. The momentum carried the demon a couple of yards past him, throwing it slightly off balance. Before it could right itself, Catt, who had swirled on one leg and catapulted her body from where she was standing to reach the demon in one movement, thrust her sword deep into the middle of its body, bringing forth a gush of hideous yellow blood. The demon's warlike scream changed into a deathly howl of pain as it tumbled to the ground, gasping for breath. Catt plunged her sword with both hands into the back of its neck. A loud groan followed as the demon slumped further until it was flat on its face in the dirt, bleeding profusely from the neck as well as the stomach. Rawin looked away. Catt stood over the creature, her sword held at the ready. But no more was needed. The demon's gasps slowly subsided until they stopped altogether.

'That was close,' Rawin muttered still dizzy from watching Catt's clinical execution of the creature that, were it not for her, would most certainly have ended his life. 'Thanks.'

'There might be more,' Catt said, combing the woods with alert eyes. 'Come away from those trees, further onto the path,' she told Rawin. As he did what she had told him, two more demons appeared from the shade of the thickest part of the wood. Unlike the first one, these two moved slowly towards the children, their height more frightening than ever as they began to tower over them. They snarled and grunted. A bubble of snot appeared in the nostril of one of them. The other grinned menacingly, sticking a finger in its ear and extracting a vile green substance which it then pushed into its mouth. Its eyes squinted as it sized up the children, wary and unsettled by what Catt had done to the other demon that now lay lifeless.

'Move slowly behind me,' she told Rawin. 'No sudden movements. Look them in the eye.' She crouched slightly and held her sword out in front of her, swaying it gently so that it pointed at each demon in turn and then in an arc back again. They inched closer, very slowly. Rawin checked the area around them while still looking back at the demons – in their eyes, as Catt had told him. 'There's a hornet's nest in the bank just behind them, in that abandoned pangolin burrow,' he whispered. 'If we can disturb them, they might attack the demons.'

'Or us,' Catt said darkly.

'They will go for the nearest threat,' said Rawin.

'Just another one of those things you just happen to know about, right?'

'Well, I did a school project on the Giant Asian Hornet. They're pretty deadly,' said Rawin with some zeal.

'We don't have a lot of time,' said Catt, still pointing her sword at the demons.

'Can you distract them?' asked Rawin.

'I'll try.' Catt spun one leg around high in front of her while swinging her sword above her head. Then she repeated the movement with the other leg, letting out a loud taekwondo battle cry that sent the demons scuttling backwards. As she did so, Rawin lent down and picked up a thick, short stick that he had spotted lying on the path and in one movement, hurled it expertly into the hornets' nest. A long silence followed. The demons looked at each other. Then they looked at Catt and Rawin and back at each other, trying to work out what had happened.

'Come on,' said Rawin under his breath, urging the hornets. 'Come *on*.'

Catt maintained her stance, watching the demons closely.

Still nothing.

The demons, now a little surer of themselves, began to shuffle forward again towards the children.

'It didn't work,' said Rawin. 'Damn.'

'Didn't it?' Catt laughed with relief as a swarm of huge hornets flew furiously out of their nest straight at one of the demons who, in a panic, turned and ran back into the forest screaming, followed by thousands of whining insects.

'Gotcha,' cried Rawin.

Enraged, the second demon advanced immediately on the children.

'Run,' shouted Catt. Rawin turned and sprinted in the opposite direction from where the first demon and the hornets had gone. But before he had gone far he turned to see Catt standing her ground as the demon charged at her, swinging its sword and grunting angrily. She managed to step aside and spin her leg up behind her, catching the demon in the stomach with her heel. He let out a small belch, but appeared not to be too bothered. He turned back and lumbered menacingly towards the girl. Rawin watched in horror. Instead of using its sword, which was what Catt had been expecting, the demon swung its free arm and knocked her flying. Her sword bounced away from her as she fell to the ground. She tried to roll over and get up but the demon was on her in a flash, gnashing and growling with rage. It lifted its huge leg and placed a foot on her chest, pinning her to the ground. She struggled, but couldn't move. The demon lifted its head and let out a victorious roar as it prepared to crush her to death. Rawin turned and ran towards the demon, which opened its mouth in a contemptuous laugh at it prepared to bat him away. As it did so, a spear entered its heart with a thud. Its laugh turned into a hideous gurgling as the life slipped from its body and it fell to the ground in a heavy heap.

Catt sprang up and looked at Rawin. 'Are you OK? What happened?'

'Er, don't know,' replied Rawin looking in the direction the spear had come from.

Out of the shadows of the forest a handsome monkey appeared, dressed all in black. He walked slowly up to the demon and gripped the shaft of the spear, placed one foot against its body and tugged firmly. In a single movement the weapon came free from the demon's body and the monkey wiped the blood-drenched spearhead on the grasses at the side of the path until it was clean.

The children said nothing at first. They simply watched in awe. The monkey moved with such grace and poise that he almost seemed like an apparition. They looked at each other and at the monkey, who behaved as if he might have done nothing more remarkable than catch a fish.

'Thank you,' said Catt eventually. 'You saved my life.'

The monkey looked with kindness at her. Then, nodding his head once very slightly, he said simply, 'You're welcome.' He walked over and sat on a fallen tree trunk, placing one foot up on a branch. He looked at the children through narrowed eyes. There was a slight frown across his forehead, but there was still a kindness in his countenance. 'I guess it was just lucky I saw you when I did.'

'What just happened?' asked Rawin.

'They were bounty hunters,' said the monkey. 'There is a price on your heads. Dead or alive.'

The children looked at each other and tried not to show emotion. Rawin raised both eyebrows and gulped. 'How much?'

'A hundred thousand pieces of gold.'

'Each?'

'Each.'

'Who wants us dead?' asked Rawin.

'I am sure you know.'

Silence. Then, 'May I ask who you are?' said Catt.

'My name is Sayola.'

'Are you in Hanuman's army?'

'I prefer to be alone.' He got up and turned towards the forest from where he had come. He put two fingers up to the side of his head and flicked them forward in a light-hearted salute as he walked away and disappeared into the shadows.

# CHAPTER SEVENTEEN

Benjakai put an arm around Sida and pulled her gently towards her. She said nothing, offering only physical comfort. She sensed that Sida had been given hope by what Pipek had told her – hope that Prince Ram might find her and rescue her. But at the same time she must have known that if he did so, there would be terrible bloodshed. Pipek had used the words 'annihilation' and 'mortal danger'.

In the distance there was the sound of cheering and the trumpeting of an elephant.

'My Lady, our master returns,' Benjakai said, without emotion. Sida narrowed her eyes and raised her head slightly, turning to one side as if to hide any feelings she might have. She gazed into the distance, her hands clasped elegantly just above her waist. Her entire being expressed calm dignity.

In an instant Pipek transformed himself into a demon and hurriedly slipped out of the garden.

The sound of demons cheering outside the garden became louder. 'Hail, hail, hail.'

'Greetings, all, greetings.' It was Totsakan's voice, strong, relaxed. 'Thank you for your loyalty and for your courage. We will prevail.'

'We will prevail,' cried the demons. 'We will prevail.'

The gates at the far end of the garden swung open, a demon at each side bowing low as Totsakan entered, now transformed from a terrifying demon into a dashing human, a formidable looking demon general at his side. They were accompanied by another demon who had also changed shape, dressed in simple traditional tunic. He wore a small gold ring in his right ear lobe.

'Mareet,' whispered Benjakai to Sida, nodding towards him. 'The other one is Totsakan's younger brother Kumphakan, another of my uncles.'

Kumphakan did not change into human form. Instead he left the others and returned to be with his soldiers beyond the gate.

'Benjakai, you may leave us,' said Totsakan. As she left, Mareet went to the far end of the garden to allow his boss the privacy he knew he wanted. His gaze drifted around the garden, but it never fixed on Totsakan or Sida.

'My dearest, how good it is to set my eyes on you once again. I trust that you are well,' said Totsakan with a warm smile.

Sida didn't answer.

He tried again: 'I hope you have been well looked after.'

'I am fine.' And then, 'Thank you.' There was no warmth in her voice.

'I have a small gift for you.' Totsakan handed a small red velvet box to her. 'I hope you like it.'

Sida hesitantly took the box and placed it on the table beside her.

'Aren't you going to open it?'

'Not now,' she said without feeling.

Totsakan stepped over and picked up the box. He gently opened the lid and brought out a necklace of delicate pearls. He held each end and moved towards Sida. 'On any other neck, these pearls would glisten brighter than the stars. On yours, your unique beauty will outshine them a thousand times.'

A soft blush rose up Sida's neck into her cheeks. She did not move. Totsakan stood behind her, lifted his hands and draped the pearls around her neck, fastening them behind her head. He stepped back. 'Turn around,' he said. Sida stood still for some seconds, but then turned reluctantly towards him, her head raised slightly and tilted to one side. Her eyes did not meet his.

'Gorgeous,' said Totsakan. 'Exquisite.' And then, light-heartedly, 'The pearls too.'

Sida stood like a statue, though an imperceptible smile tested the corners of her mouth.

Totsakan turned and breathed a deep sigh. He looked away, but addressed Sida firmly. 'My affection for you is infinite. That means I am willing to wait ten thousand years for you to return my love. Since you have come into my life, I can think of nothing else.'

'I did not come into your life. You took me, against my will.'

Totsakan shut his eyes as if in pain, though he did not move. After a minute he turned calmly: 'It was destined.'

'I am not a plaything of fate,' Sida replied sharply.

'Perhaps not. You are also not a fool. So you know what is good for you.'

'I know that you are not good for me.'

'And I suppose you think that weak husband of yours is.'

'He is not weak.'

'He is a coward and a fraud. The first sign of a man who has no integrity is when he believes what his inferiors say about him. Surround a man with sycophants and his morals will choke in a cesspool of vanity. Everyone, including those chattering, seditious monkeys, says Prince Ram is the personification of virtue and so he believes it. Sadly, so do you.'

'Because it is true.'

'You know so little. About him. About life. I can guide you.'

Sida let out a scornful snicker. 'You? Guide me? What person is happy to be guided by her jailer? You have no idea about guidance, about loyalty, about the integrity that you are so quick to accuse others of lacking.'

Totsakan lifted his head and shut his eyes as if trying to control himself. 'I will show you what your hypocritical husband is capable of.' He turned to Mareet. 'Mareet, bring

Suparnakha.' The lackey saluted and left through the gate.

Sida kept her head turned away from Totsakan.

'Ram thinks he can win you back. He doesn't know how much blood will be spilt if he tries to do so. Do not underestimate me. I might be kind and gentle with you, but I have vast and insuperable powers that I will use to shield you from him and his immoral horde of baboons. I will not hesitate to kill them all. Those ridiculous children too.'

'Children?'

'Yes, children. So cowardly is your husband that he has now enlisted children to help him. Ha! What gutlessness! If he hides behind them, I will gladly execute them. I won't ask my soldiers to do it. I'll do it myself. I'm not afraid of killing. If I had not learned to kill, if I had not killed, I would not be here.'

'Sir!' Sida cried. 'Have you no heart, no soul?'

'Madam,' he said coldly, 'I do not. Such is the pain I have endured and such is my power as a result.'

Sida shut her eyes, but she could not hold back the tears. Tears of anger, of fear.

The gate swung open again and Mareet entered, followed by a female demon. Sida did not turn to look. Totsakan strode up to her and spun her round with one hand so she was facing the demon that had just entered the garden.

'Look,' he shouted at Sida. 'Look.'

She opened her eyes slowly.

'This is my sister Suparnakha. Look at her.'

Sida saw that the demon had no nose and just one ear. She was hideously scarred.

'This is the doing of your husband. Ugh, I cannot call him that. He does not deserve to be your husband. That impostor, that charlatan, Prince Ram. He set his brother on to her and this is what he did. Disfigured for life. Why do that? Would it not have been better to kill her?'

'That is not true,' countered Sida. 'Your sister tried to steal Prince Ram away from me but he wouldn't leave me. Ever. Your sister wouldn't take no for an answer and tried to kill me and Prince Lak saved me. You see, you and your sister don't understand love. It is not a game where you point to someone and say "I want you" and then they go with you. Or you kill to get what you want. What nonsense did your mother teach you?'

'You see,' cried Totsakan angrily, 'he lies to you, you believe his lies and now you think I too will believe them. What my mother taught me is that you cannot build a love on lies. I will save you from being the slave of that dishonest knave.'

'I will never be saved by you. Never. I will never do what you want me to do. Never.'

Totsakan laughed loudly, a dark, curdling laugh. 'You poor girl. Look at you,' he said coldly. 'One day, when they ask you if you became mine, who will believe you, when you have been with me for so long? Who will be sure that you have not become my wife? I am not just anyone. I am Totsakan.'

# CHAPTER
# EIGHTEEN

Rawin and Catt watched the suave monkey called Sayola disappear into the shadows. They looked at each other and shrugged. They were both slowly getting used to the idea that extraordinary things kept happening to them and that they had almost no understanding of how or why. And in this case, who. So they trudged on through the forest – now side by side – as they set out to find Ram's chalet.

Eventually, they managed to find the clearing that Catt recalled was the place she, Hanuman and Sukreep first met up with Ram when he had shot an arrow into a tree near them. She remembered that Sukreep had given some kind of coded call that alerted Ram to their presence. But she knew she couldn't imitate that. So she called Sukreep's name. She had to do it a few times before she heard someone approach. 'Hello, dear Catt, hello. I told them you would find Rawin.' It was Sukreep. 'I must say it is a relief to see you. I didn't doubt you, but I did worry about you. Come, there is food and company,' he said.

They made their way along a short narrow path through a thicket of trees towards the chalet, which Rawin and Catt could now see more clearly. Simple flickering lanterns lit the space with a warm glow as the natural light began to fade. Sturdy stilts that held up the entire structure were hewn from the trunks of the *payom* trees of the forest and the platform was made of shiny smooth teak. It was taller than most traditional Thai chalets but was still perfectly proportioned, with a steep roof covered in intricate leaf thatching. Towards the rear of the interior the building accommodated raised platforms on each side where there were enclosed sleeping quarters. In the middle of the floor there was a low table laden with plates of rice, fruit and fish as well as coconuts and jugs of water. As they approached, the children could see Ram, Lak and Hanuman seated cross-legged on the floor. Over at one side, on a pretty purple cushion, JaoJuk sat quietly watching everyone else, his face the picture of innocence.

'Welcome,' said Ram kindly. 'Please join us. Eat. Relax. You must be exhausted.'

'Thank you,' said Rawin first. 'I'm Rawin, by the way.'

'Yes, I have heard much about you, Rawin,' said Ram. 'Come, sit. Tell us what you two have been up to.'

'Hello JaoJuk,' said Rawin. JaoJuk nodded sweetly but didn't say anything. 'Thank you for helping me,' Rawin continued. 'That motorcycle was brilliant,' he laughed. JaoJuk nodded again.

'You're a star,' said Catt to JaoJuk. 'Seriously.' JaoJuk looked at her almost angelically.

Sukreep steered them to a bucket of rain water over to the side where they were able to wash their faces and hands before joining the others at the table.

Hanuman sprang up and headed over to Rawin. He clasped the boy's cheeks between his hands affectionately. 'Let me look at you, young man. I am so glad you are safely with us at last.'

'Thank you,' said Rawin politely.

'Where did you find him?' Ram asked Catt.

'Lost in the forest.'

'I wasn't lost.'

'You just didn't know where you were,' joked Hanuman. 'We are all lost in some way or other.'

Everyone laughed heartily.

'Tell us about the motorcycle,' said Ram.

Rawin looked over at JaoJuk who looked away as if to indicate that he had had nothing to do with any motorcycle.

'Well,' said Rawin. 'JaoJuk and I have this little arrangement.'

Hanuman and Sukreep laughed. Both had seen what that 'little arrangement' was able to achieve when Rawin and JaoJuk had conjured up the drone that saved Catt from being slain by the demon Channarong. Now Ram watched cheerfully as Catt smiled knowingly along with them, though he didn't know what it was that amused them. Not wishing to delay the merriment with questions, he implored them to sit and eat. The last of the daylight had faded by then and the happy scene deep in the forest glowed with twinkling lanterns and hummed with cheerful conversation. Rawin felt happy for the first time since they had been brought to this world.

'Hey, Rawin,' said Hanuman, 'catch.' Hanuman threw a heavy coconut at the boy, but just before it would have hit him, Hanuman flashed his long tail over his head and caught the coconut. 'Phew,' said Hanuman in mock fright, 'that was close.' Everyone laughed. Rawin, who at first looked a little worried, joined in the fun.

Then Hanuman jumped up and pulled a hideously ugly face and hunched his shoulders to make himself look scary. 'Me Channarong. Me greatest,' he cried out and hobbled repulsively towards Catt and stood over her. 'Me kill you, little girl,' he grunted like a demon. Catt smiled modestly. 'Channarong, Channarong, Channarong,' chanted Hanuman, pretending to be a crowd of demons and swaying with his back hunched and his arms dangling at his side, 'Channarong greatest.' Then abruptly he flipped over on his back and kicked his legs in the air. 'No, no, not kill me. You not little girl. You big girl. Very big girl. Bigger than Channarong. I go now, very fast.' Whereupon he cartwheeled across the chalet floor, wailing as everyone laughed out loud.

'Is that what happened?' laughed Ram. 'You fought off a demon, Catt?'

'Well,' she smiled humbly. 'With a little help from my friends.' She looked over at Rawin and then at JaoJuk. Rawin was laughing. A tiny smile formed in the corners of JaoJuk's mouth.

Ram raised his glass as if to announce a toast. 'Catt and Rawin, it is truly lovely to have you with us. Oh, and you too, little JaoJuk,' he added turning to the child. 'Hanuman and Sukreep have brought me great comfort and support and now they assure me you will do so too.'

There was a brief silence. The children looked at each other. It was Rawin who spoke first. 'Well, Prince Ram, it's a little complicated. As you can see, we are from another world and we don't really know why we are here. Sukreep says we are 'destined', but we are not sure what that means.' He hesitated for a few seconds and then added: 'Catt seems to understand it better than I.'

'Allow me,' said Sukreep politely, looking at Ram for his assent. He then turned back to the children. 'Perhaps it will help if I tell you why we are here – Hanuman and me. Then you might be able to see where you fit in.'

'Please, by all means do go ahead,' said Ram with authority.

'Children,' began Sukreep, 'Prince Ram was exiled from his kingdom to this forest by his father, the king. For fourteen years. The details are not important, but Prince Ram – being a loyal son – obeyed his father's wish and came here with his beautiful wife Sida and his devoted brother Prince Lak.' Sukreep held out a hand in the direction of Lak as if to introduce him. 'Because Prince Ram was of high birth, the gods provided him with this chalet so that he, Sida and Prince Lak would have proper shelter. The forest is not always safe, as you know.'

'We know,' Rawin, said nodding with exaggerated feeling. 'We know.'

The others laughed.

Sukreep continued: 'As you also know by now, the Spectre Totsakan abducted Sida. She is now imprisoned by him in his capital city, Langka.'

'Yes,' said Catt, 'we have seen the city. We also saw someone who we were sure was Sida.'

Ram sprang up. 'You have seen her?'

'Yes, at least we think it was her,' Catt replied.

'Where?'

'In a garden just beyond the walls of the palace.'

'Hanuman,' said Ram forcefully, 'you should go to find it first thing in the morning.'

'I shall,' said Hanuman dutifully.

'I would like to go too,' said Catt quickly, a little concerned that Ram had not automatically included her.

'Me too,' said Rawin, though less forcefully.

'I am sure Hanuman would not object,' Ram said, in a way that Rawin thought was half-hearted.

'No, no,' replied Hanuman eagerly. 'You would be most welcome to come along. Would you remember how to get there again?'

'I think so,' said Catt. Then she looked into the darkness of the forest. 'But not at night.'

An awkward silence followed. Rawin wondered why Ram hadn't specifically asked him and Catt to show them the way. After no one said anything further, Rawin changed the subject. 'Meanwhile, Sukreep, would you mind continuing with your story.'

'Yes, yes, of course,' said Sukreep. 'Right, where was I? Oh, yes, after Sida was abducted, the princes came across Hanuman in the forest. Prince Ram immediately knew that there was something special about Hanuman. Not just the way he looked, but also the way he conducted himself.' Sukreep stopped and then turned to Hanuman. 'You were there, nephew. Tell the children what happened.'

'Ha, ha,' chuckled Hanuman cheerfully. 'Prince Ram approached me and said he could tell there was something different about me. How he knew, I do not know because my powers were not evident. Anyway, my mother had told me that if anyone ever notices that there is something special about me, I should know that meant there was something special about him – and she said you should immediately offer to serve him. Which I did.'

'Yes, Hanuman,' interrupted Ram, 'but you demanded something first, didn't you?'

'Ha, yes,' laughed Hanuman, as if he had been caught out. 'I did. You see, there was a time when I had behaved not as I should have. My powers were strong and I, well, I did some things that were disapproved of and the gods put a curse on me that took away my powers. They said that the curse could only be removed if someone very virtuous stroked me three times from head to tail.'

'I am sure you can guess what happened next,' said Sukreep cheerfully. 'So, you see, this is why the grateful and mighty Hanuman, with his powers reinstated, is now the loyal lieutenant of the virtuous Prince Ram.'

'Enough now,' Ram said. 'You have a big day tomorrow. Scout the city and bring back intelligence so that we can prepare the rescue mission. You should not engage in any fighting. If you see Totsakan, don't approach him. Hanuman, if you can get to talk to Sida, give her this ring. She will not know you, but she will know this ring.'

'But what if we get a chance to save Sida?' asked Catt impulsively.

Ram breathed in and filled the space with an almost deafening silence. Then he turned slowly and looked at everyone: 'Sida is *my* wife. Totsakan is *my* enemy. This is *my* war. I know this Totsakan monster well. When the time comes, Totsakan is *mine* to kill.'

No one said anything. It was as if a father had disciplined his children. Sukreep ushered Catt and Rawin away. He took them up to one of the raised platforms of the chalet where there were spaces for them to sleep separated by a bamboo screen. He gave them each a rolled-up mat to lie on and a small pillow for their heads. JaoJuk had said he would be fine on his own, that he preferred it that way.

After everyone settled down for the night, Rawin whispered Catt's name through the screen.

'What?' she responded, also in a whisper.

'What are you thinking?'

'Nothing, really. Just how to find the city tomorrow.'

'No doubts?'

'About what?'

'You know – whether we are doing the right thing.'

'Don't start that again, Rawin, please.'

'But we've got to think it through. I get the feeling we are just drifting along with events.'

'Maybe that's because we don't really have any choice,' said Catt dismissively.

'We do. You know we do.'

'I'm OK with drifting along.'

'You know what worries me,' said Rawin.

'What?'

'They never did get round to telling us where we fit in. And they told us why Hanuman is here, but they didn't tell us about Sukreep.'

'True. But why does that worry you?'

'You don't know the story, then?' asked Rawin.

'Not that bit.'

'So you don't know that Prince Ram killed Sukreep's brother and placed Sukreep on the throne, and that's why Sukreep sent his army to fight for Ram?'

# CHAPTER NINETEEN

Shade and light danced across the chalet as the surrounding trees fractured the rays of the morning sun. Catt emerged from her sleeping nook and saw JaoJuk doing yoga on the edge of the platform. She smiled at him. He didn't move but raised the corners of his mouth just enough to convey friendly acknowledgement of her greeting and then shifted into a cross-legged pose and closed his eyes dreamily.

'Sleep well?' came a welcoming voice from nearby. It was Sukreep.

'Yes, thank you,' Catt replied. 'It's very peaceful here in the forest. The night was so silent. Not like Bangkok. It was almost too quiet to sleep.'

'I know you miss it,' said Sukreep kindly. 'One day you will be able to go home.'

Catt didn't respond for a minute or two. Then she said: 'Mr Sukreep, you have been very caring about me and Rawin. Thank you for that. I suppose that's because it was you who brought us here.'

'I was just the emissary.'

'For whom?' asked Catt softly.

'Virtue,' he replied.

'You mean, like righteousness?'

'Yes.'

'Is the hermit Rishi righteous?'

'He knows what is righteous, who is righteous.'

'Does he know other things?'

'I think he knows everything.'

Catt thought for a while and said: 'Mr Sukreep, you said Rishi would be able to tell us how to go home.'

'Yes.'

'You were right, he did. He promised us we would be able to. But he said something that Rawin and I did not understand.'

'What was that, precious girl?'

'He said, 'You will not defeat the evil one unless you go home, but you cannot go home until you have defeated the evil one.''

Sukreep frowned but didn't say anything.

'What does that mean?' Catt asked.

After a long silence, Sukreep said: 'I do not know. I am sorry. But what I do know is that the wise Rishi firmly believes it is our duty to do this.'

'Duty to do what?'

'Serve righteousness.'

'You mean serve those who tell us they are righteous?' came a voice from the side of the platform. It was Rawin. He joined Sukreep and Catt sitting on the floor. There were bowls of rice soup spread out on the low table. Sukreep looked at Rawin with sad eyes.

'Not those who *say* they are righteous, Rawin,' said Sukreep. 'Those who *are* righteous.'

'And how do we know that a man is righteous?' asked Rawin.

'From what he does.'

'Is it OK if what he does is that he kills?' asked Rawin calmly.

'Rawin,' interrupted Catt firmly, but she didn't say more.

'Children,' said Sukreep after a brief silence, 'there is much that we do not know in life and much that we do not understand. But we are able to know what we must do. For example, we know that we should love and respect our parents and other members of our family. We know too that we should do our duty, whatever we are called upon to do.'

'Is it your duty to serve someone who killed your brother?' said Rawin coldly.

Sukreep looked like he had been struck by a dagger in the heart. He opened his mouth to speak, but before he could, Ram bounded on to the platform from the clearing in front of the chalet. 'Morning, everyone,' he said cheerfully. 'I hope you all slept well. Eat, please eat. Brother Lak has prepared a hearty breakfast.'

'Thank you. It does look very good,' said Catt quickly to break the dark mood before Ram detected it.

'Come, come,' said Ram, 'the rice soup is very tasty. Sukreep, please go and help your nephew prepare for his trip.'

'Yes, Sir,' said Sukreep, and he sprang up and headed around the back of the chalet.

The children ate heartily. They were very hungry and the rice soup was, as Ram had said, very good. He left them without saying anything more. Catt looked at Rawin but he didn't meet her eyes. He looked out towards the forest as if he was trying to understand something very complex. Catt decided she wouldn't try to say anything, but she felt a heaviness in her heart.

Soon they were on their way – the two of them together with Hanuman who seemed eager to make quick progress in the search for Langka. The children had not come to the chalet direct from the hill above the city – they had first gone to Totsakan's cave – and so they had only a vague sense of where to go. They were pleased when Hanuman showed firm leadership and headed boldly into the forest.

The journey was longer than Rawin and Catt had expected. Their previous excursions through the forest had been so fraught with dangers and unexpected incidents that they had lost all sense of time and space. After a few hours Hanuman suggested they rest. They found a circular clearing in the forest where a fallen tree served as a bench. Rawin took some fruit out of his backpack and offered it to the others. 'Prince Lak insisted we bring this,' he explained. They quenched their thirst from a stream of crystal clear water nearby.

Munching through an apple, Hanuman turned to Catt. 'You remember when that monster Channarong nearly killed you?'

'I've been trying to forget that,' chuckled Catt.

'Well, you need to make sure you don't get into a mess like that again.'

'Maybe ban umbrellas?' quipped Rawin. 'Catt would never have been beaten if Totsakan hadn't blotted out the sun.'

'Yes, but what if there is no sun to reflect off your sword? Or what if you drop your sword or it's knocked from your hand?'

'I'll run,' said Catt.

They all laughed.

Hanuman stood up and stretched his arms out in front of him. As he did so, Catt and Rawin watched in amazement as his arms got longer and longer. Then he placed his hands under his chin and pushed upwards, which made his body grow taller. Then he kicked his right leg out and it grew. Then the left one. By now he was about 9 feet tall. 'That's about right,' he said, looking down on Catt and Rawin. 'Just one more thing.' He grabbed his nose between his thumb and forefinger and twisted it until it was round and twice the size it was and very ugly. Then he put both forefingers in the sides of his mouth and pulled in opposite directions until his mouth was grotesquely wide. 'How's that look?' he laughed. 'You can call me Channarong.'

Catt and Rawin looked aghast and chuckled nervously.

'Now come,' said Hanuman waving his hand at Catt. 'Stop me from killing you.'

Catt looked at him uncertainly and then walked cautiously over towards him. The two stood facing each other in the middle of the clearing. Hanuman signalled with his hand that she should come closer. 'Come on. Hit me.'

'Hit you?'

'Yes.'

'Where?'

'Anywhere. Try to kill me before I kill you.'

'Pretend?'

'No. Try. Properly. Don't worry, you won't succeed.'

Catt threw a glance at Rawin who smiled nervously but cocked his head to indicate that she should go on. She stood dead still and looked back at Hanuman. Then in a movement so fast Rawin hardly saw it, she spun on one leg towards Hanuman, pivoting through the air as her foot came within inches of the monkey's demon-like face. More quickly, however, Hanuman held up one arm, parrying Catt's outstretched leg and with the other arm threw her to the ground. She grunted as the breath left her lungs.

Annoyed, Catt lifted herself slowly from the ground and faced up to Hanuman again. He braced himself, though he was smiling. 'Come on. Again.'

The girl launched herself, spinning like a top twice in mid-air, her legs rotating so fast that they appeared as a blur to Rawin. Hanuman crossed his arms in front of his face and took the full force of the blow as Catt's leg completed its rotation with immense speed. Hanuman didn't flinch. Catt dropped to the ground like a stone, falling onto her back. 'Ugh,' she said, half from exertion and half from frustration.

'OK,' said Hanuman, 'you don't want that happening too often.'

'True,' said Catt dejectedly, getting up off the ground.

'So, what should you have done?'

'Not sure.'

'Come, I'll show you.' Hanuman smacked his face a couple of times and wriggled his body and hips until he returned to his normal shape and size.

'That's better,' said Rawin with a laugh. 'You had me worried there for a minute.'

'Now,' Hanuman went on, 'it's your turn to be the demon.'

'Wait,' cried Catt, 'you're not going to make me look like that, are you?'

'Don't worry,' laughed Hanuman, whereupon he crossed his arms over his chest and gripped his shoulders and squeezed. In seconds he was less than half his size. 'Now, you're the big demon and I'm little you.'

Catt let out a gasp that was half shock and half laugh.

'You're nuts.'

'You are what you eat. Come on, let's fight.'

Catt threw a puzzled look at Rawin and turned back to Hanuman who was standing in the ready position as if he was Catt ready for a fight.

'Come on, Channarong,' said Hanuman, 'kill the little girl.'

Catt did her best to wade into Hanuman like a demon, swinging her arms and legs and lunging her body at him. In a split second Hanuman sidestepped and slipped round behind her, double-kicking her behind both knees. Catt crumpled like a rag doll. Then Hanuman pivoted his whole body on one foot and swung the other at frightening speed a fraction of a centimetre from Catt's face as she remained slumped on her hands and knees.

'Hey, careful,' shouted Rawin, getting up from where he had been seated on the tree trunk.

'It's OK,' said Catt. 'I'm alright.'

'Of course you are,' said Hanuman. He gave both his thighs one firm smack with both hands and grew back to his normal size. Then he held out his hand to her. She took it and he pulled her up. 'Remember, go for the back of the knees. Double kick. Once they are down, then you can kick at the head.'

'Goddit,' said Catt.

Hanuman put an arm around Catt's shoulders as they walked back to the tree trunk to rest. Rawin watched them with a slightly puzzled look on his face. He was still wondering if Catt was OK. And he hadn't fully recovered from thinking Hanuman was going to kick her in the head. She sat down and dusted off her clothes. She had fully regained her composure and smiled at Rawin reassuringly.

Before anyone was able to say anything more they heard the sound of thundering feet coming towards them.

'Demons,' said Hanuman with alarm. 'Probably a scouting unit from Langka. Quick, Rawin, get down to the river and hide. Catt, stand with me.' Rawin did as he was told and disappeared into a clump of ferns. Catt and Hanuman drew their swords and waited as the sound came closer. 'There's a lot of them,' said Hanuman.

Through the trees at terrifying speed came the first demon, grunting and snorting angrily. In a flash Hanuman swept his sword across its midriff, bringing forth a blood-curdling scream as the demon's guts spilled out and it thundered to the ground, convulsing.

'More coming,' cried Hanuman as three more demons hurtled into the clearing and came to a halt in front of them. They looked at the first demon that lay in an ever-widening pool of oozing yellow blood. Their eyes shifted from the monkey to the girl and then back to the monkey as they tried to size them up. Then they looked at each other as if awaiting guidance. 'You know what to do,' whispered Hanuman to Catt.

Hanuman leapt into the air and grabbed a branch above him with his left hand while swinging his sword menacingly in the direction of the demons. As they looked up at him anxiously, they failed to notice Catt, who had sheathed her sword, moving at lightning speed around behind them. Rawin watched from his hiding place but couldn't be sure that what he was seeing was actually happening. It was so fast he thought he must have been imagining it. Shimmering from the speed with which she moved, Catt delivered devastating double-kicks across the backs of the knees of all three demons in rapid succession. They dropped one by one, and as they lifted their heads to try to work out what had happened, Hanuman launched himself from the branch he was holding and flew through the air slicing each of the demons' throats in turn. He half-laughed out loudly: 'That's my girl.'

But it wasn't over. There were more; still a little way off, but approaching fast. Catt noticed that Rawin had left his hiding place and was scampering up a tree nearby. She saw him quickly gathering vines and twisting them together. Hanuman was listening intently to the sound of the advancing demons. 'There must be at least five or six of them,' he said. 'Not good.'

'We can do it,' said Catt drawing her sword and feeling its weight as she cradled it in her hands. She looked towards where they could hear the sound of the demons approaching. 'Come if you dare,' she growled. Hanuman looked admiringly at her and drew his sword. They stood shoulder to shoulder, legs astride. The drumming of the demons' feet sounded like thunder. The grunts and snarling became clearer. Then it was the breathing. Heavier, louder. Through the trees no more than thirty yards away they came. Not five or six, as Hanuman had thought, but about twenty of them, stumbling and bashing against each other as they galloped forward, snorting and hissing with rage.

'Catt, Hanuman, here, quick,' shouted Rawin. He was standing on a branch about 20 yards behind them holding on to other branches around him. Beside him hung a knotted rope of vines. 'Come, up here.'

Hanuman looked at the demons and turned. 'Girl, follow me.' He began to scamper at full speed towards the tree where Rawin was standing. 'Come, come.' Catt obeyed. Hanuman took off and seized the hanging vine rope with both hands, swinging up into the trees. As he did so, he spun himself over and clutched the vines between his feet, dangling with his arms free as he swung back. 'Jump,' he called to Catt. She leapt gracefully into the air, with her arms up, clasping Hanuman's hands in hers like a trapeze artist as he swung back again up into the tree. As she reached the highest point of their swing she let go of Hanuman's hands and dropped on to a sturdy branch, spun round and squatted like an alert squirrel. Hanuman, meanwhile, let go of the vines and flitted up through branches as only a monkey can.

On came the demons, almost falling over each other with bloodlust. They poured across the clearing and into the space beneath Hanuman and the children, looking up, roaring and gnashing their teeth and scowling with their hideous faces. As they did so, the ground beneath them began to swallow them up. They thrashed and screamed and wailed, but down they went, not one by one, but almost all together until they were gone.

'Quicksand,' said Catt excitedly. She turned to Rawin. 'How did you know?'

'Well,' Rawin said, 'I noticed that the grains of sand around here are elongated rather than spherical and that the stream down there was actually being fed by an alluvial spring. That combination creates gaps between the grains and you get ...,' he held out his hand as if introducing the scene below them, '… quicksand.'

'Of course,' said Catt with affectionate awe. 'You would know that, wouldn't you.'

# CHAPTER TWENTY

Hanuman offered Rawin a hand and then swung down from the tree with the boy holding on to him. Catt followed.

'You're a smart lad, Rawin,' said Hanuman, letting go of his hand once Rawin was safely beyond the quicksand. 'Thank you.'

Rawin smiled modestly.

'Let's hope we don't come across more scouts like that lot,' said Hanuman. 'Maybe it means we are getting close to the city. Come, time to move on.'

It wasn't long before they began to hear the distant sound of voices, occasional laughing and the hubbub of market life. Hanuman led them to the end of the forest and, with one hand gesturing behind him, signalled that they should follow cautiously. Soon they could see the walls of the city about a hundred yards off. The moat around it seemed much wider than the children remembered from when they spied on the city from the hilltop the previous day. In the centre of the wall that faced them was a gate, but no bridge across the moat or any other visible means to reach it.

'Mmm,' murmured Hanuman, 'I wonder how they cross it.'

'Elephants,' said Rawin.

'Where can we get one?' replied Hanuman. He laughed. The children chuckled too.

'JaoJuk should have come with us,' Catt said. 'I wouldn't be surprised if he could magic up an elephant.'

Rawin felt in the pocket on the side of his backpack for his phone and pulled it out. 'No signal,' he announced.

'Well, never mind,' continued Hanuman, 'let's take a closer look and see what magic we can make of our own.' Catt looked at Rawin with a quizzical expression. Rawin whispered to her with a smile: 'He has powers, remember.'

Hanuman led them stealthily along the edge of a ditch that provided them some cover so they couldn't be seen from the city. There were no lookouts or sentries on the wall, but they assumed someone – or something – might be keeping an eye out. There were enough clusters of shrubs and brush to protect them as they progressed to within a few feet of the moat.

'Right,' said Hanuman, 'you stay here until I get back. Won't be long.' The children watched in disbelief as Hanuman shrank down to the size of an ant and sped off across the remaining dry land and pitched himself into the water. A v-shaped wake formed behind the now tiny monkey as he sped towards the city walls.

The children sat in silence after Hanuman had disappeared from sight.

'I feel a bit helpless,' Rawin said eventually.

'Unhelpful, more like it,' Catt said. 'I hate sitting around waiting for someone else to do something.'

Rawin looked at her and sighed: 'Yes, I know.'

Another few minutes passed. Then Catt stood up but remained stooped to keep out of sight. 'Come on. We can't just sit and wait.' She started creeping towards the water's edge. Rawin followed.

'You have a plan?' he asked lamely.

'Not yet, but there must be a way.'

As they reached the water, a bird-like creature with a long graceful neck drifted up to them. Rawin looked at Catt.

'It's a swan from the mythical Himmapon Forest,' Catt said. 'You can see carvings of them on the roofs of buildings all over Thailand.'

'How do you know that?'

'My father is a professor of architecture, remember.'

'OK, that's useful. Is it friend or foe?' asked Rawin.

'Friend,' said the swan.

Catt and Rawin looked at each other astonished. When Catt looked back at the bird, she noticed that it was staring directly into her eyes.

'Come on,' said the swan. Just two words, so melodic that it felt to Catt like the sound of a loving mother beckoning her child. She looked back again at Rawin who nodded his head forward. 'Both of you,' said the swan.

Catt waded carefully into the water and breast-stroked gently to the bird. 'Hold on to my wing,' said the swan. 'Now you,' she said, turning towards Rawin. The boy took off his backpack and held it up with one hand so that it would stay dry. He drifted up to the swan and took hold of its other wing. 'Mind my feet,' said the swan as she began to paddle forward towards the city wall. The children looked at each other in contented resignation.

'My name is Meeya,' the swan told them.

'Hello Meeya,' the girl said. 'I'm Catt. This is Rawin.'

'I am so pleased to meet you, Catt and Rawin. We have been waiting for you to come.'

'We?' asked Rawin.

'My brother and I.'

The children looked around but there were no other swans. Aware that they were confused, the swan explained: 'My brother, my twin, and I were separated and cursed by the evil that has plagued our land. He was turned into a monkey and I, well, you can see what happened to me.'

'Ugh, that must be sad for you,' said Catt.

'Yes, we were always together. But now we cannot be. I am imprisoned in this moat and he is alone in the forest.'

'Wait,' said Rawin quickly. 'His name isn't perhaps Sayola, is it?'

'Yes,' said Meeya, 'It sounds like you might have met him.'

'Met him!' laughed Rawin. 'He saved our lives.'

'That sounds like him,' said Meeya affectionately.

'Tell us, Meeya,' Catt said, 'what did you mean when you said you had been waiting for us to come?'

'For centuries our land was at peace and the people lived and worked without strife or hostility. But grandparents passed down to their grandchildren a warning that the day would come when this peace would be shattered and conflict would stalk the land. And they said it was written that when that happened a boy and a girl would come and restore what was lost.'

'Written?' Rawin asked.

'By the sages, the wise hermits. They knew.'

The swan continued to paddle while the children held as loosely as they could to her wings so as not to hurt her. They said nothing for a short while. Then it was Rawin who spoke again: 'Are you talking about us?'

'You are exactly as the grandmothers described in their stories,' said Meeya.

'What did they say?'

'That the girl would be brave and the boy would be smart.'

The children went silent. Meeya paddled on.

'And now that we are here, what happens?' asked Rawin.

'I don't know,' replied Meeya, 'but I do know that something inside me said I should help you do whatever it is you are trying to do because in your own time you will help me. And Sayola.'

'And what do you think we are trying to do?' asked Rawin.

'Reach the other side of the moat.'

'And then?'

'I don't know.'

'Yet you are willing to help us?'

'Yes.'

'But how can you be sure that what we are going to do will restore peace to your land?' asked Rawin. Then after a short pause he said irritably: '*We* don't even know what we are going to do, so how can you be sure that you should help us? We might be on the wrong side.'

'The grandmother's tales did not say who would be right

and who would be wrong. Only that there would be no peace until the boy and the girl came. And now here you are.'

'That doesn't make sense,' Rawin shot back. 'Did Sayola save our lives for the same reason? Just because we are a boy and a girl? We might be a bad boy and a bad girl and not even know it ourselves.'

'Rawin,' said Meeya with gentle affection, 'you do not look to me like a bad boy. In any case, it is what you do, or don't do, that is good or bad. A person who is not always good can sometimes do good. A person who is mostly good can sometimes do bad things. Do we have to choose a side?'

'That's my point,' said Rawin calmly. 'By helping us you *are* choosing a side, but you don't know which side we are on, because *we* don't.'

Catt interrupted quickly. 'Oh, Rawin, can't you see? Meeya believes in us.'

'We should only believe in what we can see,' he said flatly.

'For me and Sayola,' said Meeya, 'all we have is belief. And prayer.'

'Well, Meeya,' Catt said. 'I am going to make sure your belief and your prayers are not futile. After all, Sayola saved our lives. We owe it to him, if nothing else. We will help restore peace to your land.'

'Aha,' said Meeya as they arrived at the other side of the moat. 'Bold and smart. Go, be safe.'

# CHAPTER TWENTY-ONE

Rawin put his backpack on the ground and squeezed out some of the water from his clothes. Catt did the same. The sun was strong and they knew they would soon dry out.

'Come on, let's get out of sight,' said Catt running towards the gateway. She tapped her sword to reassure herself. Rawin put on his backpack and followed closely as they entered the city. They stayed close to the wall and stopped as soon as they were through the gateway, scanning what lay ahead. Two demons were sitting side by side on wooden stools grunting cheerfully and quaffing foul-looking liquid from huge mugs.

'Gate guards,' whispered Rawin.

'Not very good ones,' Catt replied. 'Come on.' She shot silently down an alley to the right of the demons and beckoned to Rawin to follow. Now they could see a busy market. Crouching low, they scampered from one stall to the next, keeping their heads down and ducking behind baskets, barrels and barrows as they went.

Hiding between the wheels of an ox cart they watched in amazement as a thronging horde of demons went about their business, almost like any day in a Bangkok suburban market.

They grunted and slobbered and snorted, but other than that they seemed weirdly normal. Some were followed closely by little demons, who Rawin and Catt assumed must have been their children.

Beyond the market there appeared to be a labyrinth of crisscrossing roads and alleyways and in the distance the children could see pagodas and bell-shaped domes reaching into the sky in a complex of palace buildings, including ornately decorated temples of varying sizes. They stretched up a hillside so that the buildings at the top were high above the city.

'We need to see what's going on in there,' Catt said.

'Yeah,' replied Rawin, 'but how are we going to get there without being seen?'

'We hide in plain sight.'

'And how do we do that?'

'See over there – that stall selling khon theatre masks. Except they aren't demon masks, they're human masks. There must be a tradition here among the demons of performing plays with humans in them, like we do in khon theatre, only the other way round, if you know what I mean.'

The children checked out the stall. There were full body suits as well as face masks for adults, but also smaller ones for children. A few adult demons and their children were rummaging through the wares on sale, some holding suits against themselves to see how they looked and laughing as they did.

'Fancy dress,' said Rawin astonished. 'They've got fancy dress suits for children to dress up to look like humans.'

'Yes,' Catt said, 'and are you thinking what I'm thinking?'

'Yes, but you must be crazy.'

'You too, because you're thinking it as well. Come.' Catt scampered past some baskets and darted between rows of scarves and shawls that provided good cover. Rawin followed.

'Do you see at the far end of the stall, there are some that would fit us just fine,' Catt said. 'There's an old Chinese mandarin suit that would look good on you.'

'Seriously?' responded Rawin.

'Yes. I promise never to tell anyone.'

'And you?'

'I want to be one of those soldiers with the armoured breast plate and the helmet that looks like a bell. Like the ones that entertain tourists at Ayutthaya. Whenever we visited there I used to stare at them and wanted to be like them.'

'You would,' sighed Rawin.

'It was my dream job.'

'No time to dream now,' responded Rawin. 'It's never going to work.'

'Have faith,' Catt replied with a smile. 'We can do this.'

'But we can't buy the outfits. The stallholder will raise the alarm.'

'Rawin,' Catt said, sounding like his mother. 'This is the one time in your life when you will do something bad.' She paused, and then added: 'We're going to steal them.'

'Ha, ha,' responded Rawin with false amusement. 'I've been bad before.'

'Really? How exciting. What did you do?'

'Not telling.'

'OK,' she said, more seriously, 'here goes.' She crept silently round the back of the stall until she reached the far side. He watched as she deftly lifted the soldier suit and mask off the hanger and slung it over her arm. Then she did the same with the Chinese one and sped like a thieving cat back to where Rawin was still hidden among the shawls.

'Right, just pull it over your clothes and put the mask on.'

They moved quickly and in a matter of minutes they were transformed into a traditional soldier and a Chinese palace official with human faces. For Catt the mask, which was of a very fierce looking guard, extended upward into a bell-shaped helmet. She had a plastic breastplate and plastic sword. Her real sword was well hidden under the costume. Rawin placed the black scholar's cap on his head and held a scroll in his hand. His backpack bulged a little under his suit, but he thought it wouldn't be very noticeable.

'Now we just have to hope demons have a sense of fun,' said Rawin. 'A couple of tiny demon kids on their way to a fancy dress party.'

'OK,' Catt said a little hesitantly, 'let's go. Try to walk a bit heavily, like a demon. You know, stomp a little bit. But also try to walk like you're happy – on the way to a party.'

'Heavily, happily. OK, here goes.'

'You know what I mean.'

Silently they headed away from the stall in the hope that they wouldn't be seen running off with stolen goods. They wound their way to the market's edge and on to a cobbled stone street that led to the palace complex.

After a little while Rawin regained enough confidence to speak. 'Sorry to say this, but you're not walking much like a demon, Catt.'

'Really, what's wrong?'

'Not heavy enough.'

'Ha-ha.'

'No seriously. You're too cool. Like you're walking on to a taekwondo floor ready to fight. Stop dreaming about being a soldier in Ayutthaya.'

Catt lifted her feet a bit more and clunked them down firmly, but also put a bit of a happy sway in her hips.

'That's better.'

They clunked on for a while, past wooden houses on stilts with steeply sloping thatched roofs. Some had balconies or front porches on the ground floor. Old trees towered over many of the houses, casting them into welcome shade under the blazing sun. Occasionally they saw demons sitting in front of their homes watching them coming down the street. The children waved enthusiastically and put an extra bounce in their steps. It seemed to work as they were greeted with friendly waves back.

As they got closer to the palace complex they saw someone, something, standing in the middle of the road. It was the size of a full-grown demon but it didn't look like a demon – not from far off. It seemed to be watching them approach.

'Act normal,' Catt said.

'Normal? We're two humans pretending to be demons dressed like humans. So what the hell does normal mean here?'

'Just carry on pretending we're going to a fancy dress

party. Walk cheerfully.'

'Difficult to do when your knees are shaking. What is that thing?'

Catt, who was slightly ahead of him, could see that whatever it was, it didn't look like just any old demon. It wasn't dressed in conventional demon pants and tunic. In fact it wore a full-length white gown. It stood dead still in the middle of the road as they approached.

'Er, this doesn't look good,' Catt said. She felt her blood turn cold.

Then the being burst explosively into action and ran straight at them. The children were struck motionless with fear as they saw that it was, like them, wearing a mask. But it was a mask that was shaped like a face but had no eyes and no nose, just a round hole where its mouth should have been. It stopped right in front of Catt and bent down, thrusting its face an inch from hers. She could hear it snorting quietly and she could smell its foul breath exuding from the creepy looking hole where its mouth should have been. She looked straight at it, but there were no eyes for her to look into. She screamed.

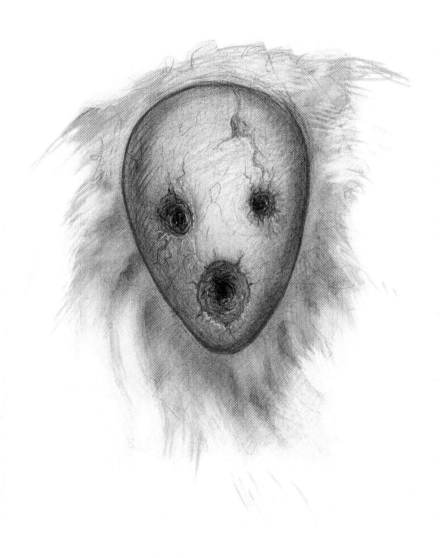

# CHAPTER TWENTY-TWO

Catt's scream seemed to stun the creature. It immediately spun round and galloped back along the road where it had come from, disappearing down a side alley.

The children stood in breathless silence for a minute, then Catt spoke: 'I have never, ever, ever been so terrified in all my life.'

'That makes two of us,' replied Rawin. 'What the hell was that?'

'God only knows.'

Rawin quickly realised that Catt's scream might have attracted unwanted attention. 'Come on, we'd better get out of here before someone comes to find out what that was all about.'

'True,' Catt said, snapping back into action mode. 'Come on. Down here.' She led the way down a narrow alley bordered on both sides by tall leafy trees that offered some shelter in case anyone came to investigate. After a while she pressed her back against one of the trees and lifted her head and eyes upwards, as if she was looking to the heavens for comfort. 'Breathe,' she said to herself. 'In. Out. In. Out.' Rawin, for whom the experience had been only slightly less frightening, stood by in sympathy. 'I reckon in the end it was more scared than you were,' he joked.

They stood there for a few more minutes. Then Rawin chuckled and said: 'I'd almost forgotten how ridiculous you look.'

'Ridiculous? Don't I look like a fierce brave soldier?'

'No.'

'And *you* don't look ridiculous?'

'Do I?'

'It's the hat. That silly Chinese scholar thing. It looks more like a helicopter propeller.'

'Well, thank you for that.'

'Seriously? I don't look like a brave soldier?'

'Only when you're not dressed up like that.'

They agreed to make their way towards the palace complex. They returned to the main street where they had encountered the strange creature and resumed their pretence of being two happy children going to a party. If anyone had been alarmed at the scream, there still seemed no sign of concern among the demons trudging along the road to and from the market. Things appeared quite normal.

When they were no more than about a hundred yards from the palace they came across a pretty park. Music and laughter filled the air.

'Catt, look,' urged Rawin. 'There it is. There's that thing.'

In the park dozens of children were running around laughing and screaming as the faceless being in the white gown rushed up to them and pretended to scare them. Except they weren't children. They were young demons dressed as human children.

'It's a fancy dress party,' said Rawin in disbelief. 'Can you believe it? A demon fancy dress party!'

'And the scary guy is part of the fun.'

'You know what – I think it probably thought we were on our way to join them.'

'Until I screamed like a banshee.'

'Now I feel sorry for it.'

'I don't. My knees are still knocking.'

They watched the party from a safe distance. Soon some

of the demon children began running up and down the wide stone stairway entrance to the palace. The guards ignored them as the children laughed and circled round and back to the party and then back again on to the stairway.

'Come on, here's our chance,' Catt said. 'Let's join them and carry on up those steps. Let's go.'

They headed first towards the party in the park and then joined a small group of demon children running towards the palace. They followed closely up the first few steps and then ran along the landing and down again and circled up the other side. As they did so, Catt noticed that the guard at that end was looking in the other direction. 'Come on,' she said, sprinting straight up the next flight of steps close to the low wall that framed the entrance. In a flash they were both beyond the guard, reaching the next landing, which consisted of an attractive mix of fountains and stone statues interspersed with shrubs and artistic topiary. Ahead of them was a large pavilion of exquisite beauty. Female demons, apparently servants-in-waiting, knelt elegantly on either side of the building chattering away to each other and apparently not aware of the children's presence as they sheltered behind the garden features.

'Stop,' Catt whispered. 'I can see Hanuman.'

'Where?'

'Shhhh.' She pointed and they watched as Hanuman concealed himself behind one of two lion statues at the entrance to the pavilion. He was watching with intense interest.

They edged closer to the doorway. They could see Totsakan inside drinking and laughing, surrounded by his harem, one of whom was lying on her side next to him. Hanuman became agitated, swinging his body back and forth behind the lion statue, his tail whipping up and down. He held his hands to his eyes, then to his ears in wild agitation.

'Now put your hands over your mouth too,' Catt said to Hanuman, who swung around in surprise. 'Monkey see no evil, hear no evil, speak no evil,' she said.

'Huh…?' began Hanuman.

Catt quickly removed her mask. Hanuman looked puzzled for a few seconds and then understood. 'Hanuman,

Hanuman,' she said. 'Stay calm.'

'But Sida is lost to Prince Ram,' said Hanuman with a mixture of anger and despair. 'Look at her.'

'No, no,' said Catt quickly. 'That is not Sida. You don't know what she looks like. I do. Those are Totsakan's other playmates.'

Hanuman turned back to look anxiously into the pavilion again.

'Sida is imprisoned in a garden on the edge of the city,' Catt went on. 'I can remember where it is. Come on.'

Hanuman cast one more anxious look at the scene inside the pavilion. Totsakan had slumped drunkenly into sleep beside the woman who lay with him. A goblet had been knocked over and red wine spilled out of it, dripping down the stairs. Hanuman scurried over to the children.

'Come on. It's this way,' Catt said. She led them silently through the small roads that separated the palace buildings.

'There's the gate,' she said eventually. 'She is in there.'

Two overweight demons were slumped on stools on either side of the gate fast asleep, snoring. Hanuman sprang forward and ducked to one side of the gateway, peering through the iron grating. Then he shrank himself down until he was small enough to fit through the gaps.

'Quick, over here,' Catt said to Rawin, grabbing him by the hand and leading him quickly into the dense foliage of a cluster of White Elephant palms, letting go of his hand as soon as they were under cover. They shuffled through the giant bladed leaves until they reached the fence that encircled Sida's garden prison. They could see clearly as Hanuman darted across the lawn to where a woman was sitting alone at a table arranging flowers. Before she was able to see him, Hanuman restored himself to his full size and approached the woman from behind.

'Sida's in for a shock,' Rawin whispered to Catt.

'Hanuman will handle it, don't worry,' Catt replied. They listened intently as Hanuman drew his hands together in the traditional sign of respect, dropped to one knee and bowed his head low. 'Good madam, do please pardon my intrusion.'

Sida spun round, looking alarmed.

Hanuman continued: 'Most esteemed and honourable lady, I beg your forbearance. You do not know me. My name is Hanuman. I come as an emissary on behalf of your revered and noble husband.'

'You?' responded Sida, 'A monkey. You speak for my husband? Is there no end to this nightmare?'

Hanuman remained down on one knee. 'A nightmare indeed, Madam. But not of my making. The evil Totsakan is the author of your nocturnal torment. I, on the other hand, have been sent to wake you from your anguish.'

'It is your turn to forgive me, monkey, but I have to be honest and tell you I have no faith that you could do anything for me except offend my eyes. Please go.'

Hanuman stood up and opened both hands, holding his head slightly bowed and adopting a look of gentle assurance. 'Madam, I understand your hesitation. If I were you and you were me, I would indeed disregard my entreaties.'

'You cannot know what it is to be me. And I thank the gods that I would never know what it is to be you.'

'How can she be so unfeeling after he has put on such a performance?' Rawin asked.

'What do you expect?' Catt said, rolling her eyes. 'That she should weep and wail like in a soap opera? You underestimate her.'

Hanuman walked around until he was in front of Sida again. 'Pray, Madam, trust me. Prince Ram sent me and awaits your return. Come with me.'

'Sir,' said Sida sorrowfully. 'I cannot go with you. If indeed you know him as you say you do, tell him to come and retrieve my body, for I have given up all hope.'

In desperation Sida turned abruptly and stumbled in disarray from the garden and through the gate. The sun had set by now and all that was left of the day was a blue-tinged silver streak across the sky. Hanuman stood perplexed for a moment, unsure what to do next. But then he followed her.

The children decided they should not try to follow because it was not yet dark enough for them to remain unseen. Instead they made their way to the far side of the garden to see if there was another route out. But first they removed their fancy dress and masks before scurrying along the walls, looking and feeling for an opening or another gate. But they couldn't find any.

'I know,' Catt said quietly. 'I can get up the wall and check out what's on the other side.'

'Up the wall?' Rawin said.

'Yeah, like this.' She looked around the garden to make sure no one could see her and then walked back several paces. Then she ran like a gymnast towards the wall and lifted one foot on to it, using that foot to propel herself upward. In mid-air she raised one arm above her head to balance her body as her other foot touched higher up the wall. Then she threw all her weight upward until she was able to clutch the top of the wall with both hands, pivoting her body until she was able to sit. She looked down at Rawin with a smile. 'See?'

'Yeah, great. Now it's my turn to run up walls, right?'

'Just a minute. Let me see what's over this side.' She swivelled her body round and sat looking out. 'It's getting dark,' she said in a half-whisper.

'Good,' replied Rawin without feeling but still worried that they might be seen. He saw Catt slide herself off the wall and heard the faint sound of her feet landing on the ground on the other side. He decided to sit and wait. What else could he do?

About five minutes later a thick rope descended slowly from the top of the wall above his head.

'Rawin, grab this,' Catt said in a loud whisper. Rawin stood up and took hold of it and waited. He tugged on it and it remained firmly in place.

'Pull yourself up,' he heard her say.

'Right,' he said to himself in mock obedience. 'Just pull yourself up.' But he knew there wasn't anything else he could do so he placed his feet against the wall and pulled himself up a little by holding onto the rope. Then he gripped the rope further up with both hands and slowly but surely made his way up, eventually flinging himself forward until he hung with his legs still dangling behind him but the upper part of his body draped over the top of the wall. After regaining his breath and his strength, he swung his body round until he was sitting looking over the other side. To his astonishment he saw that the rope stretched out for several yards below and appeared to be wound around the body of a demon leaning against a tree, either asleep or dead.

'Is it…?'

'It's OK,' Catt said, standing next to the demon. 'It's just dead drunk.'

'Well, that's a good thing,' Rawin said, launching himself from the top of the wall and landing firmly on both feet before rolling over to break his fall.

'Yep,' said Catt. 'At first I thought I might have to fight it, but then I saw the jug lying there. And when I got closer, dah-daaa, I saw it had this rope coiled around its body,' she continued, throwing her hands open for dramatic effect. 'It must have taken a break from something it was doing and ended up as drunk as a skunk. Anyway, it didn't move when I unravelled the rope. Keeping this end still wound around it meant I didn't have to weigh it down myself while you pulled yourself up.'

'Genius,' Rawin commented, dispassionately.

'It's what you would have done, Mr Einstein,' she quipped. 'Anyway, let's get moving. It looks like there's a path here leading to the moat. I could see the water from on top of the wall when there was just a tiny bit of light left in the sky. Maybe this demon and its rope had some business over there.'

So the two set off down the path, leaving the demon still fast asleep.

Meanwhile, Hanuman, now outside the garden, watched as Sida slipped hurriedly through the door of a nearby building, which he thought must be where she slept. He scampered silently through the courtyard and approached the building. He peered through tiny gaps in a carved wooden screen. He could just see Sida slumped on a low wooden bed covered in silk throws and pillows. She buried her head and wept.

Hanuman's saw a group of demon ladies-in-waiting who approached Sida, chatting among themselves. Then they started taunting her: 'What is the matter with you, spoiled woman? You are the chosen love of our master, the mighty and majestic Totsakan. Yet you spurn him. How can you do that? How can you turn your back on such great love from such a great being? Are you mad?'

'Leave me,' cried Sida. 'Leave me.'

'You do not deserve him, yet he waits patiently for you to return his love,' said one of the ladies-in-waiting.

'I don't love him,' shouted Sida. 'I will never love him. Don't you understand?'

'If you carry on like this, you ungrateful wretch, you will awaken his wrath. Where once there was the fire of love, there will be the flames of fury. He will tear you to shreds. And you will deserve it.'

Sida clutched the pillow in her hands and sobbed uncontrollably. The ladies-in-waiting shuffled around her, shaking their heads, muttering darkly.

Eventually Sida appeared to have fallen asleep and the ladies-in-waiting settled down themselves and were soon asleep.

After a few minutes Hanuman saw Sida stir gently and lift her head, looking around. Seeing that the women were asleep, she quietly rose and crept silently towards the door and out into the night. Hanuman decided not to approach her, fearing she might be startled and wake the demons. He moved without a sound several paces behind her as she headed back to the garden and through the gate. She walked slowly up to a stately *sok* tree near a lotus pond and fell to her knees. The sound of her words drifted through the night air and entered Hanuman's soul: 'Oh, my king, my king,' she intoned. 'Your wife is about to die. And you will not see her die. Alas, I tried to protect myself and wait for you. I didn't have a chance to say goodbye to you, for now I will be gone. I won't ever be with you again.'

Sida lifted her hands to the top of her head in obeisance to the gods. Then she bowed to the earth.

'Dear gods, please protect my prince and Prince Lak. Let no trouble or sorrow befall them. Please tell them I was mortally wounded by the words of the evil giant. Now I pay my respects and declare my allegiance to you, immortal gods everywhere, and entrust myself to you as I take my leave to go to heaven.'

Then she turned and pulled down a branch and lifted herself up into the tree. She removed her scarf and bound it around a sturdy branch above her and then firmly around her neck. She closed her eyes and jumped.

# CHAPTER TWENTY-THREE

JaoJuk sat cross-legged on the shiny wooden floor of Ram's chalet. He seemed to be bored and was playing with a small sack of gold which he tossed from one hand to the other. The sun's rays spread like gleaming knife blades through the surrounding trees. Away from the building, Sukreep was stirring something in a pot on a fire. Lak was writing on parchment with a crude pen shaped from a sharpened stick which he dipped occasionally in a rough clay jar containing charcoal ink.

'JaoJuk, I've got something for you,' came the voice of Ram emerging from the trees. He held out a wooden bowl containing a collection of succulent pieces of fruit. 'I know you have a sweet tooth, don't you?'

JaoJuk smiled coyly, as if Ram had revealed a secret. But the child was quick to take a handful of the tasty temptation.

'And,' Ram went on with enthusiasm, 'There's this too.' He handed JaoJuk a small mug of 'red water', which JaoJuk sipped happily.

'Not too much of that, JaoJuk,' Sukreep called from where he was cooking, 'or you won't eat the meal I've made for us here.'

'That's OK. I'll eat his share,' Lak said. 'I'm starving.'

From beyond the clearing, through the woods, came the 'password call' Ram had agreed with Hanuman to herald the arrival of an ally.

'Ah,' said Sukreep, 'that must be Hanuman and the children back already.'

The coded call was repeated.

'I'll go to greet them,' Lak said, leaving his writing materials behind and striding off into the woods.

A few minutes passed before they heard Lak shout: 'Brother, look out. It's a trap. Demons. They imitated the code.'

Ram dashed deeper into the chalet and came out armed with his bow and arrow. 'Quick, Sukreep, your sword.' He tossed Sukreep's sword in an upright position through the air so it was easy for Sukreep to clutch the hilt as it reached him. 'Rouse Chompoopan and the other soldiers.'

Sukreep rushed into the woods behind the chalet to where he knew the monkey army were camped some distance away.

Ram could just see his brother running flat out through the woods with a large group of demented demons pursuing him.

'Oh, brave and loyal brother,' said Ram to himself. 'Do not sacrifice yourself for me.' He sprinted into the woods a little ahead of where he could see the demons running after Lak. With graceful agility he sprang on to a log and launched himself into the branches of a nearby tree where he placed his feet firmly on a horizontal branch. He reached over his shoulder into his quiver and in a split second slotted an arrow into place against the string. He stretched it back and unleashed the deadly missile. It flashed through the air with a menacing hiss and lodged in the brain of the biggest demon at the front of the charge. The creature's legs buckled instantly beneath it, ploughing into the ground, its body tumbling in a cloud of dirt and foliage until it came to rest in a heaving heap. The other demons behind it came to a halt, snorting and gasping as they looked around to try to make sense of what had happened. Lak disappeared further into the woods ahead of them. Ram meanwhile had hidden behind a thick tree-trunk.

A shout came from an imperious looking giant behind the demons. He started giving orders and soon got the demons to carry on their chase. From his hiding place in the tree, Ram could see that the demon now in charge had the face of an experienced and fearless warrior. His eyes flashed with cold anger and his chin was held high so that he looked down on everyone and everything around him, like a contemptuous despot. Ram also saw that, unlike the other demons that were armed with simple swords, the leader carried a sturdy bow and a quiver of arrows over his shoulder.

'Inthorochit,' Ram said silently to himself. 'Son of Totsakan, bravest and deadliest general of the demon world. At last we meet.'

Inthorochit squared his shoulders arrogantly and breathed so that his huge chest filled out, as if he had sensed that his most deadly enemy was watching him.

'Go, brother, go,' whispered Ram to himself. 'Very clever.' For he knew what Lak was doing. He was drawing the demons away from the chalet and into the adjoining fields where the monkey army had been resting. He was so sure that this was Lak's plan that he scrambled down from the tree and headed back past the chalet to join Sukreep in the fields beyond. By the time he reached them, Sukreep had already roused the monkey army, preparing them for battle.

'At a rough guess I would say there were about thirty or more of them,' he told Sukreep. 'There is no sign of Totsakan's deadly brother Kumphakan among them, fortunately, but the arrogant son Inthorochit is at the front.' Then he turned to the soldiers and addressed them loudly: 'Our enemy Totsakan has sent his fearless son and a unit of brainless demon-soldiers to attack us. Prince Lak has diverted them and will lead them from the woods over there into these fields. Prepare to destroy them.'

Chompoopan stepped forward and addressed the army. 'Brave and loyal soldiers, pluck fear from your hearts and mould it into courage. Prepare now for battle.'

Sukreep looked at Chompoopan and raised his right fist, stabbing it forward in a gesture of support.

A cloud of dust rose from inside the woods a few hundred yards away and the sound of thundering feet and jeering demons carried across the fields where the monkey army gathered, now ready for combat.

'OK,' shouted Chompoopan. 'Let's go.' He led the army across the fields, through a gentle dip and up the other side and brought them to a halt facing the edge of the wood as the dust and noise spilled out into the open. Lak was running ahead of the demons, striding like a long-distance runner nearing the finishing line, for he knew where he was and what was about to happen. As he broke loose into the field, pursued by the demons, the monkey army raised its voice like one man: 'Charge!' Monkeys, waving swords, scampering and ducking and diving in a disorientating dance, descended upon the demons.

The sound of battle carried across the plain as demons and monkeys attacked each other, swords flailing, cries of pain and triumph rising through the dust of the pitched battle. Chompoopan pulled back from hand-to-hand combat and quickly consulted with Ram. They decided it was necessary to retreat and prepare for a renewed assault. 'Come back. Regroup,' shouted Chompoopan. The monkeys obeyed and briefly the fighting ceased. The demons, grunting and muttering, looked around for instructions from their leader. The monkeys re-assembled in lines about a hundred yards away, chattering eagerly as they listened to Chompoopan outlining the next phase of the battle.

As they shuffled into position ready to charge again at the demon army, Inthorochit stepped up onto a rock at the rear.

'Prince Ram, listen to me,' he shouted. 'You are wasting your time and your breath. And the lives of your pathetic army. You might think you can win this battle – which you can't – but your fate is much worse than that. Go on, fight if you like. Not only will you lose this war, but you have already lost your pitiful wife.'

Ram stepped to the front of the monkey army. Lak stood beside him proudly. 'We are not afraid of you,' he shouted. 'You are full of brave but empty bombast. Like father like son.'

'Ha-ha-ha,' laughed Inthorochit scornfully. 'You are the one whose words are empty. In fact your whole life is empty now. You see, your little wife has agreed to be my father's little wife. The wedding will begin when I get back to Langka with your head.'

'You lie,' Ram said. 'She would never agree. She would rather die than give in to that monster.'

'Please yourself, fool. Oh, and by the way, we've also caught those ridiculous children, the ones from the other world that for some inexplicable reason you thought might help defeat my father. Where did you get such a ludicrous notion? They are probably dead already, but if not, I'll get them to say goodbye to your head when I deliver it on a plate to my father.'

'I will not listen to your lies and your boasting,' Ram shouted, striding forward. 'Come on, fight me. Just you and me, here.'

Inthorochit let out a loud, contemptuous laugh and took an arrow from his quiver. He placed it in the nock and pulled back the string to full stretch. He lifted the bow and aimed the arrow at the sky above the monkey army and unleashed it. The monkeys watched curiously as the arrow soared above their heads changing in mid-air into a writhing serpent and fell into their midst. Monkeys scrambled in panic as the serpent lashed out in every direction, its fangs sinking into the leg of one unfortunate soldier who screamed and fought until his life ebbed away as the snake slithered around thrusting its head out in search of another victim. The other monkeys wailed with fear and ran in every direction. Inthorochit launched another arrow, and then another and another in split-second succession, each rising into the sky above Ram's simian army and then falling as deadly serpents into their frenzied ranks. The demons cheered and beat their chests with their fists. Ram knew he wouldn't be able to bring Inthorochit down with one of his own arrows from where he was.

'I've got to get closer,' he said to Chompoopan and began scurrying alone towards the left flank of the demon army. He was immediately seen by the demons, many of whom began to advance on him. There seemed no way out of the trap they were in. Inthorochit continued to rain more snakes down on the monkeys, which by now were in such disarray that they were beginning to look like easy prey if the demons advanced on them. Everyone – Ram, Chompoopan, the monkeys, and even the demons looking back – watched in stunned marvel as Inthorochit unleashed his deadly arsenal of serpents on the hapless monkey army.

But as Inthorochit pulled his bow string back for another shot, it disappeared. Not just the string, but the bow and the arrow in it, as well as the quiver of arrows on his back. The once arrogant demon now stood with his left hand held forward and his right hand up against his shoulder. But both hands held nothing. Fresh air. His face creased in dismay. He looked fiercely at his left hand. And then at the right one. He felt over his shoulder for his arrows, but there was nothing there. He spun around in confusion to try to make sense of what had happened. His eye caught sight of a movement on top of a mound on the edge of the woods. He looked intently at it. Then the demons did. And the monkeys too. Everyone on both sides of the battle stood rooted to the ground staring in one direction. Then the demons turned and fled wailing into the woods. Clearly visible on the crest of the mound was a small child with his hair tied in a top-knot, standing firmly with both arms pointing directly at Inthorochit. A light puff of smoke rose from the child's hands.

'JaoJuk!' Ram said to himself. 'You tiny, huge hero!'

# CHAPTER TWENTY-FOUR

Hanuman had never thought in all his life that he would become paralysed by something he saw. His bravery had always been unlimited, his strength unbounded, his determination unbending. But now he could not move. He watched motionless as Sida's body swung beneath the branch and her voice rasped as she choked. It seemed to him that all time had ceased, that what he saw went on forever, like a nightmare from which he could never awake.

Then his mind cleared as if someone had clapped their hands in front of his eyes. He sprang into action. He darted forward with lightning speed and lifted her convulsing body in his arms, taking her weight from the scarf that wreathed her neck. He reached down and took the sword from its sheath and in a single movement sliced through the garment. He staggered back, still holding Sida's limp body and laid her on the ground. Shaking with heartache and distress, he felt her delicate wrist for a pulse and watched her chest for signs of breath. After what felt like forever, he murmured: 'The gods be praised. Oh, lovely lady, loyal and precious wife of the Lord Ram. You live.' He prostrated himself beside her, his hands pressed together in obeisance.

Sida stirred, then looked at him and pressed her eyes shut. Her hands went to her throat and fumbled, feeling for the scarf. Her elegant, slender neck was marked with a red gash, but she could tell she had not succeeded in taking her own life. She turned away from Hanuman and raised herself on one elbow, and then slowly stood up. She turned back to the monkey who had saved her life and said: 'You idiot, you foolish monkey. What have you done? What madness or evil possessed you to do this? Can you not see how I suffer? I am a captive, a slave, a hostage. I drink my own tears every day. I tried to bring my torment and misery to an end. And you, you unfeeling monkey, why must you interfere? You have stolen even that from me, robbed me of the one thing that could rescue me from this agony.'

'No, no, your majesty. With respect, you don't understand,' said Hanuman desperately rising yet keeping his body bent in respect and his hands together against his forehead. 'Your brave and faithful husband is gathering an army even now, as we speak, to rescue you. The death you seek is soon to be defeated by the life of the truest love.'

'Monkey, you speak in poetry but your pretty words disguise your ugly intentions. If you are my husband's soldier, how come I do not recognise you?'

'I had not come to be the servant of your lord until after you had been abducted, my lady. That is why you never saw me. However, I do not expect you to trust me, Madam. But perhaps this might change your mind,' said Hanuman less poetically. He held a ring out for her to see. 'I am sure you recognise this.'

Sida stepped closer and looked with suspicion at the ring and then at Hanuman's face.

'I do recognise it,' she said coldly. 'And how did you come to be in possession of my ring? Did you steal it?'

'Madam, no, I did not steal it. Totsakan took it from your hand when he kidnapped you and threw it at a bird that came to try to rescue you, to chase it away. Your husband retrieved it and asked me to bring it to you to convince you that my mission is an honourable one. He asked that I accompany you back to him so that you might be reunited.'

'Never! Totsakan has put you up to this, to make you

trick me and win my trust. Just like you tricked me by saving my life. Do you take me for a fool?'

Hanuman held the ring up in his right hand and raised his head to look admiringly at it. 'This ring, made of pure gold, is worth nothing if it is not returned to your finger by the man whose love for you knows no bounds. Oh, Lady, oh Madam, know how true, how timeless, how eternal is his love for you. Without your love for him and his for you, there can be no love on Earth at all, not anywhere, not between anyone. The very heavens have been cast into darkness since you have been separated, the angels weep, the sun threatens to extinguish itself, the Universe shrinks. No heart can ever again be filled with love's bliss.'

'Monkey, stop. You will use up all the words created for love. Leave some for those lovers who are still together lest they be unable to tell each other how they feel.'

'Dear Lady, if you cannot be moved by these words, then hear this. Your lord, my master, told me about when you first met. He had come to participate in an archery contest at your father's castle and you hid in a window when he arrived and your eyes met and you both fell immediately in love. Only you and he know this secret. He told me this story so that you would know I am his servant.'

Sida took the ring from Hanuman, gasped and clutched it to her breast. Then she fell to her knees. 'No one else knows this.' She paused and then sobbed: 'Oh, husband, dear brave husband, you have been trying to come to rescue me. How could I have doubted you? And you have sent this monkey to bring me hope. Oh, good man. Forgive me.'

'Dear Lady,' said Hanuman, 'your loyal husband will not need to forgive you, for there is nothing to forgive. He will know that your trust could not, indeed cannot, be won cheaply. But all is well. Now come with me. I will take you home to him.'

'Oh, faithful servant of my husband, it is true that my trust cannot be easily won, but it is also true that my dignity cannot be lightly besmirched. What further humiliation must I endure? Abducted and brought here by a demon and now I must be taken back by a monkey? Really? Why did my husband not bring an army and rescue me himself instead of sending a monkey? The only way in which my dignity and his honour can be upheld is if he comes here and plucks me with his own hands from the grip of that evil monster.'

Hanuman could tell immediately from the way she spoke that he would not be able to change Sida's mind. So, he quickly sprang back and bowed. 'Madam, I am honoured to carry this message to my master. Be assured, we will be back.'

He straightened up, turned, and ran with his head high and his chest out, bursting with satisfaction that he had accomplished the mission Ram had set for him. He had found Langka and Sida and he would now be able to bring him the good news that she eagerly awaited his arrival to rescue her.

As Hanuman reached the gate of the garden he saw burning torches held aloft by a band of demons shouting and pointing at him. He staggered back, but he was immediately surrounded. He looked desperately in every direction, hoping to see some avenue of escape, but they quickly crowded in on him, their shouting and snorting getting louder. He could feel the heat from the flames of their torches. Then they parted ahead of him and through the gap they had created stepped an imperious looking demon-warrior, his face contorted with rage, his hands planted firmly on his hips. The other demons fell silent as he strode slowly and menacingly up to Hanuman and clutched him by the throat.

A little way off, still on her knees, Sida watched in horror and whispered to herself. 'Oh, no. Inthorochit.'

# CHAPTER TWENTY-FIVE

Inthorochit's massive hands tightened around Hanuman's throat. 'What are you doing here?' he yelled violently into the monkey's face. 'Who are you?' He lifted Hanuman off his feet and shook him. Hanuman choked and spluttered. He tried to shrink himself but he couldn't. The demon's hold on his throat prevented him from reshaping his body. Inthorochit stripped Hanuman's sword from its sheath and tossed it aside.

'Chain him,' he roared to the demons.

'What is your mission, monkey?' he said more calmly, but coldly. He held his grip around Hanuman's throat and narrowed his eyes, looking deeply into Hanuman's. 'What tricks are you playing, tricky monkey?' Hanuman could not speak.

Several demons carrying heavy chains threw them around Hanuman's neck and waist as well as his ankles.

'Bring this despicable creature,' commanded Inthorochit, turning and marching through the gate. 'My father will know what to do with this thing.'

Demons surrounded Hanuman, tormenting and kicking him forward, forcing him to stumble after Inthorochit. When he dropped to one knee, finding it difficult to move with the chains around him, they kicked him again until he staggered on. This continued as the grotesque procession followed Inthorochit to the palace.

Totsakan had already been alerted by courtiers that his son was bringing a prisoner. He stood tall in the doorway of the pavilion where Hanuman and the children had seen him earlier. His harem and other attendants had drifted away into the darkness behind him. Kumphakan stood at his brother's side as Hanuman was presented to them.

'My lord,' said Inthorochit, bowing, 'I discovered this foul fellow in the garden with Sida. He has not spoken yet, but he is clearly up to mischief. Not just monkey mischief. Something much more serious than that, I am sure.'

Totsakan didn't reply. He waited as Hanuman hobbled clumsily into his presence, still firmly ensnared by the chains. He was forced to sit awkwardly a short distance from Totsakan, head lowered.

'I recognise you, monkey,' said Totsakan coldly. 'I saw you in the presence of that coward Ram, who hides behind children and monkeys. Did he send you here?'

Hanuman looked at Totsakan with contempt and said nothing.

'Come on, speak.'

Hanuman stayed silent.

'Would you like some help with that?'

Still no response.

'Take him to the stadium,' ordered Totsakan. 'Bring the rogue elephant. Let's see if he remains silent when he meets him.'

Demons kicked and pushed Hanuman in the direction of a small stadium that was used for jousting and gladiator sports. They took the monkey into the middle of the arena, removed his chains and left him there alone.

Totsakan led Inthorochit and his courtiers into the spectator area where they stood in a raised dignitaries' enclosure at the head of the seating.

'Bring in the rogue,' commanded Totsakan. At the far end of the arena a wooden gate was raised, revealing a huge elephant with tusks as thick as tree branches. It edged forward, looking around suspiciously. When it saw Hanuman it stopped and stamped one giant foot several times on the dusty arena floor and rocked its enormous body back and forth. Then it let out a crazed trumpeting call that sent shivers down the spines of every creature – human, demon and animal – within miles. The monkey remained dead still, watching the elephant intently.

Then two demons entered the arena. They had drums slung around their shoulders which they beat slowly as they walked towards Hanuman. The elephant stamped and trumpeted again, watching the demons as they got closer to the monkey and their drumming got louder and faster. One came right up behind Hanuman and kicked him in the back, sending him sprawling. This alerted the elephant, which now began to approach Hanuman. He noticed there was a yellow-coloured froth foaming in the elephant's mouth.

'You're crazy, poor thing, aren't you,' he said quietly as he eyed the elephant. 'They've been driving you mad.'

Two more stamps of its front feet and it charged. Hanuman sprang to his feet and darted to one side just as the elephant arrived, sending the giant animal scrambling past him. One tusk swept so close to his head that he felt a rushing sound. The elephant swung in the direction of the two drumming demons but they disappeared through another wooden gate on the edge of the arena, which slammed shut behind them. The animal came to a halt and turned back to look at Hanuman.

'Speak!' shouted Totsakan. 'What is your business in my city, monkey? Speak or die.'

Hanuman did not even look at his tormenter. Instead he kept a firm eye on the elephant which delivered another blood-curdling trumpet and began to charge again. Hanuman waited, dead still. Closer, closer, closer came the elephant, faster and faster. Then as it bent its head down so that its tusks were the right height to bore into Hanuman, the monkey hopped almost casually onto one of the huge, curved tusks and grabbed hold of the top of its trunk to steady himself while the elephant hurtled on, shaking its head in confusion.

As the elephant slowed down, Hanuman swung up on to its neck, like a *mahout*, and gripped tightly with his legs while the huge creature tossed and thrust its body in a vain attempt to unseat him. Trumpeting in angry frustration, the elephant lifted its head high and waved it back and forth in an attempt to swat the monkey off his neck. Hanuman held firm and whispered into the elephant's flapping ear: 'I am sorry for you, oh proud, sick creature, but I am afraid I must come first.' He swivelled forward, holding his body in place with his legs firmly gripping the elephant's neck and grabbed one of its tusks firmly in both hands. Then with his legendary strength Hanuman snapped the trunk in half, lifted the piece he was holding with both hands and plunged it into the elephant's forehead.

There was an almost instant silence as the elephant stopped shaking its head and came to a halt, stood still for a short while and then slumped in a massive grey heap. As its lifeless body began to spread out on the dusty arena floor, Hanuman hopped off triumphantly.

Angrily Inthorochit reached for his sword.

'Wait!' commanded Totsakan. 'Monkey, come here.' He beckoned Hanuman to come closer.

Hanuman walked slowly up to the dignitaries' enclosure, which was high above the arena floor, and stood before Totsakan and his son. He said nothing.

'Monkey,' began Totsakan, 'I could do with a soldier like you. Come and fight beside me. You will be given anything and everything you want as a reward.'

For the first time since being captured Hanuman's face filled with expression. But he did not speak. He just laughed.

'Do not mock me,' cried Totsakan.

Hanuman laughed again and grinned arrogantly at the demon.

'Seize him,' shouted Totsakan.

Several demons ran out into the arena. Hanuman did not move. They grabbed him by the arms and looked up at their master for further instruction.

'You will regret this, monkey,' said Totsakan. 'Bring cloth and oil,' he ordered the demons. Two ran off and came back with a bundle of white cloth and a clay container. A third demon stood by, holding a flaming torch.

'Set his tail alight,' commanded Totsakan.

Hanuman looked back at his tail, but did not try to get free.

The demons wrapped some of the cloth around the end of his tail and poured oil on it.

'Light it!'

But before they could do so, Hanuman's tail grew longer.

'Add more cloth.'

The demons added more cloth and poured oil on that too.

Then Hanuman's tail grew longer still.

'Monkey, do not fool with me,' shouted Totsakan. 'Add more.'

The demons did so.

And Hanuman's tail grew even longer.

'Enough!' boomed Totsakan. 'Light it.'

The demon with the torch guided it on to the oil-soaked cloth at the end of Hanuman's very long tail. It flared into flame. Then Hanuman shrank his tail back to its normal size, unsettling the demons around him. They let go of him and he darted off to the far end of the arena, with some of the cloth attached to his tail burning behind him.

He stopped, turned and looked at Totsakan and Inthorochit. He grinned with disdain. 'I will be back with my master. You will die and we will free Sida.'

Then he swung himself up into the seating area of the stadium and ran along with his burning tail behind him. The seating caught fire and spread as Hanuman ran triumphantly up and down the rows of seats, setting the entire stadium alight. Then he swung himself up on to the roof. The fire spread there too.

'Insolent, treacherous monkey,' growled Totsakan. 'You will die for this.' Then the master of all the demons, King of Langka, and his son watched in horror as Hanuman swung from rooftop to rooftop across the city as one building after another collapsed in flames. Soon the entire city was engulfed.

# CHAPTER TWENTY-SIX

The last of the dusk light had gone when Catt and Rawin set off towards where she thought she had seen the moat, now on the other side of the city from where they had entered. They followed a wide, well-trodden path that wound through tall grass for a while before they heard the sounds of activity and signs of flickering light cast from torch flames. They stooped a little to ensure they were below the height of the grass as they crept on slowly to investigate. Then they saw the moat. Catt had been right.

A circle of flaming torches provided enough light for them to see what was going on. Several demons were milling around at the water's edge, grunting and pointing at a massive wheel. A thick rope was coiled around the middle of it, like a giant cotton reel, and extended into the moat a short distance from the water's edge. On each side of the wheel there were huge crank handles. Two of the biggest demons the children had ever seen were gripping them with both hands. Another demon that appeared to be in charge grunted what must have been an order and the two giants began turning the handles. Slowly but surely they managed to get the wheel turning and as it did, so the rope tightened and from the water rose a wooden structure that stretched out into the middle of the moat. The children were able to see that the rope had been connected to a series of small wheels that ran the full length of the wooden structure.

'It's a block and tackle pulley system,' Rawin whispered. 'It delivers a mechanical advantage that maximizes the kinetic force of the wheel by a vector equivalent to one lifting movement multiplied by the number of pulleys in the system, each lifting the same weight with half the effort.'

'Ah,' Catt said. 'I see.' She threw him a little smile.

'It's true.'

'I don't doubt it for a moment.'

'These demons are not as stupid as they look.'

'Wait,' Catt said quickly. 'Look. There's another one rising from the other side.'

'Wow. Cool,' said Rawin.

The two wooden structures met in the middle of the moat.

'A bridge!' Rawin said.

'That's brilliant. We can get across without swimming or trying to find Meeya to take us back, because she's on the other side of the city. It's also the perfect way for Prince Ram and the monkey army to get across when the day comes. They might have to do some wheel-turning, but you can explain how it works.'

'I thought in the story that Hanuman grows his tail to make a bridge across the water to Langka.'

'The story?' Catt replied. 'Seriously, Rawin? Where were *we* in the story when he did that?'

'OK, OK. Sorry,' Rawin said, shrugging his shoulders and raising his hands in a sort of surrender.

Just then the two demons with ropes coiled around them ran over the bridge to the other side. It was difficult to see what they did there, but soon they returned, trailing their ropes behind them. Attached to the ropes were large bamboo barges, which the demons were pulling along. As they got closer, the children could see that the barges contained piles of barrels and boxes, some open, others with lids.

'Supplies,' Rawin said. 'This is how they supply the city. There must be food and other things in there.'

'Other things like… weapons,' Catt said. 'Look.' She

pointed at the second barge.

It was weighed low in the water by a large pile of axes on long wooden poles.

'Deadly,' was all Rawin could say.

'They are preparing for war,' Catt said.

As they watched, they became slowly aware of a golden haze spreading across the sky. They were about to remark on it when they heard screaming. They spun round. The golden haze was a reflection in the night sky of orange flames coming from the city.

'Oh God,' said Rawin. 'There's a fire in the city.'

'Hanuman,' Catt said. 'I hope he's OK.'

'And Sida,' replied Rawin. 'Quick.'

They ran back to the city wall. They heard more screaming and the voices of demon children wailing in terror.

'Oh God,' Rawin said again.

Just then they saw what they realised must be the main gate to the city, complete with a portcullis that was being pulled up to allow hundreds of terrified demons to burst through. Some were carrying small demon children. They ran wildly towards the moat.

'Come on, let's go through there,' Rawin said. 'No one's going to stop and ask us what we're doing here now. It's every man for himself.'

'Wait,' Catt shouted. 'Look.' She pointed toward a rooftop of a building in the city. 'Hanuman!'

The children watched Hanuman swinging from one rooftop to the next, tail aflame, leaving behind him a spreading inferno. Burning gables crashed onto fleeing demons below. Every now and then something exploded while hissing and crackling sounds spread across the city and the sky turned from orange to red.

'He's laughing,' said Rawin. 'Hanuman is laughing.'

'Oh God.' It was Catt who said it this time.

'Those demon children. The fancy-dress ones. They must be in there somewhere, gone to bed. Oh, no. Poor things. And Sida. What could Hanuman be thinking?' Rawin asked in distress.

Hanuman continued to spread the flames as he crossed the city's outline silhouetted against the red sky. Black clouds billowed up over the city. Coughing and choking mixed with the screams. Once, twice, Hanuman stopped to look back at his handiwork and to laugh with contempt at those who thought they could imprison or kill the cleverest monkey in the world.

Demons teemed out the city gate towards the moat. The bridge was now up and hundreds began to rush across to safety.

'Rawin,' Catt shouted over the growing noise. 'We'd better get out of here. There's no way we can go back in there to find Sida. Come on. Now.'

Rawin turned to look one more time at the rampant monkey. 'Hanuman,' he said in dismay. 'Oh, Hanuman. What have you done?'

'Come *on* Rawin,' Catt said.

The children ran swiftly alongside the throng of demons heading for the moat bridge which was now fully in place. No demons seemed to even notice them. All were fixated on escaping. Parents clutched children in their arms, others carried meagre belongings in sacks. All huffed and grunted as they poured onto the bridge.

The children were much more agile than the demons. Rawin still had his backpack and Catt her sword, but these didn't slow them down.

'It's lucky that they raised the bridge tonight for some reason,' Rawin said. 'Must just have been a coincidence.'

'Unless they've heard that Prince Ram's army is planning an attack so they're bringing in plenty of weapons and supplies,' Catt said.

They reached the other side of the bridge near the front of the fleeing creatures. Rawin noticed that there was a block and tackle system and crank on the other side exactly the same as the one they had seen operating on the city side of the moat. Two gigantic demons stood beside the wheel watching the chaos coming across the bridge. At the water's edge there was another barge like the two that had been pulled across the moat. But there was no rope attached to this one.

'You know the rope we nicked from the drunken demon to get over the wall? I bet that was supposed to be used to pull this barge across,' he said. 'That guy's going to be in trouble when they find out what happened to him.'

The children didn't stop to watch but took advantage of the confusion and darted unnoticed into the woods beyond.

'We've got to get to Prince Ram mighty quickly,' Catt said.

'But what are we going to tell him? That Sida might have burned to death in a fire started by Hanuman? How can we tell him that?'

'Well, we don't know that that is what happened,' Catt said, more calmly.

'He certainly looked like he was enjoying himself,' Rawin said. 'Hundreds of demons must be dying in there. This is terrible.'

'It's war,' Catt said, more coldly than she had intended.

'War? None of the demons we saw today looked like they were at war. The war is between Prince Ram and Totsakan,' Rawin said bitterly. 'Over a woman.'

'Not just a woman,' Catt snapped. 'A person. Someone who has been very badly treated. Yes, she's a woman, but that's not the point.'

'Prince Ram and Totsakan are fighting over her precisely because she is a woman. They both want her.'

'That's not her fault. It's theirs. And in any case we know who she wants to be with. Her husband. Not her vile abductor. Prince Ram is right to want to rescue her,' Catt insisted.

'But it's not right that so many should die because of this. Why is it always like that? Why are wars always between kings? Those who suffer the most aren't the ones who start wars. And they never get anything from them − except die miserable deaths. Or fiery deaths in this case. It's wrong. Wrong, wrong, wrong.'

'Rawin, life is not maths or physics. It does not obey the laws of nature. Maybe you do, but life doesn't.'

'Life *is* nature. What else is it?'

'Love, jealousy, anger, greed.'

'Then I don't want to be alive.'

'You can't help it.'

'I can. I refuse to live this life.'

'What do you mean?' Catt asked worryingly.

'This life here. This Ramakien life, or whatever it is we are doing here. We never wanted this – and now it's turned nasty. Very, very nasty.'

'But we've been through all that. We have no choice. We have to do what we were brought here to do.'

'No. No. I don't think that's right. You remember what Rishi said: "You cannot defeat the evil one until you go home." So I'm going home.'

'But he said we cannot go home until we have defeated him.'

'Yeah, whatever.'

'Oh, come on, Rawin. That's not an argument. Whatever! What is that supposed to mean?'

'OK, fine. Rishi didn't say which of those two things has to come first. I'm going home in order to defeat the evil one. It sure doesn't feel to me like it should be the other way round. We are not defeating evil here. We are part of it. That fire is evil. The good guys lit that fire.'

'Rawin, listen, we have to go to Prince Ram to tell him what has happened. He will know what to do.'

'You think so?' Rawin snapped back. 'You go then.'

'And you?'

'I told you. I'm going home.'

'The cave?'

'Yes. That's the only way we know out of here.'

'But we've been there. It didn't work.'

'It worked for you the first time. Unless you were lying.'

'Oh, Rawin, why would I lie to you?'

'I don't know what to think anymore.'

'Well, don't think that. It's not fair. And it's not true.'

'OK, then, I'm going to try again.'

'Don't. Please stay with me.'

'No.'

'I need you.'

Rawin flinched. Then: 'No you don't.' And he ran into the darkest part of the woods.

# CHAPTER TWENTY-SEVEN

Fire burned more fiercely in the hearts of Totsakan and Inthorochit than the one they had watched engulfing their city. They stood at the top of the steps in front of the king's pavilion. Smoke rose from every corner of the city below as the last of the flames continued to lick at what was still left to burn – wooden pillars here and there, the scattered remains of thatched roofs that had fallen as building after building had collapsed in the blaze. They were joined by Kumphakan, whose anger was as cold as ice.

'They will pay,' said Totsakan. 'All of them. The monkey first, and then his spineless boss. I will not rest until I have had my revenge.'

'And I won't rest either, my brother, until that day,' Kumphakan said, 'for it is I who will avenge this cowardly deed. No death at my hands will bring me greater satisfaction.'

'Is Sida still in her garden?' Totsakan asked of no one in particular. He did not wait for a reply from the few courtiers who had remained with him. 'She would have been safe there,' he said with confidence. Mareet assured his master that she was unharmed. He said he had sent three more soldiers to guard her and two handmaidens to be with her as the fire raged. 'Benjakai went to be with her too,' added one of the other courtiers. 'She is devoted.'

Totsakan turned his attention back to what was left of the city. He looked out over the scene of devastation without emotion. The charred bodies of those demons that had not managed to escape littered the streets.

'Where is my other brother? Bring Pipek to me,' commanded Totsakan.

Mareet hurried back into what was left of the palace in search of Pipek.

'Inthorochit, send soldiers to bring back those who have fled,' Totsakan said. 'We will show no fear, in case Ram and his minions think they can beat us. Order everyone to come back.' Kumphakan went to gather those soldiers who had not fled the blaze and were able to do as Totsakan had ordered.

Shuffling quickly through the ruins a little way off came Pipek with Mareet behind him. He approached his older brother cautiously. He could not tell what he might do, so extreme was the rage written all over his face.

'You sent for me,' said Pipek.

Totsakan barely acknowledged his brother's presence. He continued to look out over the smoking rubble around them. He did not look at Pipek when he spoke. 'Why?'

'Why what, brother?'

'Why has this happened?'

'Your enemies will not stop until they have what they want.'

'Or until they are dead.'

'Perhaps.'

'Perhaps? Perhaps! Brother, is your wisdom so great that you know my enemies can fight even if they are dead?'

'Brother, war is not just fought between warriors. It is also a struggle between hearts. What is in your heart does not die when you are killed. Maybe you will never know this until you restore your heart.'

'Do *not* talk about my heart.'

Pipek did not answer.

'Take a break from your navel-gazing, Pipek, and do something practical. Come on, fortune-teller, tell me how my city will be rebuilt. What gods will help with this?'

'It can be done,' replied Pipek cautiously. 'But beware of their motives.'

'Don't speak in riddles, little brother. What dishonest motives would a god have who might help to rebuild my city?'

'The gods move in mysterious ways, brother. They don't reveal their intentions. We only understand their motives after they have acted.'

'Ha,' laughed Totsakan. 'I am not afraid of the gods. Let them do whatever they like. But let them first rebuild my city. For I am a king and I will have my capital back. Now!'

Pipek bowed his head, closed his eyes and brought his hands together in prayer. He said nothing. Then he slowly opened his eyes and looked up. 'The stars are well aligned,' he said to his brother.

'Command them!' shouted Totsakan.

'I don't have that power. We must await their pleasure.'

'Rubbish!' barked Totsakan. He looked up into the sky. 'Gods, listen to me,' he demanded. 'I am Totsakan, once the servant of Isuan, the supreme god. Do not dare deny me my wish. Rebuild my city!'

Gradually the sky began to cloud over and lightning split the heavens. Thunder echoed in the hills and rumbled across the plain. Heavy rain descended on the city, snuffing out the last of the fires that still burned. Slowly the crumbled ruins of the buildings that had graced the beautiful capital began to form into new shapes and structures. Mareet marvelled. Pipek paid no attention. Totsakan stepped forward and regained his demon form, holding his arms aloft. 'I am Totsakan,' he shouted into the skies. 'I am invincible. The gods obey me.'

In the distance, cheering could be heard from the other side of the moat, gradually getting louder. Those who had fled started running back over the bridge, yelling and crying with joy. Some stopped in awe as they watched their city re-emerge from the ashes, astonished that it now appeared even more splendid than before. Soon a chant rose from the masses, getting louder and louder: 'Long live Totsakan. Long live the King. Long live the King.'

'Brother, come closer,' Totsakan said to Pipek. 'Now you have seen my awesome power. Nothing can stop me.'

'I see your power,' Pipek said flatly.

'But,' said Totsakan, 'you too have a power. You foresaw this even before I did. When you prayed, you spoke to the gods, didn't you?'

'I only looked for the signs. That isn't power. I see only what is inevitable, even when I don't understand or like what I see.'

'Don't you?' Totsakan asked, sweeping his arms over the resurrecting city.

Pipek nodded solemnly.

'Yes, little brother, you do like it. And now tell me what will happen next. I have had dreams. You know how to interpret dreams. Tell me what my dreams mean.'

Pipek looked cautiously at his brother. 'I can try, my lord.'

Totsakan breathed in impatiently.

Sensing his brother's irritation, Pipek said: 'Tell me your dreams, brother. I will help if I can.'

Totsakan hesitated. He looked around to see if anyone could hear. But there was no one. Mareet was still staring in awe at the city's recovery and had all but forgotten his duties. Other manservants hovered around, but they too were focused on the miracle happening in front of them.

'This is my dream,' Totsakan began. 'I have it most nights. Two vultures fight. One is black, the other white. The white one kills the black one. I have this dream over and over. What does it mean?'

'Brother,' Pipek began. 'I have long had a terrible foreboding. No matter how much I resisted it, I kept feeling that something terrible will happen to our beloved Langka. I believe your dream is part of the same bad omen.'

'Bad omen?' Totsakan snapped. 'Why does it have to be a bad omen?'

'It's not for me to decide.'

'But you say what the dream means. So you decide whether it's good or bad.'

'I can only tell you what I see.'

'And what do you see, brother?'

'I must warn you. The black vulture in your dream is you. The white one is Prince Ram.'

'What?' Totsakan shouted. 'Are you saying Ram will kill me?'

'Not only that. Your kingdom will be destroyed.'

'Huh, disloyal brother, what nonsense! Ram has already tried to do that. Being too cowardly himself, he sent his clever monkey to do it. But look. Look now. Is Langka destroyed? What do you see?' He swept his arms in front of him to show the city restored in greater glory.

'That was just the beginning, brother,' said Pipek.

'And tell me, fortune teller, if this nonsense you speak is right, how can I stop this from happening? Am I to die? Is Langka to be destroyed?'

'There is a way.'

'And what way is that?'

'You should give up Sida. Let her go back to her husband.'

Totsakan gasped. His eyes narrowed as he leaned closer to his brother and stared into his eyes. 'What?' he barked.

'Let Sida go.'

Totsakan began to breathe heavily and the words came out of his mouth like venom from a cobra. 'Liar. Deceiver. Traitor. Get out of my sight before I am forced to kill my own brother. You have instantly surrendered everything you own, including your wife and daughter. They will be Sida's servants, bowing at her feet, from now on. You are nothing now. Exile is your reward for this infamy. Go.'

Pipek bent his head in anguish. But he did not speak.

Watching hidden behind a pillar, Kumphakan bowed his head in sadness.

Totsakan watched as Pipek turned and shuffled away. Then he screamed: 'Never! Never! She is mine!'

# CHAPTER TWENTY-EIGHT

After leaving Catt, Rawin walked with determination deeper into the forest, not sure where he was but hoping he might see a familiar path. His mind was spinning with emotion. He no longer believed they were on the side of 'good', if ever he believed it. Was Prince Ram really a good person or was he an arrogant bigwig who had never known what it was like not to have everything he desired? Why had he brought so many others into this so-called war between good and evil? It wasn't a war, he said to himself, simply an argument between two men about who would get the girl. Instead something personal had been turned into a battle between right and wrong with armies representing both. Good enough for a timeless myth, but really just about private desire.

At the same time he felt a weight in his chest so heavy that he thought he wouldn't be able to stay on his feet. He and Catt had disagreed a few times since they arrived in the Ramakien universe, but they had always managed to get over it. But this time it felt like they could never bridge the gap between them. Worse, he now feared he might never see her again, not in this world and not in their own. He hadn't even said goodbye.

He realised he couldn't see much in the dark, not just because by now it was probably the middle of the night, but because he kept having to blink to clear his eyes. I'm not crying, he kept telling himself. After trudging aimlessly through the woods for some time he fell to his knees beneath the weight of his heavy heart and allowed himself to cry properly, big rolling tears and sobs until it was all out.

Eventually he managed to recover enough to start thinking straight. He rummaged around in his backpack and turned on his phone. The battery life was now down to 17% and though he had a charger, where would he ever find somewhere to plug it in? He opened the text message app and copied the location he had sent to Catt and JaoJuk when he was plotting to escape by motorbike from Totsakan's cave. He then pasted it into Google Maps and asked for directions from his current location. The cave was 9.1 miles away. Estimated time on foot: 3 hours and 4 minutes. Although the map showed a dotted blue line to the red destination marker, in front of him Rawin could see only darkness. He powered off the phone and pushed it back into his bag. As he did so he felt his eyes go heavy with tiredness. The adrenaline that had pulsated through him over the past several hours had worn off and his body now needed rest. He felt around him for a space to lie down. His last thoughts were of profound sadness and despair, but not fear. And soon he plunged into a deep sleep.

Hours later a shaft of sunlight pierced Rawin's eyes and he woke slowly. He rubbed his face to get rid of the bleariness left by tears and sleep. Then he realised he was very hungry. He couldn't remember when he had last eaten, but it must have been at least 18 hours earlier, maybe more. He looked around him and quickly spotted some healthy-looking papaya trees on the edge of the forest. Fortunately much of the fruit had fallen, so he scooped one up and gnawed his way through the thin skin and into the delicious orange flesh, gobbling frantically to still his hunger, spitting the small black pips out as he went, since no one was there to comment on his manners. Then he noticed a cashew nut tree nearby and split open several ripe-looking pods and wolfed down the nuts inside. A stream nearby provided him with plenty to drink and soon he was revived and ready to make his way to the cave.

He powered up his phone and saved an offline version of the route the Google Maps showed and set off with new energy. As he went, he felt himself grow more and more determined to return to Bangkok and to deal with whatever new challenge that might involve, since he hadn't forgotten Rishi's words. He wondered if they were an instruction (you are *not allowed* to) or a statement of fact –it would *not be possible* to go home without first defeating the evil one. He would soon find out, he thought to himself.

After a few hours he began to recognise his surroundings. It was hillier and there were rocky outcrops here and there. Eventually he saw the huge rock face and the entrance to Totsakan's cave. He approached slowly, keeping himself hidden in the surrounding bushes as he went. He stopped for a few minutes and kept absolutely still. A blue pitta swooped past and sat on a branch watching him curiously. But there was no other sound, so Rawin crept forward and entered the cave. It was dark and dank and there was no sign of life. He took three or four steps into the cave and waited. Still nothing to worry about. So he took out his phone and switched on its torch, cautiously shining it around the cavern. Then he eased over to the right where Catt had said she had seen the gap in the roof of the cave leading up to Bangkok. He looked up and shuffled forward, occasionally looking behind him to make sure he was still alone. He shone his phone to light up the roof but it didn't help. He struggled to see anything. His heart began to pound. There was a tinge of excitement at being able to see his mother and uncle and just to be able to walk normally down a street without fear. Even go into a 7-Eleven and buy a sweet or a drink. But he also felt a deep sense of loss which at first he could not explain. Then he knew it was about Catt. He was leaving her.

One foot slipped on a wet stone and he fell, hitting the side of his thigh against another rock. Instantly realising he must stay quiet, he clamped his teeth together and hissed through them to give vent to his pain. He lay still for a few minutes and then got up, rubbing his leg where it hurt. When he looked up again, there it was. A shaft of light, just as Catt had described and through on the other side the distinct shape of one of the two golden bell-shaped domes that flank the entrance to the Temple of the Emerald Buddha. The bright sun reflected off the domes and he could see deep blue sky beyond. Rawin realised he had been holding his breath. He felt faint.

But he soon became focused on the practical question of how he would get up to the gap in the cave roof. He shone his phone torch at the wall and saw that it was irregular with indents and small outcrops that he could use to climb it. He gulped as he looked up and then down at his feet and realised that if he fell, he would be very badly hurt. No soft landing, he thought to himself as he felt the hard, jagged rocks beneath his shoes. He could already feel the bruise developing on the side of his thigh from when he fell. He looked up again and down again. He felt waves of indecision sweep over him.

He pocketed his phone and felt around for a place to take hold. His hand slipped over a smooth rock that offered a firm hold. He found another. With his left foot he managed to find a small outcrop that served as a step. He pulled himself up and fumbled for another step a little higher. Slowly he climbed the wall into the narrowing gap. As he climbed, so the light from above made it possible for him to see better. He felt more confident as he moved up slowly but surely. The view of the golden domes became clearer. He closed his eyes for a second and opened them slowly to see if it was really happening. Yes, he thought to himself, yes, as he looked up at the light beckoning him.

'Those who refuse to accept what the gods have decreed must die.'

Rawin froze. A voice. From below. It was Totsakan. Oh no, no, no.

'It is the will of the gods,' came a second voice. It was Mareet.

Rawin dared not move. He stared at the rock in front of him, afraid to even look up or down in case even the slightest movement could be heard.

'The gods have bequeathed Sida to me,' said Totsakan. 'If she will not accept it, I would rather kill her myself than let her go back to that arrogant idiot.'

Rawin held his breath. Don't move. Not a hair. Nothing. Try not to even breathe.

'Master, I have an idea. May I speak?'

'What is it, Mareet?'

'If Sida were dead, would Prince Ram not forget about her and leave us in peace, find himself another pretty girl, as you say?'

'Not a good idea, Mareet. As much as I would like Ram off my back, I don't think that would be the best solution.'

'Aha, master,' said Mareet. 'Prince Ram needs only to believe she is dead.'

'Believe?'

'Sir, she does not have to be, how should I say, *actually* dead.'

'Go on.'

'Well, Prince Ram and his brother are easily fooled, as you know, my lord. He can be shown a body that he believes is her.'

'Mareet, you were a very good deer, I am told, and you even imitated Ram's voice very well. But you can't pretend to be Sida, dead or alive,' laughed Totsakan darkly.

'Not I, my lord.'

'Who then?'

'One who knows her so well she can take on her likeness.'

'Benjakai.'

'Correct, my lord.'

'Mareet, I like that. Not only can Benjakai trick Ram, she can help pay the price for her father's treachery.'

'Thank you, my lord.'

Rawin's hands were beginning to ache. His legs were cramping. He kept his eyes shut tightly. If he made the slightest move, he would almost certainly be killed.

'Now, Mareet, there's another matter I want you to turn your mind to.'

'I am at your service, my lord.'

'That girl.'

'The little human with the big head.'

'How well put, Mareet.'

'My lord, she thinks she can vanquish you.'

'You're right. She needs to be taught a lesson.'

'Do you want her slain, my lord?'

'No, no. That will be my pleasure. But I first want her to suffer. I want her to crawl to me and beg for mercy.' Then Totsakan laughed. 'Ah, but there can be no mercy for small ignorant creatures who disobey the gods. She will die slowly and painfully. Let her bring her shiny little sword that blinds my soldiers. I will kill her with my bare hands.'

Mareet laughed too. 'Will you allow me to kill the boy, my lord?'

'Yes, Mareet, you can do that. He is not worthy of my attention. Swat him like a fly.'

There was a short silence. Then Totsakan said sternly: 'I want to be alone.'

'Your wish is my command, my lord. I'll wait outside the cave.'

Rawin heard Totsakan's footsteps move further into the cave. After a few minutes he heard the demon make the same low chant and deep groan he heard when he was his captive. He remembered how Totsakan had held an urn in his hands when that happened. After another few minutes, silence.

Just as Rawin thought he could no longer hang on, he heard Totsakan's footsteps returning. 'Mareet, come on.'

The henchman re-entered the cave. 'Master,' he answered obediently.

'I'm ready for Ram now. Let him try to kill me. His arrows will be like straws. Let's return and await his futile attempt to take Sida from me.'

The voices of the two demons slowly died away until Rawin could no longer hear them. Unable to hold on any longer, he dropped from where he was clinging to the rock face and fell to the ground. Fortunately he had not climbed very far and he managed to land on his two feet and break his fall by rolling. It was very painful, but in the back of his mind was the knowledge that however much he hurt now, it was nothing compared with what would have happened had he let go two minutes earlier.

Swat him like a fly! Rawin did not know whether to feel humiliated or indignant. Slowly he felt a surge of outrage. Then he realised why. It wasn't that he had been compared to a fly. It was what Totsakan had said about Catt. He intended to make her crawl to him and beg for mercy and then he would still kill her slowly and painfully.

'Never!' he said. 'I would die before I allow you to do that.' He looked back up at the gap in the roof of the cave and then turned firmly towards the cave entrance.

*You cannot go home until you have defeated the evil one.*

# CHAPTER
# TWENTY-NINE

I t did not take long for Rawin to find the path that a few days earlier he and Catt had taken when they had gone from Totsakan's cave back to Ram's chalet. His senses were now as sharp as a deer's. He could see more clearly, hear more clearly, think more clearly. It must have been adrenaline, he thought to himself. He wanted to fight. Now. Right now. He even thought for a moment that he would see if he could track down Totsakan and Mareet and challenge them. They couldn't have gone far. But he knew that would be crazy. So he channelled his anger into covering the ground to the chalet as quickly as possible.

It was around midday and the sun felt hot when the path took him out from under the shade of the trees. He could see hills stretching off into the distance, some covered with woods, others with gently swaying tall grasses. He recognised the hillside where Totsakan had snatched him on the back of his elephant. He recalled with warm pride how he and JaoJuk had rescued Catt from the giant demon Channarong by sending in a drone. And the sound of her courageous speech telling Totsakan she was not afraid of him. 'If you try to hide, we will hunt you down,' she had said. No wonder Totsakan hated her. He had a feeling that the day they would meet again was near.

After a few hours, he became concerned that he might not be on the right track. Once in a while he had seen something that seemed familiar, but he was now feeling less confident. So he decided to stop and see if his Google Maps app could work out where he was and maybe where the chalet was. He thought of calling Sukreep, but he decided to keep that as a final option. He wanted to save as much battery as he could.

He sat down on a fallen tree and took his phone out, tweaking the map on his screen to zoom in and out in the hope that he might recognise some landmark. He tried it on 'Satellite' mode and then on 'Terrain', which allowed him to see hills and streams. As he did so, he heard the unmistakable sound of a twig snapping under a foot very nearby. He felt the blood drain from his face as fear gripped him. He stayed still and listened intently. Nothing. He waited. Still nothing. Just as he began to recover, he heard it again. Closer this time. He felt he was about to cry out loud. Scream. Beg. Anything to take away the shaking that began to invade his body. Totsakan. No, Mareet. He had come to 'swat him like a fly'. They say even grown men cry out for their mothers at the moment they think they are going to die. He would have done that, but his throat had choked shut from the terror that gripped him. Instinctively he swung round to face whatever it was that was about to end his life. From behind a tree stepped Sayola, holding his spear pointing to the ground. He smiled.

Rawin tried to speak but he still couldn't get his voice to work. Tears of relief filled his eyes. He shook as the fear seeped from his wracked body, turning him from rigidity to jelly in less than a second.

'It wasn't me you were expecting, then?' Sayola asked light-heartedly.

'No,' croaked Rawin. He cleared his throat and tried again. 'No.' Better this time. Then, 'It was my last moment on Earth. That I was expecting, I mean.'

'Good thing it was me, then,' smiled Sayola. 'What are you doing here all alone?' He strolled languidly over to where Rawin was sitting and sat down slowly next to him on the fallen tree. 'These woods can be dangerous, you know.'

'Yep. I know. I know.'

Then a short silence.

'So?' continued Sayola.

'It's a long story,' replied Rawin with mock humour.

'I've got plenty of time.'

Rawin didn't know where to start. He remembered that Sayola's twin, Meeya, had told him and Catt that some evil force had separated them – turning him into a monkey and her into a swan. Rawin also remembered that when they met in the forest the first time Sayola knew exactly how much bounty had been on their heads – a hundred thousand pieces of gold. And he seemed to know who wanted them dead. Rawin swallowed hard as he recalled how close Catt had come to being killed by a demon. Only Sayola's perfectly aimed spear had saved her; the same spear that the handsome monkey carried now.

'Um, I'm not sure where to start,' Rawin said.

'Wherever you like,' Sayola replied.

'Well, how about this?' Rawin said, with fresh enthusiasm. 'I've met your twin sister.'

Sayola seemed to flinch. It was the first time Rawin could recall seeing him show any emotion. After briefly hesitating, Sayola replied. 'Tell me more.'

'She lives in the moat around the demon city of Langka.' He looked closely at Sayola but it wasn't clear if he already knew this. So he went on. 'She misses you.' Sayola flinched again. 'She helped me and Catt; that's my friend from Bangkok. You remember her, right? You saved her life. We needed to get across the moat, so Meeya took us. We talked.'

'What did she say?'

'She told us that an evil force had done this to you and her.'

Sayola nodded faintly.

'And she said she was expecting us. Me and Catt. "The boy and the girl" was how she described us. She knew she should help us because your grandmothers had told stories about how evil would come to your land and that when the boy and the girl came then the evil could be defeated.'

'And you are that boy and girl?' asked Sayola flatly.

'Well, I wasn't sure. But Meeya was sure we were. And

she, well, she inspired us.'

'How did she do that?'

'She helped us. And then she said she believed we would defeat the evil force and this would help her. And you.'

'And you believe that?'

'I didn't at first.'

'Now you do?'

'Yes.'

'What changed your mind?'

'Her faith. Not just her faith. She also convinced me that you don't always have to act only on what you know. I mean, on facts. Facts are important, of course. But sometimes you've got to listen to your heart because you might not ever have all the facts and if you keep waiting for all the facts then you end up waiting forever. So you need to have faith in an ideal but also faith in yourself. We need both.'

Sayola remained silent. He looked aimlessly toward the ground, his head slightly bowed.

After a few minutes, Rawin asked: 'Do you believe that you and your sister could be reunited, like you were before?'

'I am not very good at hoping.'

So deep in thought were the two that they hadn't noticed shadows moving in the trees a short distance away. But then they heard the sound. A dull thump, thump.

Rawin stood up, alert.

Sayola was already up. He lifted his spear and looked intensely in the direction of the sound. 'Elephant,' he whispered.

Yet again Rawin's heart began to pound. The forest was dense around them so they couldn't see the elephant, if that's what the thumping was. Then they saw it. Mareet was walking beside the animal that carried the chilling figure of Totsakan in all his demonic glory on its neck. At the precise moment that they saw them, Totsakan and Mareet turned and saw Sayola and Rawin.

'Hah!' shouted Mareet. He turned and ran directly at them, swinging his sword.

'Wait,' Totsakan shouted. 'Don't kill them yet.' He turned his elephant and directed it quickly into the small clearing where Sayola and Rawin stood in fear. Rawin looked at Sayola who held his spear in both hands levelled at the enemy. Mareet ran frighteningly fast around behind them to cut off any avenue of escape while Totsakan brought his elephant to a halt in front of them.

'So, boy, where is the girl? Has she left you?' teased Totsakan, still aloft on his elephant. 'And who, may I ask, is this monkey? A new friend?'

Neither Rawin nor Sayola spoke. They remained transfixed by the gigantic menace before them. Sayola looked behind them and knew Mareet would be able to stop any attempt to run. Mareet laughed: 'Go on, try to run, monkey. My sword hasn't drawn blood for quite a while. I'd love to give it a chance to enjoy the feeling again.'

Rawin was holding his backpack limply at his side. Slowly he slipped his hand into the side pocket and took out his Rubik Twist, which he hid behind his leg. Then he bent over and dropped to his knees and began to cry. 'Please, please,' he wailed. 'Don't hurt us.' He buckled over and used his body to hide his hands, which very quickly got to work on the Rubik Twist, turning, twisting, shaping.

'Oh, stop snivelling, pathetic child,' Totsakan said. He laughed again and looked over at Mareet. 'Do you feel sorry for him, Mareet?' Both demons laughed loudly. As they did so, Rawin slipped his phone into his other hand.

Then he said loudly in a pleading voice: 'Yes, this is my friend. His name is JaoJuk. Please don't hurt him. JaoJuk is a kind monkey.'

'JaoJuk, hey?' Totsakan chuckled. 'Nice spear, JaoJuk. Are you one of Hanuman's tricky soldiers?'

Sayola looked at Rawin, who whispered, 'I've got a plan.' Then he looked up at Totsakan and called again: 'JaoJuk and I like to play puzzle games together, that's all. He's not a soldier. He's like me. We are gamers.'

Totsakan laughed: 'Who is the trickier one out of the two of you? Is he also able to use magic to make a machine with wheels to run away from me? Did he tell you about that, monkey? In a minute I will allow Mareet to punish him for doing that. He'll never do something like that again.'

Sayola remained silent, not knowing what to think or say. At the same time Rawin managed to flip his phone deftly around in his hand while his arm hung by his side so as not to draw attention to it. Then he touched the phone icon on the home screen with his thumb and, pretending to rub his eyes with his other hand, looked down and saw the 'Unknown caller' number that he knew was Sukreep's. He touched it and waited, shaking with fear that Totsakan or Mareet might see what he was up to.

'Why do you not speak, monkey?' Totsakan asked. 'Did someone cut your tongue out?'

Just then Rawin heard his phone connect. He was sure it would be Sukreep, but he had to stop him from speaking because he was sure Totsakan would hear. So before Sukreep could even say 'Hello', Rawin started saying loudly, as if he was speaking to Sayola, 'JaoJuk, JaoJuk. You do not have to speak to the Demon King. Come on JaoJuk, play one last game with me now because I think the demons are planning to kill us. Just listen to me, JaoJuk.'

Sayola looked at him with confusion all over his face. Rawin estimated that enough time had elapsed for Sukreep to hand the phone to JaoJuk.

'Right, you remember our game, JaoJuk?' said Rawin loudly, addressing himself to Sayola, but really to the phone hidden at his side. 'Show the Demon King what you do when I say a word.'

'Intriguing,' Totsakan said. 'Come on JaoJuk, play the boy's little game one more time before he dies.'

'JaoJuk, now, the word is: Tiger!' shouted Rawin. 'Tiger.'

In an instant the Rubik Twist was transformed into a raging tiger that immediately charged at Totsakan's elephant, snarling aggressively. The elephant reared in alarm, sending Totsakan falling over its back on to the ground. Mareet rushed to help his master up as the animal stampeded into the forest. Then the two demons ran frantically into the woods behind it, chased by the gnashing tiger.

Sayola looked horrified as they disappeared from view and turned to Rawin. 'Um, how did you do that? Faith? Did you have faith in yourself?'

'No,' said Rawin with a triumphant smile, returning his Rubik Twist to the pocket of his backpack. 'I had faith in a little guy you're going to love when you meet him.'

'Can't wait,' said Sayola, and the two trudged off together into the woods, headed for Ram's chalet.

# CHAPTER
# THIRTY

Catt felt desolate. Rawin was right. What Hanuman had done was evil. And you cannot defeat evil with evil, she thought. So now Rawin was gone. She felt terribly, terribly guilty for saying that the deaths of hundreds of demons was 'what happened in war'. What was she thinking when she said that? Now she felt utterly alone, physically and morally. She walked almost robotically back towards Ram's chalet, barely thinking about where she was going or what she would say when she got there.

The time passed quickly. All she was aware of was that disjointed thoughts kept swirling in her mind and she never arrived at a single coherent one before they went round and round again in circles.

Soon she arrived at the chalet. She still didn't know the code to call out so she just walked towards the building defiantly. She even heard herself think, If someone shoots me by accident, I don't care.

As she neared the chalet she felt someone was watching her. Then she saw JaoJuk on the platform standing dead still, arms crossed, looking at her. He showed no emotion.

'JaoJuk, hi,' she said, slightly nervously. Why did JaoJuk do things like that? she wondered. Couldn't he at least wave or smile? Or blink, even. It would be creepy if it weren't for the fact that the child was actually very sweet in many ways. She couldn't remember if she had ever seen JaoJuk smile, but she felt as though she had. There was something about that child that felt right, but she didn't know what it was. After all, there were no clear signals about what was going on inside that little head.

JaoJuk nodded a greeting.

Catt thought, if JaoJuk isn't going to say anything, I'm not going to make an effort to talk to him. So she prepared to look for Ram and the others. She took one more quick look at JaoJuk who was still watching her. 'What?' she said.

'Rawin is OK,' said JaoJuk. 'He phoned. We made a tiger.' He then slipped away and sat on a low wooden stool as if the conversation had ended.

Catt felt irritated. She doubted she would get anything more out of JaoJuk. She sighed loudly. 'A tiger?'

'Catt,' came a voice from inside the chalet. It was Sukreep, who came up to her. 'Boy, am I glad to see you. Where are the others?'

'Oh, Sukreep, Sukreep,' Catt began, almost tearful. All those swirling thoughts were still swirling. She didn't know where to begin or what to say. But being with someone she could talk to had uncorked the bottle of emotion inside her. She just wasn't sure what was going to come out.

'What is it, my child?' said Sukreep. 'Where are the others?' he repeated. He approached the girl and clasped her upper arm with one hand comfortingly.

'Frankly, I don't care where Hanuman is. I don't care if I never see him again,' she said.

'Oh dear. What's happened?'

'Rawin has gone. Back to our universe.'

'Not,' said JaoJuk.

'JaoJuk!' Catt shouted angrily, 'What are you talking about? What is that supposed to mean? 'Not'. That doesn't mean anything.' Tears filled her eyes.

JaoJuk raised an eyebrow and pouted, but didn't say anything.

'You see,' Catt said with dismay, turning to Sukreep and then back to JaoJuk.

Sukreep came to the rescue: 'Rawin used the telepathy,' he said.

'Telephone. Tele*phone*,' Catt barked. 'It's a tele*phone*.'

Sukreep waited patiently and then continued: 'I could tell he wanted to talk to JaoJuk, so I passed the...' He hesitated for a second. '... the tele*phone*... over to him. JaoJuk just nodded and pointed at the sky and then we heard a rushing sound, like a powerful wind. It only lasted about a second and then it was over. And then JaoJuk gave the phone back to me but the call had ended.'

Catt turned to JaoJuk, 'Ugh, JaoJuk, come on,' she said emphatically. 'What happened? Is Rawin OK?'

'Rawin is OK,' said JaoJuk, and then he hopped off the stool. 'His tiger saved him.' Then he ran off into the woods.

Catt just stood there shaking her head, her hands on her hips.

Sukreep led her to another stool and told her to sit down. 'Why are you alone? Why did you say that about Hanuman?'

'Sukreep, Hanuman is a murderer,' Catt exclaimed.

'Oh, Catt, what are you saying?' Sukreep asked, his face contorted with distress.

Just then the princes appeared from the back of the chalet. They had heard voices and had come to investigate.

'Did you say murderer?' Ram asked.

'Yes,' said Catt, now a bit calmer. 'He set fire to Langka. The whole city burned. Many died. It was horrible.'

Ram's face hardened. He looked out into the woods as if searching for an answer to the questions that tumbled through his mind. Then he turned back to Catt. 'Tell me what happened.'

Catt told the story of how they had seen Hanuman trying to persuade Sida to come away with him. And how later she and Rawin had seen him dancing across the rooftops of the city, setting fire to everything his tail touched. 'He was laughing,' she said. 'Laughing.' Then she buried her face in her hands and began to sob.

'This is madness,' Ram said. 'Sukreep, what could your nephew have been thinking?'

'Master,' responded Sukreep, 'this is very disturbing. I

won't rest until I have discovered the truth.'

Lak asked the question that everyone else feared to ask: 'And Sida? What happened to her?'

'I don't know,' Catt said. She had stopped crying. 'Not everything was destroyed, and many demons escaped. We saw them cross the moat. But we never saw her.'

Just then their conversation was interrupted by a loud voice from the forest. It was Hanuman, chanting the coded call. Everyone went silent.

Lak took charge: 'Approach, Hanuman,' he called out loudly.

Hanuman came out from the woods and saw that everyone was looking at him with the sternest expressions he had ever seen. He stopped and surveyed this unwelcoming party. He knew in an instant what it was about. He had himself reflected on what he had done and there was no way he could justify it, but he tried to rescue himself anyway. He looked at everyone as innocently as he could and said: 'Langka has been rebuilt. The gods restored it.'

At once Catt turned and ran at him and began pounding his chest with her fists and shouting, 'Don't try to excuse yourself. What you did was unforgiveable. You know that. Oh, why, why?' Her eyes were closed as she pounded him, as if she could not bear to see him. He simply stood still as she did so. Then she fell to her knees and pounded the ground two or three times and then curled up into a ball and began to sob loudly again.

Ram rushed to her and knelt beside her. As he did so, Rawin and Sayola stepped unseen from the woods nearby. Rawin put out a hand to stop Sayola from getting closer. Together, in silence and unnoticed, they witnessed the scene unfold.

'Precious child,' said Ram. 'Your crying will not go uncomforted, for those tears are shed by eyes that have witnessed a monstrous injustice.'

Rawin wiped his eyes. Sayola looked at him sympathetically and then back at the spectacle before them.

'Come, child,' Ram went on, 'swap your sadness for fresh courage. Turn your eyes once more on the perpetrator of this terrible crime and demand penitence, for I give you my word, if contrition is unforthcoming from this scoundrel, I will here and now, personally sever his head from his shoulders.' Then he stood up and walked towards Hanuman, who went down on one knee and lowered his head.

'Hanuman, brave but foolish soldier. You have grown arrogant from the power you wield. You have forgotten what it is like not to be the quickest in body and mind. You deserve no mercy other than that of one who is more powerful than you, quicker in body and mind, and above all not arrogant like you. Look at this girl, for it is she of whom I speak. If she forgives you, so shall I. If not, prepare to die.'

Hanuman turned to Catt, who had slowly, reluctantly risen and stepped over to stand before him: 'Catt,' said Hanuman humbly, 'what our master Prince Ram says of you is indeed the truth. Your powers are infinite and your humility unbridled. You have sacrificed everything to assist us in our struggle and have put your own life at risk. All I can do is to beg you to believe that my heart is weighed down with regret for what I did. Only your forgiveness can ease my burden.'

'Oh, Hanuman, you will never know what your foolishness has brought upon me. Not only was your action evil in itself, but it also sabotaged the bigger fight against the evil of Totsakan. You do not know this – no one does yet – but when Rawin saw what you had done, he decided to abandon the fight against the monster and return to our universe. If the grandmothers were right to say that the evil that stalks this land would be defeated when the boy and the girl come to join the side of righteousness, you will be forever remembered as the one who overturned that prophecy. I am still here, but I cannot do it without him. My purpose is broken.'

'Brave one, fear not.' It was Sayola. Everyone turned to see him standing side by side with Rawin. 'The boy, as everyone calls him, is here, with renewed faith. And I think he might be able to mend your purpose – and your heart, for I think that too might be broken.'

'Rawin!' Catt shouted, running to him. Looking slightly embarrassed, Rawin smiled bravely, for he had been fighting back the tears while he watched. As Catt reached him, it looked like they were about to hug each other, but they stopped, looking embarrassed. After a second, she raised her hand and they gave each other an exuberant high-five.

Rawin then spoke to everyone: 'I overheard Totsakan talking to his henchman Mareet. They didn't know I was in his cave. The Demon King has vowed that he will capture Catt and make her beg for mercy. And then he said he will kill her anyway. There is no doubt in my mind any longer that Totsakan is evil. I swear now that I will fulfil my destiny to help defeat him and the evil he has brought to this land.'

Lak, Hanuman and Sukreep cheered. Catt looked relieved at Rawin and nodded. Ram smiled warmly and opened his hands to include all who stood around: 'Let us eat and sleep well, for tomorrow we will march on Langka and bring an end to the reign of the evil Spectre.'

# CHAPTER THIRTY-ONE

otsakan's elephant stopped running once it became clear that the tiger unleashed by Rawin and JaoJuk was no longer in pursuit. Totsakan and Mareet eventually caught up with it at a stream where it had waded into the water to drink.

'Cowardly, stupid brute,' Totsakan complained. 'You don't deserve to live.' Without hesitating, he drew an arrow from his quiver and shot it with stunning accuracy in the head just in front of its ear. The elephant did not move, but its body contracted slowly, like a deflating balloon. Totsakan unleashed a second arrow that entered the elephant's brain next to the first one. The animal's back legs folded and the creature rocked backwards, letting out a long, plaintive roar of agony before it fell over on its side in the water. It did not struggle, but one foot moved pathetically up and down before it settled limply into the water. A copper-coloured cloud of blood spread from the wound through the water.

'Mareet, come on. We are finished with this disloyal cretin. I don't tolerate betrayal.' He knew that Mareet would now be more loyal to him than ever. Totsakan loved loyalty.

The two demons crossed the bridge in silence back into Langka. They had not spoken much but Totsakan cursed from time to time about how Rawin had now twice used some mysterious magic to escape captivity. He ranted angrily and it was clear to Mareet, even though Mareet was not a very perceptive creature himself, that his master was now jittery about his unpredictable and powerful enemies.

Still, the sight of a restored Langka filled Totsakan with renewed pride and he began to walk more upright, his head held higher.

'So greatly do the gods approve of my kingdom that they have rebuilt Langka to shine more brightly, to stand more proudly,' he said, surveying the city and its bustling citizens before him. 'Sida will not doubt my greatness after this.'

'We will silence all those who torment us, master,' said Mareet. He felt good when he said things that his master loved to hear.

'Yes, come on. Bring Benjakai to my palace. She is no doubt fawning over her mistress.'

Mareet went to carry out the wishes of his master. Totsakan restored himself to human form and poured himself a drink before sitting on an opulently upholstered grand armchair at one end of a carpeted reception room off the main hall of the palace. The late afternoon sun streamed in through tall windows but the room was comfortably cool. He liked what he saw and raised his glass as if to toast someone. But he was alone and he felt happy drinking to himself.

Soon there was a timid knock on the tall doors at the far end of the room.

'Enter,' Totsakan commanded.

The doors opened slightly and stopped.

'Enter,' thundered Totsakan.

The doors opened further, revealing Benjakai dressed in an elegant but simple full-length maiden's gown, her hair tied back with a colourful silk scarf. Her head was slightly bowed, her shoulders down.

'Come closer,' Totsakan ordered.

Benjakai shuffled into the middle of the room, about 10 yards from where Totsakan sat. Her eyes were wet. Mareet entered and closed the door behind him.

'How is your mistress?' asked Totsakan in a small-talk way.

'She is fine, thank you, my lord.'

'You love her, don't you?'

'I do, my lord.'

'I am glad to hear that.' Then after a pause, 'The true test of love is sacrifice, isn't it?'

'I don't know, my lord.'

'Well, it is. Too much love is for self. Real love is selfless.'

'Yes, my lord.'

'Like the love you have for your father.'

Benjakai did not respond.

'You will miss him, won't you?'

'Yes, Sir.'

'Young lady, my sweet niece, I know you well. And I know you have a heart full of love. This fills me with joy and pride.'

'Thank you, Uncle.'

'And I would like to give you an opportunity to express your love. The love you have for your father, the purest love that a young woman can have.'

Benjakai looked puzzled and remained silent for a few seconds. Then, 'How may I do that, my lord?'

'You see, dear Benjakai, your father spoke out of turn. He believed he was doing the right thing, that he was using his powers to foretell the future. But he went too far.'

'I am so sorry to hear that, my lord. I am sure he did not mean to do that.'

'You're right. So, let's help him. Let's find a way to help him correct his mistake.'

'I would very much like to do that, my lord. What did he say that he should not have said?'

'Ah, young lady, you ask too many questions, the answers to which should not fall on your young, inexperienced ears.'

'I am sorry, my lord.'

'What I can tell you is that your father believes Sida is a danger to our city, to all of our lives. He said something terrible would happen because of her.'

'How so, my lord? One so serene and gracious cannot surely be dangerous.'

'Ah, you're right. She is those things – and many more. It isn't she, herself, that is a threat to us. It's her presence here in Langka.'

'Is that what my father said?'

'Yes, it is what your father said. And he concluded that only if she is no longer here will our city and our way of life be safe. Even now, Ram and his army are preparing to march on our city. They speak of what they call "the final battle".'

Benjakai opened her mouth to speak, but stopped, afraid that she might, like her father, speak out of turn. Totsakan noticed. 'Yes, young lady, he said what you are too afraid to say. He said Sida would have to die to save Langka.'

Benjakai lifted her hands to her mouth and cried out, 'No, no, no, please.'

'I can see how much you love her.'

'With all my heart, lord.'

'Then can you cut your heart in two? One part with which to love your father, the other to love your mistress?'

'No, no, your lordship, I love them equally, both with the same heart. There is no quota for love. To love one you do not have to take away love from another. In fact the more I love my father, the more I love Sida. And the more I love Sida, the more I love my father.'

'Well, young lady, that's very touching,' he said. 'I am glad you feel that way, for it is with that heart, so full of love for them both, that you can repair the damage done by your father.'

'How so, my lord? Tell me. I will do anything.'

'You have your own powers, my dear niece. Now is the time to use them. Transform yourself into the appearance of Sida and pretend that you are dead. Let Prince Ram see the lifeless body of his wife. Once he does so, he will leave us alone. Langka will be safe from him and his army. Your father's prophecy will be negated.'

Benjakai thought for a few seconds but did not speak.

'And you would be reunited with your father. And prove your loyalty to me.'

Her face lit up and then darkened. In her eyes and across her forehead danced a thousand clashing thoughts. Happiness, fear, sadness, confusion, longing.

'Good,' Totsakan concluded, as if she had agreed. 'Go on, then. Mareet will help you. Looking like Sida, you will float your body across the moat to the other side where Ram and his forces are gathered. When he sees that you – Sida – are dead, he will turn away and leave us in peace.'

# CHAPTER
# THIRTY-TWO

The dawn crept over the low hills beyond the forest, sending rays of pale sunshine through the trees, gradually lifting the dark that had settled over Ram's chalet in the night. JaoJuk was meditating cross-legged on the edge of the platform while Sukreep busied himself around a raging fire barbecuing cuts from a wild boar he shot the previous day. He had also prepared an omelette from duck eggs. The smell of tasty food soon brought everyone else out and before long they were all well-fed and ready for the day that lay ahead. They did not speak much to each other. A mood of apprehension hung over the small group as they thought of the battle that was to come.

Rawin helped Sukreep clear away the remains of the meal and waited for a moment when they could be alone. 'Sukreep,' he began cautiously, 'I am sorry to bring this up but something has been worrying me for a long time,' he began.

'What is it, boy? Feel free to ask.'

'Well, I read in the book... OK, I know you keep saying the book is not the same thing as your life. But help me understand. In the book, Prince Ram kills Phali, your brother.' He waited for a few seconds, then asked sadly, 'Did he?'

Sukreep breathed in deeply and looked sideways at Rawin. 'Why has this been worrying you, Rawin?'

'Because killing someone is serious. It's bad, isn't it?' replied Rawin firmly. Then he added: 'If my brother was killed I would want to know who did it and why.' He paused. Then: 'Don't you think that?'

'Young man – may I call you that, for your mind is so much more mature than your physical being – not a day goes by when I do not think of my brother.'

'I can understand that,' Rawin said, sympathetically. 'It must be painful for you.'

Sukreep put a hand on Rawin's shoulder and led him to a big log at the edge of the woods that was used as a bench. 'Come, sit down.' He breathed in deeply, as if seeking clarity. 'In life, things happen that we can never understand.'

'We can try,' Rawin replied. 'We should always try to know the truth, shouldn't we?'

'Yes,' Sukreep sighed, 'but sometimes we cannot accept the truth and we won't believe what happens in front of our own eyes. Sometimes it's too painful so we deny it. We even tell ourselves that something didn't happen – or it didn't happen the way others say it did. I do not know about the book you talk about, but I do not blame Prince Ram for my brother's death.'

'Who do you blame?'

'I blame the gods.'

Just then, JaoJuk appeared from behind a tree. He looked into their eyes, first at Rawin, then at Sukreep and then, magically, into both at the same time. Then using the fingers of both his hands he drew a rectangle in the air in front of them. It expanded and filled with pictures, like a film. They gasped. Rawin gripped the log they were sitting on. Sukreep raised his hands to his face and pressed them firmly against his cheeks. Both stared, mesmerised.

*Seated in the lotus position, the god Isuan looked up as Phali and Sukreep approached him, bowing respectfully. Isuan handed Phali a trident and beckoned to a deva. The deva approached as if to attack Phali, who waved the trident. A glowing avatar escaped the body of the deva and in a flash entered Phali, whose body gyrated with increased power. The deva cowered in surrender and Isuan raised his hand to end the challenge. Phali bowed and stepped back, caressing the trident. Then Isuan summoned a beautiful young maiden to step forward. Isuan gestured to Sukreep who took the maiden by the hand and bowed in gratitude. Then Isuan called the god Narai and pointed at Phali and said something to Narai. The scene faded away and another showed Phali sitting on a throne. The young maiden sat at his side while Sukreep sat alone forlornly to one side.*

Rawin turned and looked at Sukreep. He wanted to say something comforting, but he didn't know what. He was only a boy. He could not possibly know how something like that would feel. But he desperately wanted to understand. 'Tell me what happened, Sukreep, please.'

Sukreep replied sombrely: 'We did something good and Lord Isuan rewarded us. A powerful weapon for Phali, a wife for me. He made Phali vow never to take her from me.'

'And what did Lord Isuan say to the other god?'

'That was Lord Narai. He told Narai that if ever my brother broke his promise not to steal my wife, he should be incarnated as Prince Ram and, um, kill Phali.'

'Wow,' said Rawin. He felt silly saying that, but he didn't know what else to say. They looked back at the picture in front of them.

*The two brothers were involved in a ferocious battle with a buffalo which escaped into a cave. Phali said something to Sukreep and then entered the cave. Sukreep sat down outside the cave and waited. The sun rose and set several times and rain fell. When blood seeped from the cave entrance Sukreep touched it with his fingers and wept. He waited while the sun set and rose several more times before he pushed a boulder across the entrance to the cave and returned to the palace. There he placed the crown on his head and addressed the people of the kingdom with tears in his eyes. Then Phali appeared, waved a hand to signal that Sukreep should go, and returned to the throne. Sukreep shuffled away sadly and disappeared into a forest.*

Sukreep turned to Rawin: 'I didn't know my brother was still alive. The blood I saw was the buffalo's but it had been diluted by rainwater. I thought it was Phali's. I was sure he was dead. So I pushed the boulder in front of the cave to stop the buffalo escaping. But Phali wasn't dead, and he managed to shift the boulder and return to our kingdom. My punishment was exile. And so here I am.'

*Inside the forest a fight raged between Prince Ram and Phali, watched by Sukreep. Prince Ram fired an arrow at Phali who held his trident in one hand and effortlessly caught the arrow in the other. As he did so his body glowed with immense energy and power. Prince Ram walked up to Phali and held out his hand and they talked. Phali shook his head, turned and said something to Sukreep, and then plunged Prince Ram's arrow into his own heart and died.*

JaoJuk stepped in front of Sukreep and Rawin, raised both hands and crossed them in front of his face before pulling his arms down sharply to his sides. The screen disappeared.

Sukreep dropped his head into his hands and sobbed. Rawin stroked his shoulder. 'I'm so sorry for you,' he said. Sukreep nodded to acknowledge Rawin's sympathy. But then Rawin could not hold back: 'What happened? Why did he do that?'

Sukreep swallowed and looked up, pulling himself together. 'Prince Ram asked Phali if he could wipe a little bit of his blood on to the blade of his arrow. He wanted to prove that he had shot him and had therefore fulfilled Lord Isuan's order.' Then Sukreep's voice choked and he could not carry on. Eventually he managed to continue: 'My brother refused and said he had to honour the command of the almighty Lord Isuan. He told me he was sorry for what he had done. And then... well, you saw what happened.'

Sukreep stood up and dragged himself away to be alone. Rawin sat, stunned.

A short way away, the others were beginning to gather their weapons, preparing to leave for the journey to Langka. Lak had gone to assemble the monkey army in the fields nearby and to bring three chariots for Ram and his entourage. Sayola, now formally part of the leadership of Hanuman's monkey army, accompanied him, his deadly accurate spear in hand.

Rawin walked back to the chalet dazed by what had just happened. Catt was practising her taekwondo techniques with her sword in both hands in graceful but deadly flashing movements that made Rawin shiver.

'Hey, Rawin,' she called out, 'you ready for this?' She sliced the air with her sword in three quick successive moves that were almost impossible to see because of her speed. Then she stopped and smiled at him, lowering the sword.

'More than ever,' he said, with greater enthusiasm than he had intended.

'Ah, good. I feel this is our time. And soon we'll be able to go home,' said Catt cheerfully.

'Yes,' Rawin joined in, 'and I feel so much better that I now know what we are fighting for.'

Catt sheathed her sword, crossed her arms and looked at Rawin inquiringly, cocking her head to one side. 'Tell me more.'

'Well,' he began, locking his hands behind his head as he looked firmly at her, 'I'm sorry I argued with you about what we were doing here and kept doubting who was right and who was wrong, who was good and who was evil.'

'Oh, come on,' interrupted Catt warmly, 'that's you, Rawin. That's who you are. That's what you do. Question, question, question.'

'Maybe,' he said, 'but now I think I've got answers, answers, answers.'

Catt laughed. 'You've finally decided that Totsakan is an evil monster because he wants to torture and kill me.'

'That, yes, but more than that.'

'What more?'

'Prince Ram.'

'What about him?'

'He didn't kill Sukreep's brother Phali.'

'I thought you said that's what happened in the book.' She hesitated and laughed again. 'Uh-uh, not the book. We are not in the book. Sorry.'

'That's true, but it's not just that. He was carrying out the instructions of Lord Isuan. He was doing what the supreme god ordered. And even then he showed mercy.'

'Unlike Totsakan, who wants to show me no mercy.'

'Exactly.'

'So we ride alongside the merciful good one to defeat the ruthless evil one?'

'Exactly.'

They high-fived each other and laughed.

'You know what else,' Catt continued. 'I long to meet Sida and tell her how greatly I admire her spirit and her courage. She has suffered so much. Even now I worry that Totsakan might prefer to take her life than let her go.'

Just then Lak returned with the three chariots that would lead the march to Langka. They were pulled by stately white horses glittering with ornate livery and jewels. Ram and Hanuman climbed into the biggest chariot at the front and Lak and Sukreep in the second. Rawin, Catt and Sayola were told to get into the third. JaoJuk sat calmly on a small bench at the rear of the chariot facing backwards, his feet swinging. Monkey footmen ran alongside the chariots. The rest of the army was already on the move across the plain on the other side of the trees. Soon they would join up, forming Ram's mighty force in its full glory.

After they had covered a fair distance, one of the scouts who roamed freely ahead sent a coded bark back to his fellow scouts warning of an enemy presence. The code was passed down the line until it reached Hanuman.

'Be alert,' he ordered quietly, 'but keep moving.' He swung athletically out of the chariot and drew his sword, loping silently ahead to join the lookout scouts. The others watched as Hanuman darted from one tree to another, hiding himself and beckoning two or three of the scouts to follow. They too moved swiftly and silently.

Then Hanuman could be heard demanding loudly: 'Who goes there?'

'I come in peace,' came a voice from the depth of the forest.

'Show yourself.'

Slowly, a slightly bowed figure emerged from the trees. It was Pipek. He carried a leather-bound almanac in one hand held up high against his right side like a learned monk. He raised the other hand in a sign of peaceful greeting.

'I am Pipek, brother of Totsakan,' he said. 'I beg to be able to speak to Prince Ram.'

'If you think you can persuade Prince Ram not to destroy your evil brother, you are seriously mistaken,' responded Hanuman.

'No, this is not my mission,' said Pipek. 'Totsakan has exiled me from his kingdom for telling the truth.'

'And what truth is that?'

'The truth that says, if he does not allow Sida to return to her husband, something terrible will happen to Langka.'

'How true indeed are your words,' came the voice of Ram, who had jumped down from the chariot and quietly joined them. 'I am told that you are a fortune teller, Pipek, but you do not need to be a wise sage to know that I will not rest until Sida is back at my side and Totsakan annihilated.'

'To this end and to you,' replied Pipek, 'I am willing to devote my service and my loyalty.' He bowed.

'If you come in good faith, Pipek, then I accept your offer. You may join with us. I look forward to hearing your wise counsel.'

'But, my lord,' said Pipek gloomily, 'I should share with you a vision that greatly disturbs me.'

'What is it?' Ram asked guardedly.

'Forgive me for not being able to see perfectly,' said Pipek, 'but I see signs of something terrible that has happened or is about to happen.'

'What?' Ram commanded. 'Speak.'

'My lord, I fear I am too late.'

'What makes you say that? What do you see?' Ram asked.

'I see the lifeless body of Sida,' he cried out, and fell to his knees.

# CHAPTER THIRTY-THREE

Sida had been imprisoned in one of the larger palace buildings at the top of the hill. She was told that Totsakan would not allow her back into the walled garden for fear she might be kidnapped – or even try to flee. Two demons were standing at attention outside the door. She stood at a window that had been covered with bamboo bars, but the palace buildings were high enough for her to be able to see over the city to the moat and the forests that stretched far into the distance that formed the horizon. She wondered when Ram would come to rescue her as Hanuman had promised. She fixed her gaze on the forest in the hope of seeing him riding at the front of his army. She realised she had done that many times already that morning, even seeing movement in the trees, then knowing it was only her imagination. Her eyes dropped and she swallowed in an effort to fight away the tears.

She heard a light knock. Turning her head elegantly she called out: 'Who is it?'

'My lady, it is Benjakai.'

'Come in.'

The door opened and the two guards stepped aside to allow Benjakai to enter. Then they closed the door behind her.

'Mistress…,' Benjakai began, but she was unable to speak.

'What is it, Benjakai? What's the matter? You look terrible.'

'Oh, Mistress Sida, my heart is broken. My eyes won't stop flooding.'

'Yes, I can see, dear one. Tell me, what's the reason for all this?'

'Little did I know how love could be like a sword that can sever a heart in two. I am in both heaven and hell.'

'Dear angel, I know of the heaven, for I have been blessed with your love. But the hell? What hell?'

'Oh, Sida, Sida, my father has been banished from Langka. Totsakan has sent him into exile.'

'For what?'

'He interpreted Totsakan's dreams.'

'Nightmares, you mean. Such a creature cannot dream.'

'My lady, you're right. For him they were indeed nightmares.'

'And what did your father say they meant?'

'He said…' Benjakai hesitated.

'Go on, my dear friend, nothing can hurt me more than what I have already suffered.'

'He said your presence here in Langka would lead to a terrible disaster. He urged Totsakan to set you free.'

'The gods bless your father then.'

'But this made Totsakan very angry. He vowed never to let you go and instead he ordered my father to leave the kingdom forever. Exiled.'

'Oh, poor you. And you love your father so much. What injustice!'

'Dear Sida, forgive me.'

'Forgive you for what?'

'This isn't my choice.'

'What is not your choice? You will never do something that will need to be forgiven. Not you, dear, precious Benjakai.'

'No, no, mistress. You are wrong. You are wrong. I will soon do terrible harm to you.'

'How, dear Benjakai, will you do that? You are gentle and loving. You are kind and just. You're not capable of doing harm to anyone.'

'Harm to one can be kindness to another, my lady.'

'Now you speak like your father. Are you a philosopher too?' Sida joked.

'No, my lady. This is not philosophy. It is the terrible truth.'

'So, who will you harm and be kind to at the same time?' asked Sida, almost playfully.

'Oh, mistress. You and my father.'

'How so?'

'Like this.' Benjakai held her hands up to her face and screamed. Her body twisted and shook and was slowly transformed into that of a demon. Her pretty face remained pretty but was now adorned with a golden headdress, pointed at the top. The full-length gown that once covered her slim body had gone. Instead, her top half was naked, apart from an ornate golden necklace that reached down between her breasts. She wore a full-length gold-coloured sarong skirt with dark red trimmings. 'I am this,' she cried. 'This is me. I am a demon. I belong to the race of demons. My father is one, my uncle is the king of the demons. I have to be loyal to him. I have to be who I am.'

Sida saw that Benjakai no longer displayed the kind smile she always showed when addressing her mistress. Instead, fangs protruded from the corners of her mouth. She suppressed a gasp and breathed in deeply. 'Benjakai,' she said softly, 'you do me no harm by being who you are. I have always known you are a demon. But you are still you. Maybe you are happier like this. Whatever you are I still love you. No, my dear Benjakai, the only harm you can do to me is to try to stop me loving you.' She raised her chin and smiled. 'And what about the kindness you spoke of? What kindness will you bring to your father?'

'This!' cried the demon. And again Benjakai transformed right in front of Sida's eyes. But those eyes would not believe what they saw. Sida held her hands over them and looked again and then she hid her eyes again and looked again and again and again. And each time she saw the same thing. Standing in front of her was her exact mirror image. Benjakai had been transformed into her, Sida.

Sida ran to a mirror at the end of the room and stood there staring at herself. She turned and looked back at Benjakai. But that was like looking into another mirror. She saw herself.

'Madam,' cried Benjakai. 'I am sorry. I am so sorry. This is the only way I can bring my father home. The kindness I will do him is the harm I will do to you.'

'But I don't understand,' cried Sida. She looked frantically at herself in front of her.

'My dear, dear, Sida. When your loving husband sees me, he will think I am you but I will pretend to be dead. He will believe you've died and he will go away broken-hearted. He will leave Langka, and Totsakan will have you forever.' She fell to her knees sobbing. 'And my father will be allowed to return to Langka. That is the deal.'

At that moment the door swung open and Totsakan swooped in. He looked at Benjakai on her knees and strode over to her. 'Very convincing,' he said coldly as he looked her up and down. Then he swept a hand across the back of her head, knocking her over completely. 'Get up, you snivelling child. Go and do what you are told.' He grasped her arm and lifted her from the floor and flung her towards the door. 'Take her,' he commanded. Mareet appeared and thrust his arm under Benjakai's limp body, hauling her from the room.

Then Totsakan turned to Sida. 'Prince Ram will have her. And I will have you,' he barked.

# CHAPTER THIRTY-FOUR

anuman turned to Ram: 'Do not believe this
fraudster, Master,' he insisted. 'He is an agent of his
evil brother. He has come to sow doubt in your
mind and to weaken your resolve. Don't listen to him. Let me
kill him now.'

'No, no,' Ram commanded. 'Leave him.'

Still on his knees, Pipek looked at Ram and nodded.
'Allow him to kill me, Lord, for I have nothing left to live for.
I have been banished from my home and will never see my
loving daughter again.'

'Are you sure it was Sida you saw in your vision?' asked
Ram hopefully.

'My Lord, I cannot say it is conclusive but what I saw
was very strong. I saw you holding Sida in your arms. But far
from this being the happy moment for which you long, it was
a moment of terrible grief.'

'Visions be damned. A few minutes ago you said you
wanted to serve me and to reunite me with my wife. Prove to
me that you are sincere. Come with us now and expel this
darkness from your mind.' He turned to Hanuman and the
others who had gathered by now. 'Come everyone. The
battle awaits us. Sida awaits me. I will not be thwarted by

visions.'

As the others began to return to their chariots on Ram's command, Hanuman quietly walked up to Pipek and put an arm under his, lifting him from his knees back to his feet. 'I will be watching you, man. Try any funny stuff and I will take your head off.' He patted his sword.

When Hanuman returned to his chariot, the children asked anxiously what had happened. 'Nothing,' said Hanuman curtly. 'Just some confused visionary who can't think straight. Keep your mind on the fight ahead.'

The journey took several hours but passed quickly as everyone's mind was fixed on the challenge that lay ahead. Catt and Rawin had earlier explained to the monkey scouts that they should lead the army round to the far side of the city, where the main gate was situated, and soon the scouts reported to Ram that they had reached the edge of the woods that bordered the plain beside the moat.

'Catt and Rawin, go ahead and see how things look. You know the area,' Ram ordered.

'I'm going too,' said Sayola, hopping off the chariot and darting after the other two children. The three of them approached the water's edge slowly, keeping low.

'No sign of the bridge,' Rawin noted.

'No, but there's the wheel that raises it, over there,' Catt said. Further along the shore stood the wheel with the crank handles that the children had seen earlier.

'Right,' Rawin went on. 'Come on, let's get over there and have a look.'

They scampered alongside the water, still keeping low, until they reached the wheel, but they could see that the bridges were down, invisible under the water.

'We will have to come up with a plan for getting those bridges up so our soldiers can get across the moat,' Rawin said. 'If they try to swim, they would be sitting ducks for the demon archers. But there is no sign of the ropes that pull the bridges up. They must be under the water too.'

At this point they were down on their haunches and elbows, leopard-crawling to the edge of the moat.

'Can you see anything?' asked Sayola.

'Nothing,' Rawin replied.

'Except…' Catt said in a cheerful voice. 'Her.'

'Who?'

'Her.' She chuckled and pointed as Meeya the swan glided towards them.

'Oh my God,' said Sayola, 'It's you, isn't it?'

'My dear brother,' said Meeya, 'yes, it's me. I miss you so much it feels like I will die if we cannot be together again soon.'

'It's going to happen soon, don't you worry,' Catt said boldly. 'Our army is in those woods waiting to attack the city and defeat the Spectre. Then the curse on you two will be lifted.'

'Just in time,' sighed Meeya.

Sayola waded a few feet into the water and stretched out a hand. Meeya rubbed her beautiful neck on his arm as they looked into each other's eyes.

'I'm going to cry in a minute,' said Catt.

'Don't look,' Rawin joked.

'It's OK,' said Meeya reassuringly. 'You've probably never seen a monkey caressing a swan before. Don't miss it.'

Catt let out a strangled laugh that turned into a sob. 'Oh, stop it you two. Now look what you've made me do.' She wiped her eyes.

'Sorry to spoil the fun,' Rawin interrupted, 'but Meeya, do you think you could do a little inspection for us under the water?'

'Anything I can do to help,' she said.

'Can you see if the ropes for raising the bridge are under there?'

Meeya swivelled and darted under the water in a flash. A few minutes later she returned with a rope trailing from her beak and extending into the water behind her.

'That's it. That's the one,' said Rawin.

Meeya passed it to him.

'Thanks. That's brilliant. Now all we need is someone as strong as two demons to turn the wheel to pull the bridge up.'

'I know just the man who can,' said Catt. 'Just the monkey, in fact.'

'Hanuman.'

They all chuckled. Rawin looped the rope around the

wheel that the demons had used to lever the bridge up. 'I'll stay here until Hanuman comes,' he said.

'Thanks for your help, Meeya,' said Catt. 'I'll head back to the others to tell them what's happening here. You two can stay and talk for a while. But sooner or later we're going to need you and your super spear, Sayola. You might have to save my life a second time.'

'It would be my pleasure,' said Sayola. 'But I hope it never becomes necessary.'

Catt scuttled off to return to the others, staying low again along the water's edge until she reached the point where Ram's army remained hidden in the woods on the other side of the short plain. Just as she was about to cross to the woods she noticed something at the water's edge.

Lying face down in the mud was a motionless body. Catt approached anxiously. 'Oh my God, no,' she stammered. 'This can't happen. No, no, no.'

She ran to the body and touched its neck to search for a pulse. But before she was able to feel anything, Ram approached with Pipek and Hanuman beside him.

'Catt, what is it?' Ram asked anxiously.

'Oh, Prince Ram,' Catt moaned tearfully.

Ram ran the remaining distance and fell to his knees beside the body, lifting it into his arms. What followed was the most haunting cry of pain ever heard in the universe, like everyone who had ever suffered the death of a loved one had poured their agony into a single voice that carried across the plains and the hills and through the forests and beyond.

Pipek rushed to his side. 'Oh gods, damn me, I beg you. This is the sight I saw in my vision. This very heart-breaking spectacle before me, exactly like this. How can I reverse this terrible, terrible thing? If only I had the power to undo the past rather than see the future.'

Ram's body shuddered as he wept uncontrollably. Hanuman tried to console him, but he turned away. He clung to the limp body in his arms as if somehow he could comfort her.

Hanuman crouched beside his master and watched gloomily as there appeared to be no end to Ram's torment. He turned to Pipek, who was clutching his chest as if he wanted to tear it open and pluck his heart out. 'Since you can see so much, wise man, can you see who did this?'

'I cannot. I don't have that power.'

'But you said you had a vision of this. Did you see nothing before this? How did it happen? Are you saying Sida killed herself? Or Totsakan killed her? Do you know nothing, Mr Fortune-teller?'

'I don't know. What more can I say?' Pipek moaned.

Hanuman walked over to Catt and put an arm around her shoulder. Quietly he said to her, 'There's something not quite right about this. Sida tried to kill herself once before, in the garden. I was there. She thought all was lost and that she would never be free. But I convinced her that Prince Ram was coming to rescue her and I know she believed me and that she had hope. Why would she now lose that hope when she knew Prince Ram would soon arrive to free her? This doesn't make sense.'

'Maybe Totsakan decided to kill her,' Catt suggested.

'Never. He has risked everything, his city, his brother's loyalty, everything, to keep her. The more I think about it, the more I am sure this is some sort of trick. Remember, it was through a trick that he was able to abduct her in the first place. He got one of his henchman to shape-shift into a deer and then imitate Prince Ram's voice. Wait. That's it. It's another one of their shape-shifting tricks.'

Hanuman walked back to Pipek and confronted him. 'Pipek, you are a demon. You know about these things. Is this Sida or someone pretending to be her?'

Ram looked up, a flicker of hope in his eyes. Then he looked down at the lifeless body in his arms again and shook his head, unable to believe that anyone could pretend to be his inimitable wife.

'Come, Mister wise demon, help us here. Is this really Sida?' Hanuman continued.

Pipek remained silent. It was clear that he did not know more.

'Well, then,' said Hanuman, 'let us build a funeral pyre and cremate our beloved Sida.' He turned and started collecting wood. Ram was too stricken with grief to pay attention. Catt could do no more than look on with a heavy heart. But she watched Hanuman with interest. She had always thought he was the cleverest creature she had met, and right now he seemed to know something no one else knew.

Time seemed to stand still. Ram began rocking with the body of his beloved wife still in his arms. Pipek was muttering inaudibly, shaking his head and now and again casting his eyes up to the skies as if to summon the gods.

Soon Hanuman, with the help of some other soldiers, had built a substantial pyre and had found a suitable flint stone with which to set it alight. He held a clump of dry grass close to the stone which he struck expertly with his sword, causing a spark to jump into the grass. It began to smoulder. 'Come, let us say our goodbyes to dear Sida,' he said coolly, and walked over to Ram. He slipped the prince's hands off Sida's body and began to drag it towards the pyre. Ram slumped into a broken heap, unable to resist or watch. One of the soldiers placed the burning dry grass under some of the smaller sticks and blew on them. The fire began to spread across the other sticks and heavier wood on top.

Before Hanuman was able to get close to the flames, the dead body in his grasp sprang to life. 'Wait, wait, stop. It's me, Benjakai. Stop.'

Everyone cast their disbelieving eyes on her as she transformed from Sida into Benjakai.

'Daughter, what have you done?' Pipek cried. Benjakai ran into his arms. 'Forgive me, forgive me. I am sorry. Totsakan forced me to do it.'

'Then Sida is not dead,' said Ram, almost as a question. 'I can live. I was ready to die, but now I have hope again.'

'My lord,' said Benjakai quickly, 'your dear Sida – also my dear Sida – is alive, of that you can be sure.'

'But you, daughter, are as good as dead to me,' snapped Pipek. 'How could you do such a thing? You betrayed your mistress and you sought to deceive Prince Ram. This is unforgiveable.' He shook Benjakai loose and stepped away from her. 'You deserve the most severe punishment there can be.'

'No, no, Father,' she moaned. 'Forgive me, please. I was wrong. I am sorry. Sorry.'

'Young lady,' Ram intervened. 'There must have been a reason you did this.'

'Oh, good lord, please have mercy. Totsakan promised me if I did this he would allow my father to return to Langka and be reunited with his family. There was nothing I wanted more in life than that.'

'Even when it came as a result of you destroying the lives of others,' said Pipek angrily. 'You have forgotten everything I taught you, child. My lord, it is my wish that she should be executed. It is the only just punishment for this crime.'

'So you are not at all a wise man, Fortune-teller,' said Hanuman. 'You claim to be able to see into the future, yet you cannot even see the misery that your own actions would bring.'

Pipek dropped his eyes and then turned to Ram. 'My new lord and master, may I ask you to decide what should be done with this deceitful woman? I wash my hands of her.'

Just then Rawin came running to find out why no one had come to help with the wheel at the bridge. He took in the scene before him and in an instant understood what had happened.

'Prince Ram, Prince Ram,' he insisted, 'I know what happened. This is Benjakai, right?' He looked around and though no one answered, it was clear to him that she was. 'I heard Totsakan and Mareet planning this. I heard them say they would force Benjakai to do this, to pretend to be Sida. It's not her fault.'

'Come to me, young lady,' Ram said gently. Benjakai walked unsteadily over to Ram and stood before him. Her head was bowed and her eyes were closed. 'If your deceit had not been uncovered by the wily Hanuman here, I would have believed Sida to be dead and she would have believed I had forsaken her. Neither of us would have been able to live with the grief. You are truly deserving of harsh punishment.'

'My lord, forgive me,' begged Benjakai. She fell to her knees and clutched Ram's hand. 'I will serve you and Sida for the rest of my days if you can find mercy in your heart.'

'No, young lady,' said Ram quietly. 'If I were to show you mercy it would not be because I would be gaining a servant for life.'

'Then from where, my lord?'

'From knowing that what you did was to mend your father's broken heart. If you are capable of sacrificing all else in order to love your father, then you are deserving of mercy. Come on, be with us. We will march on Langka now. I will be reunited with my loving wife and you with your loving mistress. That will make three happy souls.'

Catt turned to Rawin and wept with relief into his shoulder.

# CHAPTER THIRTY-FIVE

Prince Ram returned to his chariot and led his army out of the woods to the edge of the moat. He turned and addressed them as their eyes combed the walls and buildings of the city beyond the moat in search of the enemy that they knew lay in wait for them.

'My brave and loyal compatriots,' he began, 'we have at last come to the moment we have waited for, when we can confront the perpetrators of evil that have brought misery upon this land, separating husband from wife, brother from sister, father from daughter. We will restore good to our world, bring back kindness, humility and mercy. But first prepare for a long battle. Reach into your good hearts and bring forth the courage needed to prevail. Long live our kingdom and brotherhood!'

The monkey army cheered and chanted, 'Long live our kingdom and brotherhood.'

As they did so, they saw Hanuman grip the handle of the huge wheel to which the bridge's ropes were now fastened. He began to turn it. His muscles bulged and his shoulders expanded until he was twice the size of the mightiest demon. Slowly he turned and turned and slowly the bridge began to rise, creaking, from under the water. The monkey army cheered him on.

'This defies all the laws of classical kinetic mechanics,' Rawin remarked.

'Everything Hanuman does defies every law of physics,' Catt chuckled.

'But it goes only halfway across the moat,' Ram observed anxiously. 'That is not enough. Our soldiers cannot risk swimming the rest of the way. The demons will fire on them as they reach the shore. It would be a massacre.'

'Anyone have any ideas?' asked Lak, looking at the others gathered around their leader.

'I know,' Rawin said cheerfully. He turned to the small child beside him who had been watching dispassionately. 'JaoJuk, this is nothing. Bridges are our specialty.' He reached into his backpack and brought out his Rubik Twist. JaoJuk looked at him and the two of them ran side by side on to the bridge as it surfaced. Water was still spilling off the edges as Hanuman gave the wheel the last few turns needed to bring it horizontal.

'What are they doing?' Ram shouted with alarm. 'They will be killed.'

'Don't be afraid, my lord,' Catt reassured him. 'They know what they are doing.'

The monkey army fell silent. Everyone watched in wonder and worry. With relief they saw the two children stop before they reached the end of the bridge. Rawin began to fiddle with the Rubik Twist. JaoJuk stood with his hands on his hips waiting. After a few minutes, Rawin bent down and put the Rubik Twist on the wooden floor of the bridge. JaoJuk cocked his head in Rawin's direction and a slight smile took shape on his lips. ... Bang! A cloud of white smoke enveloped them.

'Oh, no,' Lak shouted, 'they've been hit by cannon fire.' He began sprinting on to the bridge. Catt called after him, telling him not to worry, but Lak didn't hear. He disappeared into the cloud of smoke and the monkey army began murmuring nervously. As the smoke began to clear, they could see three figures standing together on the bridge – the sturdy frame of Lak, sword in hand, and beside him Rawin and next to him JaoJuk, hands still on hips. They were all looking towards the city, their backs to Ram's army.

'My God!' Ram gasped. 'I've seen JaoJuk in action before, but this is amazing.' As he did so, the monkey army began to cheer, for everyone could see a second bridge now connected to the one Hanuman had lifted, providing access all the way across the moat to the gates of the city.

'Brilliant!' Ram said, and then, 'Advance!' He flicked the reins of the horse that pulled his chariot and led his troops on to the bridge. The sound of an army loudly on the march echoed across the water and bounced off the walls of Langka.

Lak and Rawin didn't wait for the others to join them. They began to run on to the new section of the bridge, heading for the gates of the city. JaoJuk stayed where he was. When Lak and Rawin were halfway across the second bridge, a spear sailed through the air from the city walls. Lak saw it coming and in a flash managed to push Rawin out of the way. But as the two of them fell, the spear embedded itself in Lak's thigh.

'What…?' Rawin muttered as he started getting up. Then he saw Lak lying flat on the bridge, the spear protruding from his leg. He ran quickly to his side and tried to pull it out. As he tugged, Rawin expected Lak to cry out in pain, but he just lay there. He was unconscious.

Having seen his brother fall, Ram leapt from his chariot and sprinted across the bridge until he reached him. He knelt down and for the second time in just a few hours held a lifeless body in his arms in heartbroken despair. As he did, he looked up at the top of the city wall where the spear had come from. Standing on the battlements of the city wall, Kumphakan looked triumphantly down on the grim scene below.

Rawin had again found it impossible to find words to comfort Ram. He stood silently staring at the brothers, wishing he could think of something he could do. JaoJuk shrugged disconsolately, his face a picture of helpless gloom. Just then Sayola reached them. He had run after Ram.

'Who… how?' he began.

Ram nodded his head in the direction of the city wall. 'Up there.'

In a flicker Sayola began to run towards the city wall at

an astonishing speed, his spear held in his right hand over his shoulder. Faster and faster until he had almost reached the wall. He threw his weapon with a grunt and watched it as it whistled through the air. Kumphakan seemed to be hypnotised by the weapon as it sailed with deadly accuracy towards his heart. In the fraction of a second before it hit him, he spun sideways and the spear thudded into his left arm. He fell out of sight.

At the water's edge Pipek saw what happened. Though he was not at all athletic, he ran as fast as he could across the bridge until he reached the brothers. 'This is my brother Kumphakan's spear. I know it. Alas, if it is not removed, Prince Lak will die by sunrise tomorrow,' he warned earnestly. 'And the only way it can be done is if you apply a certain medicinal herb to the wound.'

'Tell me quickly, where can I find it?'

'It grows in the forest a long way from here. Too far for an ordinary being to travel to in one day. A miracle is needed.'

By now Sayola had come back. Ram turned to him. 'Hanuman,' he said. 'Take Pipek with you and tell him where to find the herb.'

Sayola and Pipek hurried across the bridge back to the army to find Hanuman. Ram lifted Lak in his arms and carried him past his chariot towards the shore, the spear still lodged in his leg. Rawin and JaoJuk walked respectfully alongside the brothers, heads bowed like mourners at a funeral. When they reached the others Sayola reported to Ram: 'Hanuman has gone. Pipek told him where to find the herb.'

Ram simply nodded and laid his brother on a grass bed that had been hastily prepared by Benjakai.

Rawin went to Catt and sat down forlornly on a log beside her. 'Has anyone gone with Hanuman?'

'You kidding?' replied Catt. 'Sayola offered to go. But do you know what Hanuman said to him?'

'No, what?'

'He said, "You are not even a real monkey, boy, and if you tried to keep up with me, all you would see is my butt disappearing over the hill".'

Rawin smiled, but didn't feel the mood was right to laugh.

A sombre silence fell. Sukreep had gone with Chompoopan to rally the monkey army and to reassure them that, while they would be without Hanuman and Ram and Lak at the outset of the battle, they should be prepared to cross the bridge and begin the fight immediately.

'Come on,' Catt said. 'We need to be at the front with Sukreep and Chompoopan. Prince Ram will wait here with Prince Lak for Hanuman's return. I feel this is our responsibility.'

'Sure,' Rawin said.

'I'll go with you,' Sayola said, holding a spear, exactly the same as the one he had hurled at Kumphakan.

'Hey, where did you get that?' Rawin asked, surprised.

Sayola just smiled. 'Those who cursed me thought they would make me suffer longer by giving me the means to fight for my miserable monkey life. Wherever I go, my spear returns to me.' Its blade was yellow with demon blood.

A loud thumping sound came from the forest. Catt sprang up and unsheathed her sword. Sayola swung round and held his spear ready. Above the treetops they could see Hanuman's head as he swiftly scythed his way through the wood, now ten times his normal size, trampling trees and everything else beneath him. He emerged in front of them clutching an enormous collection of trees and bushes under each arm.

'Back already,' Catt said. 'Hundreds of miles and back in less than an hour.'

Hanuman observed the astounded faces that looked up at him. 'I didn't know which was the right one, so I brought the lot,' he explained matter-of-factly.

Catt turned to Rawin: 'See, another law of physics broken.'

'At least he didn't bring a whole mountain,' Rawin laughed.

Pipek pointed at one of the bushes in Hanuman's grasp and said: 'That's it.'

'Oh, good,' said Hanuman, who flung all the remaining trees and bushes into the forest behind him, bringing trees down as he did. Then he returned to his normal size.

Benjakai rushed forward and took the herb, grinding it on a stone. She mixed it in a lotus leaf with some water from the moat and offered it to Ram as everyone else watched breathlessly. 'Here, Master, apply this to the wound.'

Ram propped his brother up against his leg and gently poured some of the herbal mixture on to the wound. Then a little more. Everyone moved in closer as if beside a hospital bed, eager to witness signs of recovery in a loved one, but trying not to stare. They waited.

Ram tried gently to remove the spear, but the wound remained tightly closed over the head of the weapon, still lodged deep in his brother's thigh. Lak remained lifeless. Ram looked up at Pipek.

'Are you sure this is the right herb?'

'I am, Sir,' replied Pipek.

Benjakai moved forward and knelt down beside Ram. 'May I?' she said as she put an arm around Lak, taking his weight from his brother. When she was holding him firmly, she took the lotus leaf gently from Ram and poured a bit more over the wound. In an instant the head of the spear appeared to loosen. Benjakai put down the lotus leaf and, with both hands, withdrew the spear. Lak opened his eyes and looked around him, sitting up immediately.

'Praise the gods,' Ram cried out as he leant forward and hugged Lak. 'Brother, you are alive, my dear, dear brother.' He turned to Benjakai: 'You are truly our beloved and loyal servant. Thank you.'

Benjakai bound the wound with soft bandages and then wiped tears from her eyes as she quietly backed off to leave the brothers in each other's arms. Hanuman looked at her with unconcealed admiration. Catt walked up to him and slapped his arm affectionately. 'Even for you, that was amazing.' Hanuman winked immodestly at her. 'And now,' she went on, 'are you ready for a fight?'

'Never been readier.'

# CHAPTER THIRTY-SIX

K umphakan had fallen heavily from the city wall to the cobbled stone street below with Sayola's spear embedded in his arm. He writhed on the ground, overcome with pain. Eventually he gathered enough strength to stand up. He reached with his right arm across his powerful body and clutched the shaft of the spear. He unleashed a terrible roar as he dislodged the head of the spear from his flesh and threw the weapon to the ground. He roared again, clutching the wound to stem the flow of blood. He was quickly surrounded by first-aiders who bound his arm with bandages and mopped his brow, drenched in the sweat of agony.

Totsakan appeared with a small entourage of attendants. He did not dwell on comforting his brother. 'Come on,' he said to Kumphakan. 'The battle is upon us.'

Kumphakan breathed in and then slapped his left breast vigorously with his right fist. 'Sir, I am ready to serve you.'

Totsakan swept down the street towards the stadium followed by his entourage, Kumphakan and Inthorochit. 'There is no time to lose. The coward Prince Ram's forces, led by children and monkeys, are preparing to cross the moat. We need to engage in battle outside the walls. They cannot be allowed to enter the city.'

The stadium heaved with the commotion of the demon army. From in front of the VIP podium where Totsakan, Inthorochit and Kumphakan now stood, thousands of demon-warriors stretched out over every inch of the stadium, swaying like a stormy sea. They chanted 'Long live the King! Long live the King!' They stamped their feet and banged their shields with their swords. 'Long live the King.' The noise carried across the city and beyond.

Totsakan raised his arms to signal he wanted them to stop. Slowly the noise abated and the army looked up adoringly at their master.

'Patriots and loyal subjects,' he began, his thundering voice reverberating across the stadium. 'Our way of life is under threat from invaders. Vermin. Vile scum that have come to infest our home and threaten our race. Your courage and loyalty stand between what we have now and annihilation from aliens who seek to steal and violate our women.'

This sent the demons into a frenzy. One of the generals shouted: 'Stop them, kill them, annihilate them.' The entire army chanted the same words.

'Now is the time for you to show your love for your motherland and your king. Be willing to die for this. Be merciless. Be unforgiving. Be cruel.'

'Merciless, unforgiving, cruel,' they chanted.

'Now, follow your glorious, brave commander Inthorochit.'

The sound of a trumpet from the city wall interrupted.

'That is the alert to tell us the barbarians are at the gates,' shouted Inthorochit. 'Archers and guards, take up your positions. The rest of you await further orders. Fill your hearts with hatred.'

On the second bridge, Hanuman, Sukreep and Chompoopan strode fearlessly shoulder to shoulder toward the city gates. Behind them walked Catt and Sayola side by side. She rested her hand on the sheath of her sword. He cradled his spear in his right hand. Ram had ordered them to demand that Sida be immediately handed over in exchange for which they would not attack the city.

At the other side of the moat, Ram and Lak stood alert in their chariot at the front of the massed ranks of the monkey army, spread out along the shore. Rawin and JaoJuk sat patiently on tufts of grass, occasionally surveying the scene ahead of them. A short distance away Pipek and Benjakai watched anxiously.

Hanuman was the first to reach the portcullis, which remained forbiddingly shut. He banged haughtily on the wooden lattice grille that stood between him and the city of Langka. 'Anybody home?' he shouted breezily and then banged again. To his surprise, the portcullis began to rise slowly.

'It's a trap,' said Sukreep hastily. 'They want us to enter and they'll attack us inside.'

'Well, enter we shall,' said Hanuman and he bent slightly to pass beneath the portcullis before it had been full raised. Then he sauntered through the stone archway, drawing his sword as he did. 'Coming ready or not,' he shouted.

Two demons rushed wildly from the city side of the archway with their swords swinging over their heads. Hanuman cut them down with two blows and continued through the archway. He stopped, looking around. Before he had a chance to see anything, arrows rained down at him. He flicked them away with his shield but he knew one would soon hit him. Slowly he eased his way back into the archway, raising a hand to signal that Catt and Chompoopan should come no further. 'They want us to come in. They've got snipers up on the roofs and walls ready to pick us off if we go in. You were right, Sukreep. They want to trap us just inside the gate.'

'But we need to pass on Prince Ram's message,' said Sukreep.

'You reckon?' asked Hanuman sceptically. 'Should we write them a letter?'

'I will go,' replied Sukreep.

'Uncle, they will kill you.'

'We must do as Prince Ram has ordered.'

'He didn't order you to commit suicide.'

Sukreep removed his sword and handed it to

Chompoopan. 'Keep this. I will need it again sometime.' He walked through the portcullis gate into the archway. As he neared the other side he raised his hands above his head to signal that he was unarmed. Hanuman and Chompoopan watched from outside, silent with unease.

'I wish to address your king,' Sukreep shouted.

In a flash four demons swept into sight, two from each side, and seized Sukreep's arms and frog-marched him out of sight. The portcullis gate started to lower and shut completely.

'Mmmm,' mused Hanuman. 'Not good.'

'Shall I go after him?' asked Chompoopan.

'I don't want to lose you too. Let's wait to see whether he manages to pass on Prince Ram's message. You never know.' Hanuman turned and walked back towards Sayola and Catt and told them what had happened. 'Tell Prince Ram,' he said to Sayola. 'Catt, come with me.' Sayola turned and sprinted back across the bridge.

The wait was not as long as they had feared. On the top of the wall above the portcullis Inthorochit appeared holding Sukreep by the throat. The monkey's face was bruised and swollen and he looked dazed.

'Bastards,' murmured Hanuman. 'You'll pay for this.'

'Idiots,' shouted Inthorochit at Hanuman and Catt, 'listen to me. You sent this pathetic creature to bargain with my father. He tells me Benjakai didn't do what she was told. So she betrayed her family and is now with you. Ha, that makes me shiver in my boots. Tell your cowardly leader that if he wants Sida he should come and get her himself. If he dares. He can also come and get the body of this weakling servant of his.' He shook Sukreep and drew his sword.

'Noooo!' cried Hanuman. 'Noooo!' Catt drew her sword, and ran towards the gate entrance. 'Come back,' Hanuman shouted at her. 'They'll kill you too. Wait!' Catt stopped. They looked at each other, unable to decide what to do. They looked up just in time to see Sukreep lean forward and bite Inthorochit on his arm. Inthorochit let out a howl of agony and let go of Sukreep's throat. Hanuman and Catt watched in awe as Sukreep ripped Inthorochit's sword from his hand as the demon bent over in pain and clutched his arm. With Inthorochit's sword, Sukreep cut down two demons that had arrived to support their boss. He lifted his foot and, with what was nearly the last of his strength, kicked them over the city wall. Their lifeless bodies fell heavily to the ground not far from where Hanuman and Catt were standing. Sukreep leapt up onto the top of the outermost battlements of the city wall, chased by several other demons. He threw Inthorochit's sword back wildly in their direction to give himself a bit of time and leapt high into the air, plunging towards the ground. Hanuman and Catt stopped breathing. Chompoopan put a hand over his eyes. But Sukreep had timed his jump perfectly. He landed on the biggest of the two demons he had killed, bouncing off its bloated belly and landing on his feet.

'Wow,' he said. 'That was close.'

For once Hanuman was speechless. He simply enveloped his uncle in his arms and held him to his chest.

'Let's get out of here,' Catt interrupted. 'That Inthorochit monster will want revenge, that's for sure. Come on. Let's not push our luck.'

Hanuman and Chompoopan put their arms round Sukreep to give his tortured body support as they scampered across the bridge. Catt glided just ahead of them, her supreme agility more breathtaking to watch than ever.

As they reached halfway, the portcullis rose and a thousand demons poured out from the city chanting 'Kill them, stop them, annihilate them.'

# CHAPTER
# THIRTY-SEVEN

Hanuman and Chompoopan managed to haul Sukreep back to the safety of the monkey army on the far side of the moat before the demons had progressed far over the bridge. Catt had reached Ram first and quickly updated him on what had happened.

'Inthorochit is acting out of blind rage,' Ram concluded. 'He has no proper plan. We can deal with this.' He ordered his troops to form four lines, two on each side of the beginning of the bridge, going back in a V-formation. 'As the demons reach the end of the bridge, move forward in fours, two on each side, and cut them down. As soon as you've taken two or three out, retreat to the end of your line and let the next soldier do the same. Preserve your strength. Do not try to kill more than a few before giving way to the next in line. Courage, brave soldiers, courage!'

The monkey-soldiers moved quickly to obey, marshalled and encouraged by Hanuman and Chompoopan. They had only a few minutes to get into the formation Ram had ordered, but the first soldiers were ready when the wave of demons arrived. Hanuman and Chompoopan led the way, one at the front on each side of the bridge. As the first demons tried to leave the bridge, Hanuman and

Chompoopan waded into them, flanked by two of their best warriors on either side. The demons had no chance. The ones that followed had to slow down when they reached the end of the bridge as the wounded and dead piled up. Some fell off the side of the bridge into the moat, but as they waded ashore they were easy prey for the monkey-soldiers.

The slaughter was fast and ugly. For every monkey that fell, as many as ten or more demons went down. Inthorochit watched the carnage from the city wall. Before long he realised that if he allowed it to continue he would not have much of an army left. So he sent down orders for them to retreat. It took a while before the order reached the front of the demon battalion, but when it did they turned fast and stampeded in disarray back across the bridge. The monkey-soldiers cheered victoriously.

'See to the wounded immediately,' Ram ordered. 'Those who have laid down their lives for us should be given dignified cremations. Pipek, please preside over the ceremony.'

Benjakai supervised the first aid teams, grinding and mixing medicinal herbs from the forest and bathing wounds with water from the moat. Beds were quickly shaped out of the abundant soft grasses on the plain. Benjakai worked with untiring commitment and compassion, watched with approval by her father, whose face was contorted with anxiety and sadness.

A team of monkey-soldiers set fire to the many demon corpses that littered the edge of the moat and began to sweep away the debris of the battle.

Ram and Lak called a meeting of their senior commanders, Hanuman and Chompoopan, as well as some other soldiers who had proved themselves to be brave and skilled in battle. He beckoned to Catt and Sayola to join them.

'We need to come up with a plan to intensify our advantage. But we cannot risk trying to get in through the city gates. The same thing will happen to us as just happened to them,' Ram said.

'We need to get them out of the city again,' Hanuman replied.

'Yes, but they won't make the same mistake again. They could just sit there and wait for us to come. Or not. As long as Totsakan has Sida, it is we who have to make the move, not them. Totsakan will know that, even if his unstable son doesn't.'

'Remember,' interrupted Sukreep, who had just joined them, his face still swollen. 'Totsakan has one weak spot. We need to exploit it.'

'First, Sukreep, tell us, are you better?' Ram said.

'Better enough to think,' Sukreep replied. 'I do not need my face for that.'

'So what do you think is Totsakan's weak spot, then?'

'Pride. He hates being humiliated.'

'And how can we use that against him?'

'Make him look like a coward in front of his people,' Catt added.

'Interesting,' Ram mused. 'Any ideas?'

'Challenge him to a fight on the bridge, just the two of you. If he refuses his followers will know he is a coward and he could never live with that,' Sukreep went on.

Ram thought for a bit. 'Mmmm. I like that. Let's come up with a proper plan. I look forward to killing this monster who has brought so much suffering to our world. But now we need our army to eat and sleep, because it's getting late. They will not try to attack us again tonight, so we should take the opportunity to rest.'

Lak stayed with his brother while Hanuman and Chompoopan left the small gathering to carry out their master's orders and to ensure that the cremations of the dead had been carried out. Sukreep limped towards the grass bed that had been made for him. Catt accompanied him and when the two of them were alone, Rawin joined them.

'Your face looks very sore,' Catt said sympathetically. 'What did they do?'

'Ah, nothing. I'm OK.'

'That doesn't look like nothing,' Rawin said. 'Here, take this.' He handed Sukreep a soft cloth that had been soaking in a herbal mix for soothing wounds. Sukreep took it and held it against the swelling around his eyes.

'You were very brave to go in there,' Catt went on.

'They beat you up, didn't they? Tortured you. I wouldn't have had the courage to risk that.'

'Ah, you do not know yourself, then, young lady. You have the courage of a tiger.'

'I'd rather fight than try to reason with them,' she said.

'Yes, I know,' sighed Sukreep. 'Quite right, for no one is as quick as you with a sword. We needed you before in this war with the Spectre, but I sense that the final battle is upon us. And that is when we will need you most.'

'But Prince Ram is here. And Prince Lak, the bravest of them all. And Hanuman, the quickest, and you and Chompoopan. You are all great warriors.'

'Yes, dear one, but the sages have told us that we cannot win this war without you and the boy.' He turned to Rawin. 'You, Rawin. The two of you.'

As he said this, the children heard the voice of the Rishi come flooding back, each word now full of a significance they could not have understood when they were spoken all that time ago: *We hoped we would not have to summon you to help in this onerous battle against the evil one before you were older, but it is now that you are needed. Otherwise all will be lost.*

Rawin looked at Catt and she at him. They both heard it. *Otherwise all will be lost.* The Rishi's voice. But Sukreep had not. He did, however, sense that they were feeling something that he was not part of, so he said nothing. But he moved so that he sat between them and put an arm around each, gently swinging his head to her and then to him and back again to her as he spoke: 'Children, as I told you once before, there are things we do not understand but which we must accept in faith. But there is one thing I know deep down in my heart which I hope you will understand. Or...' he smiled, 'accept in faith.' He continued: 'And that is, a war cannot be won by swords alone. Your heart needs to be good. If you have a bad heart, you might win many battles, but you will never win the war.'

'I will accept that in faith, dear Sukreep,' Rawin said with a smile, 'because even though I do not know it to be true for myself, what I do know is that for you it is true. And therefore it must be true.'

'OK, OK,' Catt laughed. 'Sukreep you have just

managed to persuade Rawin – who until this moment has only ever believed in science – to accept something in faith. That's enough for one day. Let's go and sleep.'

They said goodnight to each other and slipped away into the darkness to find somewhere comfortable to spend the night and to build up their strength for the next day – when swords and good hearts would be needed.

By the light of a burning torch nearby, Ram was reading through a letter he had written on thin parchment which he planned to have delivered to Totsakan the next day. It read:

*Nontok,*

*You might be surprised to discover that I know who you are. You might think that you have hidden your origins from the world by strutting around like a king. But you are not a king. A malignant tyrant cannot be a king. You can pretend to be a king. But you do not have the kindness of a king, nor the moral code of a king. And above all you do not have the courage of a king.*

*But now you have an opportunity to prove you have courage by meeting me on the bridge so that we can fight, hand-to-hand, just you and me. If you defeat me, then I will have no further claim over the hand of Sida. If you refuse even to fight me, then you will confirm that you are a coward. And Sida could never, ever love a man with no backbone.*

*Face me on the bridge. Bring whatever weapons you choose. We will end this long war once and for all without further loss of life. Apart from one of us.*

*Signed, Prince Ram, Prince of Ayutthaya, rightful and true husband of Sida*

Ram decided he would read the letter one more time in the morning and left it on the upturned log he had used as a table. He took the torch with him into the tent in which he and Lak would spend the night. Sentries kept watch over the moat bridge while everyone else embraced the sleep they desperately needed after the long march and the hard-fought battle of the day.

Once silence had settled over the monkey army, four demons slipped unheard into their camp. They were members of Inthorochit's special forces, able to swim the moat on the other side of the city, quickly cross the open country and approach their sleeping enemy from the far side of the forest where there were no sentries. They combed through the camp looking for anything that might prove useful to their commanders in their plans for the next day's battle. As they did so, their leader scooped up a strip of parchment with writing on it and stuffed it inside his tunic. And then they were gone.

# CHAPTER THIRTY-EIGHT

T otsakan stood on the highest balcony of his palace from where, on the other side of the moat in the gathering dusk, he could see the fires that burned the bodies of his fallen soldiers.

'Fool,' he thundered. 'Inthorochit you fool. Fool!' He swept enraged from his balcony and strode down the hallway, entering the room where Sida was imprisoned. She was standing at the window looking out over the moat. She too had witnessed the consequences of Inthorochit's folly. But for her, it had brought hope, not the despair of her tormenter. She did not turn to look at Totsakan, but even from behind he could tell from the way she held her head that her spirits had been lifted by what she had witnessed.

'Don't gloat,' he snarled. 'They will never defeat me.'

'They've made a good start,' Sida replied buoyantly.

'That coward, Ram, who you claim to be your husband and saviour, will soon burn like that. If there is anyone left to light the fire.'

'Ha,' snapped Sida, 'I see your words become stronger as you become weaker.'

'Don't mock me.'

'You mock yourself.'

'I am not afraid of a man who hides behind monkeys and children.'

'You keep saying that. But from what I have seen, those are rather clever monkeys. Better soldiers than yours.'

'Never.'

Sida hesitated for a few seconds. Then she said, 'Tell me about those children. You mentioned them before.'

'A boy and a girl. He can do magic and she thinks she is good at fighting.'

'How nice. I hope to meet them one day.'

'I intend to kill them before you can do that.'

'Oh,' interrupted Sida, 'you're scared of them, aren't you. I can tell.' She chuckled contemptuously.

'Hold your tongue, woman.'

'What is it about you? You're scared of my tongue, I know you're scared of my husband, and you're scared of monkeys and now of children. Are you scared of the dark too, oh brave King Totsakan?'

He strode angrily over to her and raised his hand ready to hit her. Sida swung around and looked him in the eye. 'Don't you dare!'

'Ugh,' growled Totsakan in frustration, turned on his heels and stormed out of the room.

In the hallway he found Inthorochit with several of his generals, Kumphakan, whose wounded arm was still bandaged, and Mareet. They were arguing amongst themselves. They were estimating their casualties and discussing how to reorganise their battalions. Inthorochit was subdued. When they saw Totsakan, they stood to attention and went silent.

Totsakan said nothing at first. He slowed his walk and went over to Inthorochit, bringing his mouth right up against his son's ear. Everyone stood dead still. The hallway was silent. Then Totsakan bellowed deafeningly, 'Why? Why? What were you thinking? Idiot!'

Inthorochit held his head up, but shame replaced the arrogance that usually played on his face. The others looked away. The palace hallways echoed the sound of Totsakan's thundering voice.

Eventually it was Mareet who spoke. 'My lord, we have

a plan.'

'It had better be good,' Totsakan shot back instantly. 'Come on.' He led them into a room where he sat upon a large, imposing chair. The others folded their legs under them as they sat on the carpeted floor. 'Tell me,' he commanded.

Eager to appear to be making up for his mistake, Inthorochit was the first to speak: 'I have already dispatched my best special forces team to check out their camp. They've gone round the back.'

'What do you hope to find?' asked Totsakan doubtfully.

'Maybe their plans.'

'Well, let's make sure they need a plan instead of just reacting to our mistakes.' Totsakan had cooled slightly, but his bitterness still laced his comments. 'We need them to take risks instead of waiting for us to offer our heads to be chopped off.'

'Yes, my lord.'

'What about the boy and the girl?'

Kumphakan spoke up: 'I have briefed a small assassination squad to concentrate a hundred percent on taking them out. They've been told to ignore everything else that is going on and to target the girl first and then the boy.'

'She's the main problem,' agreed Totsakan. 'What's the plan for her?'

The commander of the assassination squad was next to speak: 'Her weak spot is her love of the boy.'

Everyone laughed loudly, slapping each other on the back. 'Love, ha-ha. She loves him?' 'Does he love her?' 'Ha-ha.' 'Puppy love, isn't it so sweeeet!'

'OK, enough,' Totsakan snapped.

'Well, as you might know, he's not much of a fighter himself,' continued the assassin. 'He doesn't take part in battle. So we find a way to lure him into danger. And when she comes to rescue him, we take her out.'

'Mmmm,' Totsakan mused, 'I like that. But there's another problem.'

'What, my lord?'

'The boy has magical powers.'

The demons began muttering anxiously. 'Magic?' 'Powers!' 'What does he do?'

'OK, shut up, superstitious idiots,' Totsakan continued. 'We need to find a way to neutralise those powers.'

'My lord,' Inthorochit interrupted. 'I think I know where his magical powers come from.'

'Speak.'

'The little one.'

'Little one?'

'There is a little one. His – or her, I can't tell if it is a boy or a girl – hair is tied in a knot on the top of its head, wears fancy clothes, looks like a doll. Every time something goes wrong for us, the child is there somewhere, not in the middle of the action, but somewhere there. It's weird.'

'Is that the little one that stood next to the boy when the second part of the bridge appeared?' asked another general.

'That's him. Her. It,' said Inthorochit.

'But it was the boy who did that.'

'No, he can't do it without the child.'

Inthorochit cleared his throat. 'Er, I didn't tell you this before, my lord, but in an earlier battle he – this child – made my serpent arrows disappear.'

'Disappear!?' Totsakan shouted his question.

Inthorochit nodded disconsolately. 'My quiver was empty.'

The other demons began to mutter to each other again anxiously. The idea of magic had unsettled them, but this was even more shocking. Inthorochit's super power – his serpent arrows – could be taken away through magic. By a small child!

The discussion went on into the night as Totsakan, his son, his younger brother and their top generals talked around and around in circles, trying to come up with a plan to defeat not just Ram and the monkey army, but three children, one more a doll than anything else. The conversation lurched between military planning and fear – fear of magic and powers beyond their control.

It was already almost dawn when Totsakan banged his fist on the arm of his chair. 'Shut up, shut up, all of you. Are you children too? Scared of things you cannot see or understand? Show me that you have bravery, like real soldiers. Or do I have to fight this war on my own?'

There was a sharp knock on the heavy wooden door. The demons almost swallowed their own tongues in alarm. They looked at each other and then at the door. They were silent with fear.

Totsakan looked at them with contempt. 'Cowards,' he said, striding over to the door, yanking it open to reveal a demon dressed in camouflage gear. The demon bowed deferentially. 'My lord,' he said. 'We have returned from Prince Ram's camp.'

'Aha,' remarked Totsakan, 'Come in. What can you tell us?'

The special forces soldier entered, accompanied by two lieutenants. 'Yes, come in.' Totsakan beckoned as the other two hesitated. They came into the room and knelt while showing due respect to the generals seated around. Totsakan returned to his chair and raised a hand to the leader of the special forces team: 'Well?'

'We found this, Master,' said the demon, holding a strip of parchment.

'Well, what is it?'

'We think it might be their plans for an attack on our city tomorrow. Later today, in fact.'

'Excellent,' commented Totsakan, now full of newfound confidence. 'What does it say?'

'My lord,' said the special forces demon, 'we are soldiers, brave soldiers in your service.'

'Yes, yes,' interrupted Totsakan impatiently.

'But we cannot read.'

'Ah, OK. No problem, brave soldier.' Totsakan looked around the table. 'Who can read here?'

'I'll read it,' said Kumphakan.

'Good. Give it to him.' The special forces soldier handed the parchment to Kumphakan, who hesitantly began reading aloud. As he did so, his voice began to croak. 'Nontok,' he began. The others in the room looked down at the floor, afraid to catch anyone else's eye. When Kumphakan reached the words '… you do not have the courage of a king' he coughed awkwardly. When he reached the end, Totsakan stood up, on fire with rage. His eyes were huge, his hands opening as if ready to strangle someone. Everyone else in the room – the most important demons in the entire demon race – looked down into their laps, afraid to allow their king to see the astonishment on their faces. No one dared move.

'Kill him!' ranted Totsakan. 'Kill them all. Go, now, attack.'

'Er, how should ...' began one of the generals.

'I don't care how,' bellowed Totsakan. 'Take every man. Attack. Now!'

# CHAPTER THIRTY-NINE

Hanuman moved slowly through the camp soon after dawn, gently stirring the monkey army. 'Wake up, wake up,' he called out warmly. 'Tonight we will barbeque boars and drink cider and celebrate. Tomorrow you can sleep late.' Then he laughed heartily. All around the forest monkeys groaned as they awoke, dusted themselves off and buckled on their armour and weapons.

Catt sat up and stroked the blade of her sword. She saw Sayola throwing his spear into a tree, plucking it out again and repeating the motion. He cast her a friendly smile and continued.

'Practice makes perfect, right,' she commented.

'Right,' replied Sayola. 'If only the enemy stood as still as this tree, though.'

She laughed.

Sukreep walked over and handed them each a bowl of rice. 'Eat. You will need strength.' After Catt had done so she went down to the water's edge and washed her face. She looked across the moat at Langka and wondered what the day would bring.

A voice cried out from deep inside the woods. 'They're coming. The demons are coming.' Catt hurried back from the water's edge and rejoined Sayola. They hurried to Ram's side. He was already consulting with Lak and Hanuman.

'They've decided to come from the rear,' Ram noted. 'That means they must have come round from the other side of the city. Is there another bridge there?'

'No, not that we know of,' Hanuman answered. 'Our scouts have been round that side many times and they've not seen anything like that.'

'Then they must have swum across. They will be tired and heavy with water. We should not let them rest. Come on, let's not wait for them. Attack first.'

Hanuman started issuing orders to his lieutenants. Monkey-soldiers were sprinting through paths in the woods in well-ordered platoons. As they emerged, they saw the demon army assembled on the gentle slopes of the hills stretching back from where they had camped. Kumphakan stood at the front, his arm in a sling. The demons look bedraggled, their wet bodies gleaming in the sun that had risen high behind them, many with their heads bowed from exhaustion.

'Prince Ram was right. They're weary from the swim,' Chompoopan said. By this time he had reached the front of the army and was preparing to lead the charge with Hanuman and Sukreep. Hanuman called out to his gathered troops: 'They have come a second time unprepared and led by a general with one arm. Move fast, be swift and deadly.' He drew his sword and darted up the slope, followed closely by an eager detachment of the bravest soldiers, barking a spine-chilling war cry.

Ram and Lak took up a position on the edge of the woods to observe the battle. Catt and Sayola watched anxiously at his side as a messenger waited ready to carry instructions to the other soldiers if Ram saw the need for a change of tactics. On his orders, Rawin and JaoJuk remained in the camp along with a handful of guards.

After the fighting had gone on for a while, Ram remarked anxiously: 'They are fighting more boldly than I thought. We are suffering a lot of casualties.'

'Prince Ram,' Catt interrupted, 'I can help.'

'You cannot risk your life going into that battle,' Ram responded.

'No,' she said. 'I can use my sword.'

'They have swords too,' said Sayola.

'Not like mine.' She drew it with her right hand and caressed the gleaming blade with the fingers of her left hand.

'Ah, yes, that sword. I have heard,' said Ram.

'Please, Prince Ram,' said Catt urgently, order our troops to retreat a little down the slope.'

'Retreat? That will give the demons fresh determination. We cannot risk it.'

'Believe in me.'

'But my duty is to my army,' Ram replied.

'Then I too will do my duty to them,' said Catt. 'And to you, my lord.'

Ram hesitated. He watched for a while longer as the demons began to overwhelm the monkey army. He turned to the messenger. 'Tell Hanuman to make an orderly withdrawal. He will know what that means.' The messenger scampered up the slope and disappeared through the ranks to the frontline. Very soon they could see one platoon fall in behind another. The front one held its line, continuing to fight, while the other fell back. The demons seemed to be puzzled and stayed where they were. They could be seen talking among themselves, clearly trying to decide what to do next. Soon the monkey army was about 50 yards off.

Without saying anything to Ram, Catt sprinted up the slope and through the monkey ranks, emerging on the other side in the open space between the two armies. She unsheathed her sword and held it horizontally in both hands high in front of her. The reflection off the sun flashed across the demon army, which became disorientated as they held up their hands to shield their eyes.

'Aha,' Ram laughed. 'Now I see this girl and her sword in action at last. Victory will soon be ours.'

Just then an enormous demon broke ranks and charged at Catt, letting out a blood-curdling scream, swinging its sword violently above its head. It was Channarong, the giant demon who had fought her once before. Catt did not move until the demon was a metre away, then she let her left hand drop the blade of her sword so she was able to swing it in her right hand. She scythed Channarong down in one movement and turned to watch the demon plough, grunting and squealing loudly, into the ground. Then she leapt on its shoulders and plunged her sword into the back of its head. She yanked the sword out and wiped it on the dead demon's tunic to remove the blood from the blade. Then she stood, legs astride, on the lifeless beast and raised her head insolently and shouted: 'Who's next?'

As the demons looked around at each other in confusion, a single arrow whistled through the air and entered Kumphakan's heart. He fell to the ground like a stone.

Holding his bow and standing at the front of his own army's ranks, Ram shouted: 'That's for trying to kill my brother with your poisonous spear, Kumphakan. May you rest in peace.'

There was instant chaos. The ranks of the demon army disintegrated in different directions as some, still rubbing their scalded eyes, fled in panic, knocking others over and precipitating a stampede back up the slope. Soon the monkey army was in pursuit, catching up and slaughtering the stragglers until there was no need to continue the fight as the demons disappeared from sight.

The monkey army cheered triumphantly and surrounded Catt in a victory dance. Ram and Sayola ran up the slope to join them. But as they reached them, one of the guards from the camp arrived breathless. 'They've taken the boy.'

'Who?' demanded Ram.

'Rawin,' said the sentry. 'Demons have taken him.'

'Where?' Catt shouted. 'Where?'

'On the bridge. They're taking him across the bridge.'

The monkey-soldiers made way as Catt, without saying a word, sprinted through their ranks faster than any of them had ever seen any living creature move. Some fell to their knees sobbing in an emotional mix of momentary relief and now despair. They watched as Catt disappeared into the woods in a flash.

'No-no-no,' murmured Sukreep. 'Not Rawin. He can't defend himself. No-no-no-no.' He followed Catt as fast as he could.

JaoJuk stood looking annoyed and flustered on the shore of the moat. The lifeless bodies of several monkey guards lay near where the bridge met the shore. There were two more on the bridge itself. Halfway across, three demons were dragging a struggling, bound Rawin to the city side. Catt's stride didn't shorten for a second as she came out of the woods, crossed the short plain in front of the moat and dashed at lightning speed onto the bridge, though in some ways it almost seemed like she was travelling in slow motion. Yards away from where the demons were dragging Rawin, Catt's foot caught on a thin vine that had been strung across the bridge and she fell heavily to the floor, losing her sword. Before she could recover, two of the demons ran up and threw a coarse net over her and pulled it tight so that her arms and legs could not move and her face was pressed hard against the mesh. She struggled and tried to lash out like a caged wild animal, but she could barely move at all. 'Let him go, let him go,' she yelled. The demons laughed. 'We knew you would come to save him.'

Totsakan appeared on the city wall above the portcullis gate. He looked pleased and stared disdainfully down at the scene on the bridge. 'Kill the boy and bring the girl to me. I have unfinished business with her,' he shouted.

'You evil beast. Come down here and fight,' Catt responded. But her voice didn't carry far, partly because her head was pressed against her chest.

The demon still holding Rawin threw him to the ground and pulled out its sword. Rawin struggled, but his arms and feet were tied and there was nothing he could do. He groaned with pain. Catt could just see what was happening. 'Leave him, leave him,' she shouted. 'Stop. Please stop.' But the demon simply grinned ruthlessly in her direction and lifted its sword.

Catt began to sob and beg. 'Please, don't do it. Please, please.'

As the demon began to bring its sword down on Rawin's neck, a stone hit it right between the eyes, sending it stumbling back. It dropped its sword and held its head where the stone had hit, grunting with pain. In an instant a monkey swung up out of the water and on to the bridge and swept down on to the demon's sword, lifting it and plunging it into the demon's throat.

'Sukreep!' shouted Rawin. 'Oh, God, Sukreep.' Only then did Rawin begin to sob with relief.

'I'll be back,' shouted Sukreep as he ran towards the two demons that were holding Catt in the net. 'OK, you're dead,' he said coldly as he unsheathed his own sword and began to approach them, slightly crouched, the sword in front of him, swinging in both hands.

One of the demons let go of the net and faced up to Sukreep with its sword. It swung wildly. Sukreep ducked and elbowed the demon in its ribs as its body hung over him. 'Ooof,' it groaned, but Sukreep wasn't big or strong enough to do much damage that way. The demon turned and approached more carefully this time. Sukreep lunged forward in a sham attack and then pulled back as the demon moved to defend itself. Then again, and again. Feint, pull back, feint, pull back. Frustrated, the demon swung wildly again. This time Sukreep sliced into its sword hand. The demon dropped its sword and howled, clutching the wound with the other hand. Sukreep was quick to end it. In a second, he had thrust his sword deep into the demon's neck. He yanked it out as the demon fell, blood spurting all over the bridge.

The other demon let go of the net holding Catt and ran full speed at Sukreep, who was still recovering his balance from the first fight, bowling him over. He went face down on the bridge, his sword spinning out of his hand. The demon kicked him once, twice in the stomach and the head and then, as Sukreep turned over, placed a huge foot on his throat. It lifted its sword to deliver the final blow. But it let out a loud yell as a swan fluttered noisily and wildly from the water and clutched the demon's foot in its beak and began shaking it as its wings flapped frantically. The demon grunted in horror at this unexpected attack, banging its foot against the floor of the bridge to try to shake the swan loose. But in an instant Sukreep had recovered, pulled himself up and retrieved his sword, plunging it into the demon's heart. It slumped slowly to the floor. The swan let go its grip and slipped away into the water.

'Oh, Sukreep, Sukreep, thank you, thank you,' Catt said,

still unable to move. Sukreep sliced through the net until the girl was free. She quickly retrieved her sword, which was still lying on the bridge where she had fallen. Sukreep ran back to Rawin and cut away the ropes that bound him. He was overcome with relief as both children sank into his arms and the three hugged each other in silence broken only by gentle sobs. JaoJuk looked on and quickly wiped a tear from his eye.

Rawin gently pulled his head back and looked at Sukreep. 'You saved our lives. Absolutely saved us. I was totally sure I was going to die.'

Sukreep looked at them both and smiled lovingly. Then he patted his heart.

# CHAPTER FORTY

Prince Ram and Prince Lak rode their chariot across the bridge and leapt off when they reached Sukreep and the children. 'Sukreep, that was very brave,' said Ram. 'And you, Catt, you almost laid down your life for Rawin.' Hanuman had come with him. 'We weren't able to help, Uncle,' he said. 'It all happened so fast. Thank the gods you are safe.'

'And thank Meeya,' Rawin added. Ram and Hanuman looked puzzled. 'The swan,' explained Rawin, 'she is the twin sister of Sayola.'

'We should reward her,' Ram said. 'How can we do that?'

'When you defeat the Spectre, that will be her reward,' Rawin told him.

'How so?'

'That is when the curse on her and Sayola will be lifted and they will be brother and sister again.'

'Then let us waste no time in achieving that. The demon army has been routed. We can enter the city unopposed.' He turned to Hanuman: 'Bring a platoon of your best soldiers to accompany us. I will go on ahead.' But before he could return to his chariot, the portcullis gate started to rise.

'Wait, my lord,' said Hanuman. 'Someone is coming.'

A tall figure dressed in full armour and wearing a mask emerged slowly through the archway carrying a sword and shield. As it came closer, they could see that the mask consisted of huge black holes for eyes and a hollow nose. A set of long jagged teeth stained with dripping blood protruded from a broad mouth.

'Totsakan!' Ram growled. 'At last you have found the courage to face me. Your ugly mask does not frighten me. In fact it is less ugly than your real face. I am not afraid.'

'Then die unafraid,' came the reply, muffled by the mask.

'Stand back,' said Ram to the others. 'He is mine to kill, remember.' He drew his sword and walked forward slowly while the others watched. The two warriors' swords crossed and stayed still for a few seconds before the fight began. The clanging sound of steel on steel rang across the water of the moat as the two danced and pranced across the bridge, forward, backwards, sideways, each attempting to land a fatal blow, each able to sidestep in time. Ram was much smaller than his foe, but that meant he was quicker. Eventually he brought his enemy crashing down with a fierce blow that sent his sword and shield spinning away. Ram moved quickly and stood over him with his sword at his throat. Blood seeped slowly from where the sharp blade lightly punctured the skin. 'Surrender, monster. Do not move. I would gladly drive this sword right through you and end your infamous life. But first show me your face, coward.' Ram deftly flicked his sword so that it slit the mask to reveal his enemy's face.

'Inthorochit!' he roared. 'What? Why?' Ram stepped back aghast and looked towards Hanuman and Lak. 'It's Inthorochit,' he called out, and as he did so, Inthorochit, rolled to one side and sprang up. He managed to make a run for the city gate before Ram realised what had happened. 'Stop!' he yelled. But Inthorochit kept running. 'Stop. Face your destiny!' Ram shouted. Inthorochit stopped and turned back to look at him.

'Go to hell!' roared Inthorochit. 'Can't you see that you're a born loser? Your own father sent you into the wilderness. Your wife left you for a better man than you could ever hope to be in your wildest dreams. And now you have lost your fight with me. Loser. Los....' Before Inthorochit could complete the word, an arrow entered his brain right between his eyes. The demon staggered two or three steps and slumped into a heap, motionless. Ram spun round to see his brother holding the bow that had unleashed the deadly missile.

'Totsakan is yours to kill, brother,' said Lak as he lowered his bow, 'but this one was mine.'

'Noooooo!' From the top of the wall came a hollow howl that seemed to make the entire city shudder. 'No, no, no.' It was Totsakan. 'You have killed my son. My beloved son.'

Ram looked up at the creature that had tormented him for so long. 'Release Sida now!' he demanded.

'Never,' shouted Totsakan. 'Inthorochit wanted me to let her go but I said no and he volunteered to face you instead. Now look. How can I let her go after what you have done? That would be a betrayal of my son. No, I will never do that. Never.'

'Then you too will die. If you stand in my way you will join your evil son in hell, where you both belong.'

Totsakan let out an agonising wail that sounded like a wounded elephant. His body convulsed several times as he mutated back to his full demon form. Then he disappeared from sight.

'Let's go,' commanded Ram. Leaving behind the chariots, he strode towards the city gate, his bow and arrow quiver over his shoulder, his sword unsheathed. To his right was Lak and to his left Hanuman. Just behind them came Sukreep, flanked by Catt, and Rawin. They too unsheathed their swords. Sayola followed, along with JaoJuk. Chompoopan went back across the bridge to bring more troops to join them.

As they entered the city through the archway beyond the open portcullis, they saw demons scurrying and cowering, none of them soldiers. Ram led the others through the market square. They remained unchallenged. Soon they had crisscrossed the city streets and saw the broad steps leading up to the palace. Ram raised his hand to bring his small band to a halt.

'Ah,' he remarked. 'They still want a fight.'

Arrayed up and down and across the steps were rows and rows of demon soldiers. At the highest point of the steps stood Totsakan in all his imperious demon glory, dressed in his finest attire, looking every inch like a conquering Caesar. Mareet stood proudly beside him. His soldiers were dressed in black and gold uniforms with multi-coloured ribbons on their chests representing medals they had been awarded for bravery.

'It's his personal palace guard,' Lak said. 'Highly trained, willing to die for their master.'

'Then die they shall,' Ram said.

'Brother, we need to wait for Chompoopan and more of our troops. We cannot take them on without backup.'

'Catt,' Ram said. 'Can you blind them with your sword?'

She stepped forward and raised the blade horizontally in front of her face. But Totsakan instantly responded by unfurling his giant umbrella above the palace, blocking out the sun.

'Ha,' he whooped, his thundering voice tumbling down the steps. 'Don't you remember? Now what are you going to do, clever girl?'

Catt pressed her lips together in frustration. 'I'll fight your best soldier, one on one,' she shouted back. 'It will have to be someone better than Channarong, of course.'

'You dare to mock my soldiers?' he growled.

'Whoa, Catt,' Rawin said quietly. 'We are outnumbered here. We've got to think of something quickly.'

'Perhaps we can try to get into the palace and find Sida without fighting our way past this lot,' Lak suggested.

'Do we know where she is being kept?' asked Ram.

'No, but Benjakai will know,' said Hanuman.

'Bring her.'

Sukreep turned and scrambled back towards the gates to cross the bridge and find Benjakai. As he did so, an advance troop of a few dozen monkey-soldiers led by Chompoopan entered the city. Sukreep told Chompoopan what had happened and urged him and the troops to hurry to the palace steps. He pointed the way and then headed over the bridge.

At the top of the steps meanwhile Totsakan bellowed out a command: 'Bring me the girl!' An order was shouted from within the ranks of the palace guard and four fearsome-looking demons stepped forward, drawing their swords. They shuffled almost stiff-legged in perfect unity, left, right, left, right, ascending the steps toward Ram and his small band.

'I'll handle this,' Hanuman said. In an instant he grew his tail until it was ten times his body length and then he rushed forward and slung it around the legs of the four demons and yanked it. All four tumbled to the ground in flustered disarray. They scrambled up again, but had lost their composure and appeared unsure what to do next. Loud muttering ran through the ranks of the palace guard.

'I said bring me the girl!' Totsakan roared.

One of the four demons broke loose and charged at Hanuman who cut it down in one devastating blow. He then spun round and drove his sword into the demon's chest. Almost in the same movement he retrieved the weapon and readied it in time to take on the remaining three which had now decided to charge at him together. Catt pirouetted into their path and scythed one down. Before the other two could do anything both collapsed with arrows embedded deep in their skulls. Ram and Lak, who were standing to one side, reloaded their bows and looked at one another. 'Nice shot, brother,' they said in unison.

An angry roar broke out amongst the other palace guards who then charged Ram and his comrades. As they did so, Chompoopan and the advance guard appeared from behind them and went straight into battle.

'Just in time,' Rawin, breathed, taking cover with JaoJuk behind one of the stone statues to the side of the stairs.

Ram, Lak, Hanuman and Catt led the fight, dodging and sweeping, slaying demons at an astonishing rate. Sayola used his spear to pick off any he thought were particularly threatening. The platoon that Chompoopan had brought was the best the monkey army could offer and they fought bravely and effectively alongside Ram and the others. Rawin watched as Totsakan waded into the battle. He was bigger than any other creature and swept aside attackers almost effortlessly.

But there was something about what Totsakan was doing that alarmed Rawin.

'He's going for Catt,' he said to JaoJuk. 'And she hasn't seen him coming.'

He was about to shout a warning to her when Totsakan brushed soldiers aside, both demons and monkeys, as he groped his way towards the girl. He swept her up, turned and lumbered up the steps holding her like a doll. When he reached the top, he turned to look down on the battle before him and held Catt up in one giant hand like he was showing off a trophy. Then he roared from deep down inside his massive chest, like a victorious ape after a fight to the death with a rival. 'One false move from anyone and I will throttle her.'

The battle had already come to an abrupt halt as everyone stood in awe of the spectacle above them. What had been a loud and ferocious battle scene had been transformed into one of eerie silence.

Rawin was the first to move. He ran out from behind the statue and shot up the first few dozen steps until he was on the first landing, close to where Totsakan stood triumphant. The demon army did not try to stop him. They watched him and then looked back at their master. At the bottom of the steps, Ram, Lak, Hanuman, Sayola and Chompoopan watched uncertainly. They had no idea what Rawin was intending to do. They feared Totsakan would kill the girl as he had threatened.

'Totsakan,' Rawin shouted. 'You remember me, I know. You did this to me once, what you're doing to Catt. You took me to your cave and I thought you would kill me. But you didn't. And that is why I know you are not going to kill Catt.'

Totsakan did not reply immediately. Then, 'I *am* going to kill her. I should have killed you when I had the chance. But you betrayed my trust.'

'I am sorry I did that,' Rawin said. He knew his words could be heard right across the palace steps, but this was no time to hide his feelings. 'I was scared.'

'You had *nothing* to be scared of.'

'Not then. But look at you now. What are doing now is really scary. So I was right to be scared of you then.'

'They made me do this,' he snarled.

'Who are they?'

'Them,' he said pointing down at Ram and the others.

'No. They didn't make you do this. They came here to ask you to free Sida. If you had done so, none of this would have happened.'

Totsakan did not answer.

'You know who really made you do this: those minor gods who humiliated you for thousands of years.'

'Ten thousand.'

'Ten thousand. For all that time you were a righteous and studious scholar and loyal servant of Isuan.'

Totsakan jerked his head up slightly, as if he had been given a slap in the face. Catt struggled but Totsakan continued to clutch her by the throat.

'And now look at you,' continued Rawin. 'Your whole life has become a never-ending battle and you have nothing to show for it but the deaths of your beloved son and younger brother and the exile of another. You were once thoughtful and diligent, now you are a monster. You rule by fear alone when someone as mighty as you could be loved and respected by your subjects.'

'Do not lecture me, child.'

'I am not lecturing you. I am just saying what you yourself know to be true. Deep down inside you are the man you were when you served Isuan so loyally. You would never have hurt a child then. You know what, I don't think you would do it now either. That's just not who you really are.'

'Ha!' scoffed Totsakan. 'To lose the one you love is worse than losing who you really are.'

'You cannot love unless you are who you really are.'

'You told me before that you don't understand love, boy.'

'Maybe not, but I understand what it means to fear losing the one you love.' Rawin's voice choked slightly.

Totsakan looked down curiously at Catt and then back at Rawin. 'I will let her go if...'

'If you do not lose Sida.'

Totsakan did not answer. He looked around him slowly and then at Ram. Then he threw back his head and looked up into the heavens and at the same time pushed Catt away. 'Go, go,' he yelled dejectedly.

Catt stumbled down the first few steps and regained her balance, looking back at Totsakan with a mixture of disbelief and relief. At exactly that moment Benjakai appeared at the bottom of the steps and ran to Ram. She pointed up to a barred window in the highest part of the palace. 'Sida is in there,' she said. Immediately behind her came Sukreep with a swarm of monkey soldiers running to the foot of the steps, ready for battle.

Totsakan pulled himself up to his full height and bellowed with rage: 'You see. More lies and betrayal.' He moved forward with immense speed and groped for Catt, who hadn't been able to scramble far from him. He managed to grab one of her legs and tried to drag her towards him. 'Come back. I will not be cheated again. Die, girl.' As he readied himself to strike at her an arrow hit the left side of his chest with such force it knocked him backward and he let go of the girl's leg. He managed to steady himself for a moment when another arrow hit at exactly the same spot. Mareet ran to his master's side but all he could do was watch in horror as Totsakan staggered and looked down at the arrows, which he grasped weakly in one hand. Then he lifted his head and looked at Ram who was still holding the bow from which both arrows had been shot. Then he turned to Rawin. 'Betrayer!' he groaned, fell on the steps and lay dead still.

# CHAPTER FORTY-ONE

Silence descended over the palace guard as they looked on in disbelief. Mareet knelt at Totsakan's side but appeared afraid to touch him. Totsakan lay on his back. A murmuring began to spread among the demons, gradually getting louder. Ram and his loyal band stood watching alertly, their swords still in hand, ready in case the demons decided to turn on them. Instead the demons began to disperse slowly, as if they didn't know what to do or where to go. Some went up towards the entrance to the palace, others just walked away down the steps and into the city. Some sat dejected on the steps. None challenged Ram or his troops. Mareet remained beside his master's body. Blood seeped from the arrow wounds down the side of Totsakan's chest and dripped on to the stone steps.

'The reign of the Spectre has ended,' declared Ram to his soldiers. 'Peace can now return to our world. Thank you for your bravery and loyalty. Long live peace and goodwill!'

'Peace and goodwill,' they responded solemnly.

'What about him?' asked Hanuman bluntly, pointing to Mareet. 'Shall I make him rest in peace too?'

'No. Leave him. The loss he has already suffered is greater than would be the loss of his own life,' Ram said. 'He can do no more harm now without his master. Let him grieve.'

Catt turned to Rawin and spoke quietly. 'What happened there?'

'I really don't know. I was just talking, hoping something I would say could stop him killing you. I was just babbling.'

'Thank you. Though it wasn't babbling, Rawin.'

'You would have done the same.' He paused, then: 'I hope.'

'The same.' As she said this she blushed and dropped her eyes. Then after an uncomfortable few seconds she asked: 'Do you think he thought you were trading me for Sida, that he could have kept Sida?'

'That's not what I said.'

'No, but it seems that's what he heard.'

'What he wanted to hear, perhaps.'

Just then they both noticed that Sayola had been transformed from monkey back to human. Before them stood a dashing young man, still dressed in black, but with long, glistening hair flowing down to his shoulders and a multi-coloured hairband in the *mat mee* silk pattern, tied at one side of his head. He looked down at his body and held his arms up slightly to inspect them, turning them over and then back, looking closely at them as if in disbelief. Then he glanced at Catt and Rawin and said, 'Meeya.' He sprinted away into the city streets towards the moat.

'They will be together again,' Ram smiled. 'And so too will I and my ever-loving wife.'

'And I with my precious mistress,' said Benjakai.

'Come on, then. We should go to her now.'

'We're coming too,' said Hanuman. 'Just in case. There might still be some crazy palace guards who have sworn to protect her with their lives.' Leaving Mareet to his misery, they headed up the steps into the palace. Pipek sat down at the entrance to reflect on the events of the past few hours while JaoJuk went and sat alone beside one of the statues.

Benjakai led the way rapidly to the building where Sida was imprisoned. The hallways of the palace were empty. When they arrived at the room where she was being held, two guards crossed their lances in front of the door and grunted.

'Tell them that they have five seconds to get out of here and, if they don't, those will be their last five seconds alive,' Hanuman said to Benjakai. She spoke, but the demon guards refused to move. Hanuman grew taller and clasped each of them by the neck and banged their heads together. They collapsed in a heap in front of the door. Hanuman reached down and dragged them out of the way and quipped: 'Sweet dreams.' He restored himself to his normal height and pushed the door open.

A shaft of radiant sunshine poured in through the barred window at the far end of the room silhouetting the elegant figure of Sida who stood looking at the doorway, her hands clasped together under her chin in a gesture that seemed to mix fear and joy in equal measure. Hanuman stepped to one side and swept a hand in front of him and bowed to signal that Ram should enter. Everyone else stood back as Ram stepped forward into the room. He dropped to one knee and announced courteously: 'My lady, I have come for you.'

To everyone else, the next few seconds seemed like hours as Ram and Sida stared in silent wonder at each other. Then Hanuman took one step into the room, took the handle of the door and closed it. 'Come,' he said to the others, 'this is their moment,' and he led them all back through the hallways of the palace. Only Benjakai stayed behind, outside the door.

As they headed out of the palace, Sukreep came between Rawin and Catt and put his arms around them, one on each side. 'This is the day we have long been told by the sages would come. Without you we could not have banished this evil force from our land. I cannot tell you how grateful I am – how grateful we all are. I am sure Prince Ram will honour you somehow before you...' He hesitated. Then: '... before you go home.'

'No need,' said Rawin. 'We only did what was written.'

'Maybe,' said Catt with a chuckle, 'but it wasn't written in the book.'

'Ah, the book, that book,' sighed Sukreep. 'I must read it some time.'

'Nah, don't bother,' Rawin laughed. 'It's nothing like what really happened.'

As they reached the steps leading down from the palace they stopped aghast. Totsakan and Mareet had gone.

'Where? What?' they all said at once.

Pipek was still sitting outside the palace entrance. They turned to him. 'Where is Totsakan's body? Did Mareet take it?' asked Sukreep.

'Totsakan is not dead,' replied Pipek sternly.

'What?!' they all said in disbelief.

'He had two arrows in his heart,' insisted Hanuman.' There's his blood,' he said pointing to the deep yellow patch on the stone.

'He has no heart,' replied Pipek.

'I could have told you that,' Catt said.

'No,' said Pipek. 'I do not mean it metaphorically. Totsakan has no heart, literally.'

'Huh?'

'He removed it. It made him immortal.'

'So, what happened then?' asked Hanuman. 'He just got up and walked off?'

'Yes, a few minutes ago.'

'This can't be happening,' Lak said.

'I am sorry, but it is true,' said Pipek. 'As long as he is separated from his heart, he cannot die. It is agony for him when he visits it from time to time so that he can feel its power in him. Pain is the price, but immortality is the prize.'

'Where is it?' demanded Lak.

'I do not know.'

'Wait. I think I do,' Rawin said. 'That's it. I saw him holding an urn. When he took me to his cave. He didn't know I could see. He held an urn in his hands and groaned like he was in terrible pain. I heard him again the second time I was there. His heart is in that urn.'

'Why didn't you tell us before?' complained Hanuman.

'I didn't know that it was his heart that was in the urn. That's the last thing I would have thought, that he could remove his heart. I thought his pain was some private thing.'

'Private!' Catt tutted. 'Really, Rawin. Sometimes you have too much respect.'

'We need to go to the cave,' said Hanuman. 'We need to smash that urn and crush his heart. Otherwise he will come back and plague our world again. Chompoopan, stay here to tell Prince Ram what has happened.'

Hanuman hurriedly led the way, followed closely by Lak, Sukreep, Catt and Rawin. As they headed down the steps into the city, JaoJuk ran after them. Sukreep saw him and stopped. 'Come,' he said, 'Up.' JaoJuk hopped on his back and held tight as they trotted fast towards the city gate.

When they emerged through the archway they saw Sayola standing at the water's edge holding the hands of a girl in both of his hands. Meeya had also been released from the curse that had turned her into a swan. The two children were looking directly into each other's eyes and laughing quietly to themselves. The girl's hair hung loosely on either side of her face, her bright eyes and enchanting smile radiating happiness.

Rawin ran up to them and apologised: 'It's so good to see you reunited, but something very worrying has happened.' He didn't wait for them to ask. 'Totsakan isn't dead. His brother Pipek says he hid his heart in his cave and while it is not in him he is immortal. This thing isn't over yet.'

'Oh, no, what are you going to do?' asked Meeya.

'We're going to get to the cave before he does and end this once and for all.'

'You mean…' began Meeya.

'Crush his heart,' Rawin went on, a little shocked at how easily those words came out of his mouth.

'We're coming,' said Sayola quickly. He had already seen the others with Hanuman heading through the woods. He grabbed his spear and the three of them ran to catch up.

The journey took several hours, but no one complained about being tired or needing a rest. They stopped once to drink from a stream, but were soon striding and occasionally trotting along the many paths that wound their way through the forest. Rawin and Catt had no difficulty remembering the way.

Eventually they saw the rocky crags that replaced the woodland in the area surrounding Totsakan's cave and soon saw the familiar cliff face. There was no time to be over-cautious, so they ran up to the entrance, entering together with their swords at the ready. Sayola was with them, his spear held in both hands ahead of him. Sukreep had already set JaoJuk down a short distance before the cave. JaoJuk, Rawin and Meeya inched slowly towards the entrance, listening carefully after the others disappeared into the darkness.

The five who had led the way swept into the cave in close quarter combat formation, one going to the left, one to the right, then standing aside to allow another to come through the middle, then repeating the movement so that all corners of the cave could be covered instantly, as well as behind them. The cave was dark and there was no evidence of the presence of another being, though a single torch burned on the right-hand side. As soon as he heard Hanuman say, 'All clear,' Rawin rushed in. 'There are torches along the walls. You can light them with that one,' he said. JaoJuk and Meeya followed.

Sukreep grabbed the burning torch and moved across the wall, lighting the other torches until the entire cave was flooded with light. Everyone still kept their weapons ready, occasionally scanning the cave for any signs of life.

'There!' Rawin shouted, pointing. 'There's the urn.'

Hanuman rushed to the cavity in the cave wall and seized the urn, turned and placed it on the floor as everyone quickly gathered round. He lifted the lid.

'Damn!' exclaimed Lak.

'Is this Pipek's trick?' wondered Hanuman.

'No, I don't think so,' said Rawin. 'Everything else rings true. I saw Totsakan and I heard him.'

'Wait!' called Sukreep, who was inspecting the rest of the cave. 'Over here. Blood.'

The others rushed to see.

'That's Totsakan's blood for sure,' Lak said.

'Here. More,' said Sukreep, who had moved a little further to the right. 'And here.'

Everyone followed him as he carefully tracked the blood trail in the flickering light of the torches.

'Wait!' Rawin said. 'This is weird.'

'What?' responded Lak.

'Look,' continued Rawin. 'The blood stops here.' He looked up at the roof. He knew it before he had even seen it.

The gap. The shaft of light. And then the sky above the buildings of the Grand Palace. 'Oh, God,' said Rawin slowly. 'Oh, God. He's gone up there.'

'What's up there?' Hanuman demanded to know. Everyone rushed to look up. Clearly visible through the fissure high up in the roof was the shiny golden pagoda towering above the temple of the Emerald Buddha.

'It's where we came from,' Rawin said, hesitantly. 'Come from,' he corrected himself.

'And Totsakan has gone there?' said Hanuman in disbelief. 'Why?'

'Revenge,' said Sukreep glumly. 'He must have realised that this is where you come from. You have defeated him here, he knows that. But he is not finished yet.'

Rawin turned to Catt. 'Oh my God. Rishi. *You will not defeat the evil one…*'

Catt joined in immediately and together they recited the words, '… *unless you go home, but you cannot go home until you have defeated the evil one.*'

# CHAPTER FORTY-TWO

'We have to stop him!' Catt said, emphatically. 'Now. We have to go now,' she said, turning to the others.

Sukreep was the first to speak. 'Go,' he said, sadly but without hesitation. 'Go. No world is safe from the Spectre. Only you can do this.' He walked up to them and took them both into his arms and held them silently for a minute. They hugged him.

'Sukreep, oh Sukreep,' said Catt. 'Thank you for everything.'

Rawin swallowed deeply. He couldn't speak.

'No, it is I who should be thankful. Eternally.'

Hanuman said only: 'This is not the end for me. Not for us. Where can I find you?'

Catt answered quickly: 'Bangkok.'

Rawin added: 'Lopburi.'

'OK,' said Hanuman. 'I will see you in Lopburi.'

Lak was solemn. 'Go with my blessing and the blessing of my brother, Ram. Our thoughts and our gratitude will always be with you.'

Rawin and Catt turned to Sayola and Meeya. But before they could say anything, Meeya looked them firmly in the eye. 'We're going with you.'

Catt looked at Meeya and then at Sayola, who looked straight back and said, 'Absolutely, we're going with you.' He held his spear up and gave it a little shake. 'This is going too.'

'Yeah, but…' Rawin began, and he looked at Meeya again. 'It might be too dangerous for you. Sayola has his spear and, well, for Catt and me, it's home. I would be too worried about what might happen to you.'

'It's true,' Sukreep added. 'We don't know what it is like there and, well, you have to admit you're not really a fighter, are you? No disrespect meant.'

'Well, it depends on what you mean by fighter,' said Meeya. Then she looked intently into Rawin's eyes. Rawin looked back and then said: 'Meeya must come with us. She will be an invaluable member of our team. In fact we couldn't manage without her.'

'What?' Catt said in disbelief. 'That's the precise opposite of what you just said.'

'Meeya has to come with us,' Rawin insisted.

Catt looked at Sayola and then at Meeya to see if they were as puzzled as she was. 'Sorry,' she said, 'Did I miss something?'

Then Sayola explained: 'You see, Meeya has mind control powers. She made Rawin change his mind.'

Catt looked at Rawin and then at Meeya, who just smiled innocently.

'Seriously?' Catt said.

Meeya shook her head around in a sort of yes-no kind of response. 'Well, it doesn't always work. Most of the time though.'

'Rawin, did you hear this?'

'Yes,' he replied. 'That's why we need her to come with us.'

Meeya whispered to Catt: 'He won't remember what he said before, don't worry. He will have a brief period of feeling a bit muddled, but it will go away quickly and everything will seem logical again.'

'Can you do this to anyone?' Catt asked.

'I don't know yet,' she said with a big smile. 'We'll have to see.'

'Well, I'm with you all on this. Meeya's coming too.'

Then Catt turned to JaoJuk. 'And you, JaoJuk?'

JaoJuk simply shook his head. 'Can't go.'

Catt stepped over to him and knelt down beside the child. 'May I?' she asked, holding her arms open. JaoJuk stepped into her embrace. 'Bye,' he said matter-of-factly. Rawin joined them. He leaned forward and held up one hand. JaoJuk met it with a high-five. 'Bye.' Rawin looked away to fight back tears. 'Please return this to Rishi,' he said, handing his Rubik Twist to JaoJuk. 'I can't use it without you.' That last word was almost inaudible. Catt swallowed deeply.

'OK, come now,' Hanuman said, 'Who's first?' He grew his body until his shoulders reached the height of the hole in the cave roof. Catt ran up Hanuman's leg and clambered up his body and on to his shoulders. Then she lifted herself into the shaft and started to climb.

'Next,' Hanuman commanded. Rawin held a hand forward to indicate that Sayola should go next. Meeya followed. And last, Rawin. Hanuman watched as they disappeared into the sunlight at the top of the shaft. He resumed his normal height and turned to Sukreep, placing his arm around his uncle's shoulder and patting him.

'The destined two are now four. They have done what they were called here to do and now they must rid their own home of the Spectre. May the gods be with them.'

Then the two monkeys and Lak left to return to Ram and Sida, now reunited forever.

# CHAPTER FORTY-THREE

T he sun glared down from a washed-out blue sky above Bangkok's Grand Palace. The air was hot and sticky. Catt clambered out of the hole in the top of the cave, stood up and looked around her. Immediately she recognised where she was – back on the flecked grey marble floors of the Temple of the Emerald Buddha, surrounded on every side by the mural paintings of scenes from the Ramakien story. She looked back to see where she had just come from, but there was no hole, no shaft reaching down into a cave below. She looked around in every direction, trying to work out how she came to be standing where she was. She felt her sword at her side, but there was no other evidence of where she had been or how she had come back. Then she was aware of a presence beside her. It was Sayola. He was standing with his mouth open, staring at everything around him. He was still holding his spear. Catt didn't see how it happened, but in an instant Meeya was standing next to Sayola and a few seconds later she heard Rawin say, 'I think I'm happy to be back. But… I'm not sure.' Catt looked behind him and around her again, but she couldn't tell how they got there. There is no time to worry about things like that, she thought. They had to find Totsakan.

'Sayola, you're going to have to hide your spear,' Rawin said. 'It's making the tourists nervous.' He nodded in the direction of the many people shuffling around the temple admiring the paintings, some of whom looked curiously at the four children.

'Oops, this too,' added Catt, touching her sword. 'Come on, let's get out of here.' She led the way quickly through the temple, out into the courtyard and headed for the exit. Sayola held his spear against his side so it was less visible.

'Look!' Sayola remarked, 'there he is.'

'Ha ha, no,' Rawin laughed. 'That's a statue.'

'A statue? Do they like him here?'

'No, no. It's just that he is fierce, so he makes a good guard. There are demon guards all over the country. There are twelve in this temple alone.'

'Well, I guess they are scary,' Meeya laughed. 'But it's a strange job for a king.'

'Well, Prince Ram always said Totsakan wasn't a proper king,' laughed Rawin.

'Come on. This way,' Catt commanded as she headed through the gateway marked 'Exit'.

On the street outside the temple they saw an old woman selling souvenirs and trinkets. She was sitting on a woven grass mat. Rawin scratched around in the side pocket of his backpack and found a 100-baht note. 'Auntie,' he said politely addressing the woman. 'Please can I buy your mat?' He offered the bank note. She looked at him and the others curiously and shrugged. She got up slowly, reached down and handed Rawin the mat and took the money.

'Here,' said Rawin to Sayola, 'roll your spear up in this. And your sword, Catt.'

Then they heard screaming. Hundreds of people were running chaotically across the street from the Grand Palace, spilling on to the open field of Sanam Luang, the Royal Park. Cars and buses screeched to a halt as people ran in panic across the road in front of them.

Then the children saw him: Totsakan sauntered arrogantly down the middle of the road, casually turning cars over, his huge arms flailing, his face taut with aggression. Drivers and passengers tumbled from their cars and stampeded towards the safety of the open field. Totsakan paid no attention and continued to walk aimlessly down the road.

'What do you think he's doing?' asked Rawin. 'He seems to be just randomly hitting anything he gets near. Lucky for us he doesn't have a weapon.'

Totsakan stopped and stared for a moment.

'What's he looking at?' Catt wondered.

'Oh, no,' said Rawin. 'I think it's that girl coming out of Silpakorn University. She hasn't seen him yet. She looks like you, Catt.'

'But surely...' began Meeya. Before she could finish her sentence Totsakan swooped on the girl and grabbed her round the neck, lifting her up.

'He thinks she's you,' Sayola said, alarmed.

'No. He's not stupid,' said Rawin. 'He's furious. And that means he is going to take it out on anyone who is like us. Any child from our world. That girl's older than Catt. He can see that. But he doesn't care.'

'But I care,' thundered Catt. She unwrapped the mat, pulled out her sword and ran towards Totsakan. Sayola grabbed his spear and joined her. Rawin followed with Meeya.

'Totsakan!' the girl shouted when she got close enough for the demon to hear her over the screaming and the traffic noise. 'Let her go. It's me you want.'

Totsakan turned and looked at Catt and then at the university student. He let go of her and she fell to the ground and lay there twisted, choking as she gasped for air. 'Come on then,' he said to Catt. 'Straight swap. Or should I crush her?' He placed a foot on the student.

'Let her go!' Catt yelled again. She ran at him with her sword held in both hands in front of her. Totsakan stepped back, ready to swing at her as she closed in on him. But before she reached him, Catt swung sideways and slid down on her knees beside the student. She put an arm under her and lifted her until she was on her feet.

'You've got to do this,' she ordered. 'Run.' Totsakan realised what she was doing and took a swipe at the two girls but Catt managed to shove the student out of the way and ducked her own head as Totsakan's huge arm passed over them. 'Now, go,' she insisted.

Startled, but now sufficiently recovered, the student scrambled across to the other side of the road until she was at a safe distance. Then she fell into the arms of some people who were watching and sobbed uncontrollably. Catt meanwhile sheathed her sword and did two backward somersaults until she was out of Totsakan's reach. He had been surprised by the speed with which she moved. A large crowd that had been watching, half in horror and half in fascination, began to applaud wildly. Sayola came and stood beside Catt, his spear ready.

'You think you're smart, girl,' Totsakan scoffed. 'I'll get you sooner or later.' Then he turned and punched the roof of a taxi, leaving a deep dent in it. The driver jumped out and ran howling towards the safety of Sanam Luang. Just then a police van and patrol car came round the corner and wove their way through the chaotic traffic, sirens blaring. When they got close to Totsakan, the two vehicles stopped and armed policemen took up positions behind them and began firing at Totsakan. The bullets bounced off the demon, but he flinched every time one hit him. He began to run along the road that flanks the Grand Palace to get away from them. Some of the policemen chased after him. Their commander stayed with the vehicles and ordered other officers to arrest Catt and Sayola. Four of them grabbed the two children by the arms and ordered them to drop their weapons. Catt argued fiercely, but she didn't know how to explain what she and Sayola were doing in the middle of a busy road in Bangkok's most visited tourist area carrying a sword and a spear.

'Lock them in the van,' the commander ordered.

A short distance away Meeya said quietly to Rawin: 'Let me handle this.' He looked at her quizzically as she stared intently at the police officer who wasn't aware of her presence. After about a minute the officer shouted to his men just as they were opening the back of the police van: 'Release them and return their weapons.'

The policemen looked at their commander and then at each other in disbelief. One asked him to repeat his order. 'You heard me,' he bellowed, 'release them and give them their weapons back. Let them go.'

Surprised but delighted, Catt and Sayola took back their hardware and walked quickly away from the policemen as if they feared there might be another change of mind. Sayola threw a glance at Meeya who winked at him. A faint smile passed across her lips. Rawin flicked his head at Catt and Sayola to signal that they should keep walking. He didn't want the police to know they were together. Catt got the message and she and Sayola walked in the direction that Totsakan had gone.

As soon as they reached the end of the road, Rawin and Meeya wove their way through the hundreds of people running in fear in the opposite direction. The children couldn't see Totsakan now, but it was clear to them that he was still wreaking havoc as he went. Amid the cries and screams of those fleeing, they could hear the police guns being fired. 'Come on, let's catch up,' said Rawin. They began to run.

They turned the corner and saw that the street that runs down the western side of the Grand Palace was littered with damaged vehicles – cars and tuk-tuks overturned or knocked to the side of the road, motorcycles abandoned by their riders, even buses left in the middle of the road, passengers and drivers having fled. People ran in all directions screaming. Rawin and Meeya could see Catt and Sayola running ahead, dodging the oncoming horde escaping Totsakan's wrath. They ran faster to catch up and saw more police vans approaching from the opposite direction. Totsakan swerved down a side street that led to the Thien Pier. By the time Catt and Sayola followed him, Rawin and Meeya had caught up with them.

'He's heading for the river,' shouted Catt, darting between cars. They couldn't see Totsakan, but they heard the commotion as he ran down the street, knocking vendors' barrows flying, scattering fried chicken, pork kebabs, fried bananas and other food across the road. Small pink plastic stools, many overturned in the chaos, littered the street. Stray dogs cowered from the noise amid the pandemonium but, cringing, still managed to gobble down some of the food scraps on the road.

As the four reached the end of the side street they saw the ferry that runs from Thien Pier to the Temple of Dawn on the other side of the river start to pull away from its mooring. Totsakan ran at full speed and jumped from the pier, crashing onto the back of the ferry. The boat dipped low in the water and then bobbed up again. As Totsakan held on, the passengers inside began screaming and wailing as they tried to get out. Dozens hurled themselves into the river and flapped around trying to stay afloat. A few lifebuoys were thrown from the ferry, but most passengers had to do their best to swim to the shore unaided. Totsakan pulled himself up and clambered along the roof of the boat until he was balanced. As more passengers threw themselves overboard, the boat's pilot maintained a steady course for the Temple of Dawn pier opposite. The majestic pagoda towered above all else on the riverside.

'My God,' Rawin shouted. 'Those people are going to drown.' But just then one of the express river boats that run up and down the city's busy waterway chugged slowly closer to where the passengers were bobbing in the water. As soon as the ferry had reached halfway, the express reversed engines and held its position as buoys and life jackets were thrown into the water. Passengers leaned over and pulled to safety those who managed to swim or paddle close enough to be reached.

'Brave,' Sayola commented.

Rawin ran down the pier until he reached a longtail boat that had been abandoned in terror by its owner. 'Come on,' he shouted as he shuffled to the back of the boat and gunned the engine. It roared into life on the third pull. The other three followed him and sprang into the narrow vessel, with Catt up front, Sayola behind her and then Meeya. Rawin manoeuvred the vessel with the steering shaft that controls the propeller as if he was born to it.

'I didn't know you could do this,' shouted Catt over the deafening roar.

'My uncle has one of these up north,' Rawin shouted back. 'Except his is a 12-cylinder 22-horse power. This has just six barrels and about seven HP.'

'Of course,' Catt muttered dryly.

The longtail boat was faster than the ferry and reached the other side of the river just after Totsakan had leapt on to the pier at the Temple of Dawn, leaving the ferry rocking slowly next to the landing platform, the pilot still sitting in terror at the wheel. Totsakan seemed fascinated with the iridescent, spiritual beauty of the pagoda. He ignored the people who fled hysterically around him and headed for the entrance to the temple. By the time he reached the foot of the central pagoda the site was deserted and he slowly wandered around, transfixed by the many sculptured figures that surrounded it, demons and elephants, some with three heads. He seemed almost calm as he wandered around the site.

Rawin meanwhile cut the engine of the boat as they drifted to the side of the pier. As it gently rubbed up against the rubber tires, they leapt off, one by one and headed for the temple. The last of the fleeing tourists were running past the ticket booth as they entered. A tourism officer tried to stop the children: 'No, no, don't go in there,' he stammered. 'You'll get killed.' He turned and watched in astonishment as the four children ignored him and sprinted towards what he regarded as certain death. Then he turned and ran for his life.

'What's Totsakan doing?' Catt whispered, now just behind Rawin. He had led the way and was peering between the small trees and outbuildings of the temple to try to get a good view of Totsakan.

'He looks like a serious tourist, examining the temple in great detail,' Rawin told her. 'At least he has calmed down a bit.'

As they discussed what to do next Totsakan walked around to the right of the temple complex and approached the Ordination Hall. The children followed, out of sight. Totsakan stopped.

'He's seen himself,' Catt chuckled.

At the Hall stood two decorated stone statues of demons guarding the entrance, their hands resting on lances. The one on the left was Totsakan, and he knew it as soon as he saw it.

Just then a line of novice monks emerged from the Hall, each holding an alms bowl. When they saw Totsakan they stopped and looked at him, but none of them said anything or showed any fear.

'What is this doing here?' he bellowed, pointing at his statue. 'Are you trying to humiliate me? I am not a guard. I am a king.'

The monks continued to stand still, but now they looked puzzled.

'Remove this!' Totsakan commanded. Still the monks did nothing.

'I am a king!' cried Totsakan. 'Show me respect,' he commanded. Then he stepped forward and lifted a hand ready to strike the nearest monk. The monk did not move.

'Wait!' Catt shouted, sprinting forward. 'Stop.'

Totsakan spun around and looked at her. 'You again,' he growled. He turned his back on the monks and started to walk towards the girl.

'What is it you want?' she asked in an annoyed tone.

'You,' he bellowed.

'Well, that's not going to happen. Not again.' She shifted her feet apart and held her sword in front of her in both hands. He swiped at her. She danced out of the way. Then he swiped again, quicker this time. Again, even quicker, she bobbed to the side and he missed. Before he could have another swipe, she slipped behind him and kicked him behind the knees. 'Thanks for the lesson, Hanuman,' she said to herself. Totsakan's legs buckled under him, giving her just enough time to jab her sword into his leg and spin away.

'You little witch!' he shouted. He squared up and started to trudge toward her, fuming.

Rawin and Meeya watched anxiously. Sayola held his spear in the throwing position but, not wishing to endanger Catt by launching it, waited to see what she would do next. He did not have long to wait. In the blink of an eye she went from standing completely still to shifting through three pirouetting taekwondo kicks in succession, striking Totsakan first in the chest, then the midriff and then in the leg where she had stabbed him a minute earlier. Totsakan tried to parry the attacks, but each time he was too slow, unable to prevent Catt landing the three blows as her body spun through the air. It was the third that hurt the most. He let out a groan that progressed into a howl of anger. 'You will not get away with this,' he roared.

While Totsakan was distracted by his skirmish with Catt, Rawin slipped behind him unnoticed and quietly steered the monks to safety back inside the Ordination Hall. Seeing that the danger to the monks had now passed, Catt backed off. Totsakan looked at her suspiciously. Then he turned and walked back to the main temple compound, looking around him. As he did so, a boy ran in panic along the stone-paved path, darting between the trees and through the manicured gardens and topiary. He scampered like a monkey over the iron railings that separated the main temple courtyard from the wider complex. Rawin quickly remembered that when they arrived at the temple he had seen the boy leading a blind woman who was singing into a microphone and rattling a tin mug for charity donations from tourists.

'Where did she go?' he asked. By now Catt and Sayola had joined him.

'Don't know,' replied Catt. 'Maybe he left her near the refreshment stand. That's where they were earlier.'

Rawin rushed down the path towards the refreshment stand where he saw the woman helplessly tapping her white stick around her. She had stopped singing and had dropped her tin mug. A few bank notes and coins had spilled out on to the ground.

'Auntie, Auntie, quick, you have to hide,' Rawin said, taking her by the hand. She bent down and felt around for the mug. 'No, Auntie, we can come back for that later. We have to hide.' He led her behind the refreshment stand and tried his best to explain what was happening.

Totsakan turned, having heard voices. He looked around, and after a while decided to go after the boy. He had no trouble climbing over the iron railing that the boy had scaled. He entered the temple complex, slowly looking left and right in search of the boy.

'Come on,' cried Catt. She hurried ahead of Sayola down the path after Totsakan. Meeya went to help Rawin with the blind woman.

Catt led Sayola round to the front of the temple. They entered through the ticket gate and ran between the buildings and many golden statues and stone sculptures in the courtyard. When they reached the pagoda that now towered above them they saw the boy running for his life round the structure. He hesitated and then darted up the short flight of stone steps to the raised base at the foot of the pagoda. As he did so, Totsakan appeared from round the other side, also on the raised base. He darted towards the boy who, in alarm, turned to his right and ran up the steps to the stairway on the outside of the pagoda. Totsakan followed. In a panic the boy nipped into the narrow stairway and began to climb. He started crying but didn't stop. He looked back in terror as Totsakan followed. The giant demon couldn't fit between the low walls that flanked the steps, so he just clambered up the pagoda, his huge body visible from the other side of the river, sending a terrified chill across the city.

'OK,' said Sayola, 'we've got to stop this.' He ran to the side of the pagoda where he could see Totsakan clearly getting closer to the boy who, now exhausted, was cowering on the small landing at the top of the stairs and hiding his face. Totsakan didn't appear to be in a hurry. Holding on to the side of the pagoda he reached out to grab the boy. But before he could do so, Sayola launched his spear. With a sickening thud it hit Totsakan's body just beneath the arm that was stretching out towards the boy. He tried to reach across himself to extract the spear, but it had sapped his strength. He groaned and then roared with anger, until slowly he was able to reach the spear. He tugged, but it would not come out. He tugged again, gasping with the pain as he did so. Then he tugged with all his strength, which caused him to lose his balance. He fell. His huge body tumbled down the side of the ancient structure and came to rest with a loud thud at its base.

'Quick,' Sayola shouted to the boy. 'Come down quickly.'

'I can't,' he wailed. 'I'm scared.'

'You can. I'll be here when you get to the bottom.'

'No, no, no, I can't,' the boy cried. He sat down and hid his face in his hands.

Just then Meeya came and stood next to Sayola. She looked intensely up at the boy but said nothing. Sayola turned to his sister and knew what was happening. A minute later the boy stood up and began to hurtle down the steep steps as if nothing had happened. When he reached the bottom he ran past Totsakan, who was still on the ground groaning, said thank you to Sayola and vaulted the iron railings before rushing off towards where he had left the blind woman, now being comforted by Rawin.

'What a team!' Catt said, with a broad smile.

# CHAPTER
# FORTY-FOUR

Totsakan dragged himself to his feet and staggered to the river where he lurched down one of the ferry landing ramps. He sat down, leaned over and splashed water on his wound. The children ran to the riverside and hid behind the wall. They saw Totsakan at last manage to pull Sayola's spear from his side and toss it into the water. He groaned in agony. Blood continued to seep from the deep gash. Then he lowered himself into the water and began drifting out towards the middle of the river.

'What about your spear, Sayola?' asked Rawin, turning to look at him.

Sayola simply smiled.

'Ah, right,' Rawin remembered. 'You've got another one already. How did that happen? The curse has already been lifted.'

'Don't know. I am as surprised as you are. Maybe because the Spectre is still alive.'

'Come on you guys,' Catt interrupted. 'You don't have to have an answer to everything. Just be glad you've got your spear back, Sayola, because I've got a feeling you're going to need it again soon.'

Then they saw Totsakan look downstream at a gigantic

cargo barge being towed by a small tugboat chugging slowly up the river against the outgoing tide. They watched as Totsakan used his massive arms to paddle out and pull himself up on to the barge. As he did so, the tugboat pilot began to shout hysterically. He ran to the back and frantically disconnected the thick ropes that were tied to the barge. He looked in horror at the giant demon sitting on the barge that only minutes earlier was his sole responsibility. Then he looked away, shaking his head in disbelief, returned rapidly to the front of the tug, opened the throttle and sped upriver as fast as his little vessel could go, shouting madly as he did so.

The children had been gripped by the sight of Totsakan boarding the barge, but quickly realised that something terrible could happen as the massive vessel now drifted downstream with the tide.

'Come on,' Rawin yelled. 'We need to get down river.' He ran round the Temple of Dawn complex into the narrow alleys of the neighbourhood behind it. The word had got round that the demon had left, so the people who had fled for their lives had started to return to their homes, shops and vending stands, all talking excitedly about what they had seen. Catt, Sayola and Meeya followed closely. Rawin rushed up to a tuk-tuk and started to talk to the driver. But he hesitated because he didn't know where to tell the driver they wanted to go. The driver, who was rolling a cigarette, looked suspiciously at the mat that Sayola was holding.

'Listen,' Catt interrupted, 'we have to be honest with you. We want you to follow the demon.'

The tuk-tuk driver looked silently at her, and then at Rawin. Then he looked at Meeya and Sayola and at the rolled-up mat. His face didn't once change its blank, disbelieving expression. Then, still without changing it, he said: 'Five hundred baht.'

Rawin and Catt exchanged looks for a couple of seconds. Then she said, 'Done.' They all climbed into the tuk-tuk. The driver revved the engine several times and then turned the vehicle into the middle of the alley and accelerated.

'Woo-hoo!' shouted Sayola over the sound of the engine, 'this is fun.'

'Everyone thinks so,' Rawin shouted. 'If you've never ridden in a tuk-tuk before, you've not lived. Millions of tourists will tell you so.'

By now thousands of people had gathered on both sides of the river to watch the heart-breaking sight of Totsakan trashing parts of their city. Many gathered on the Memorial Bridge and the Prince Pokklao Bridge looking down in awe as Totsakan drifted slowly downstream below them. Most of the traffic was unaware of what was happening, so there was the normal flow of tour boats, ferries, river taxis, speed boats, longtail boats, barges and other vessels ploughing their ways and wares up and down the river.

As the barge drifted downstream with the last of the ebbing tide it scraped against the concrete walls on the Chinatown side of the river, pulling down a row of fragile wooden houses, which collapsed into the water. Then it crashed through a string of private piers and landing platforms along the riverside. As the vessel rubbed against the concrete, the sound was deafening – like the scream of an animal in excruciating pain, getting louder and more distressing as it went on, seemingly without end. Totsakan remained seated on the tarpaulin on top of the thousands of tons of cargo in the barge's hold and showed no emotion as he watched the destruction it caused. The screams of people in the collapsing houses could barely be heard over the terrible noise of the barge grinding its way along the wall. Then the noise stopped abruptly as the barge drifted back into the middle of the river, now facing sideways. It continued downstream at this angle for some way until the river curved south again.

On the other side the four children hung on tight as their tuk-tuk driver seemed to take his mission to heart. After passing behind the headquarters of the Thai Royal Navy, he swerved into every alley he could find that led to the river so they could monitor the progress of the barge downstream. Then when the road no longer hugged the riverside, they raced back to the frontage roads that skirted the riverside neighbourhoods. Then back down another alley to the waterside, and then back out again. In and out, to and fro they went, between houses and offices and monuments and temples. Whenever they were able to see the river they jumped out of the tuk-tuk to get a better look from the wall and then jumped back in and raced on. It was slow progress at great speed, but they did manage to keep up. At the Taksin Hospital they turned down the street that led to the river. When the tuk-tuk could go no further the children jumped out and ran to the water's edge.

Totsakan was still sitting on the barge as it drifted slowly but unstoppably into a row of luxury double-decker cruise boats docked at the River City Pier, the departure point for pleasure trips up and down the Chao Phraya. From where the children were standing it seemed as if they were watching a slow-motion disaster movie. The weight of the barge pulverised everything in its way. Huge pieces of the cruise boats bent and buckled upwards and then snapped and collapsed into the river. The staff on the boats, who were preparing for their daily sunset river cruises with happy tourists, ran screaming for the shore, some leaping into the water. Many on the lower decks disappeared from sight amid the tangled wreckage as the sound of splintering wood and snapping steel shattered the air up and down the waterfront. Totsakan stood up on the barge as it carved its destructive path through the boats, eventually drifting back into the middle of the river.

'Oh God, no,' Catt said slowly and deliberately. 'No, no, no. This is terrible. Terrible.'

'It's not over yet,' Rawin said grimly. 'Look. The barge is heading for Iconsiam.'

'What's Iconsiam?' asked Meeya.

'It's the city's most famous luxury shopping mall,' Rawin explained. 'It's got a 5,300 square metre pleated glass façade, 24 metres high.'

'Rawin, enough technical detail, please,' Catt snapped. 'We need to get down there. Back to the tuk-tuk.'

When the barge drifted on the tide near the Iconsiam pier, Totsakan stepped off into the water and, after wading the last few yards, climbed onto the landing platform. He stood surveying the modern architectural wonder before him, gazing admiringly at the spectacular glass façade that displayed the names of some of the world's best-known luxury brands. Hundreds of shoppers who had been enjoying the classy food and drink amenities on the forecourt began to scream and run to the sides of the building to escape. Then

Totsakan's eye caught sight of two window cleaners standing on a small basket-like platform that hung by steel cables from the top of the building. He stepped forward and thrust an arm over the side of the platform, pulling one of the two men out and flinging him with one hand to the forecourt, sending tables and chairs, glasses and plates flying and shattering across the patio. The other man was so terrified he jumped. Those people on the forecourt who hadn't yet managed to get away wailed in horror.

Then Totsakan took the cable in both hands and scaled the glass façade like a rock climber. Inside the mall shoppers watched in panicked horror as the giant demon climbed the glass front in full view. When he reached the top, he clambered over the railing and on to the upper deck. People ran screaming for cover. After surveying the scene, he walked up to the next façade that confronted him, the spectacular Apple Store from where the world-famous Apple logo glowed illustriously over the river. Customers, unaware of what had happened over the past few minutes, drifted around the store like patrons at an art gallery.

After staring for a while Totsakan strode up to the façade and raised his arms, slapping them with great force against the glass, which shuddered like a thunderclap. Inside a scene of such hysterical chaos erupted that Totsakan himself seemed shocked. Shoppers stampeded in every direction, some trampling over one another, screaming and wailing frantically as they tried to get to the exits. Totsakan turned and ripped a metal bench from the floor of the patio and hurled it with enormous power at the glass front. It shattered, sending huge sheets of glass cascading into the store. Screaming shoppers desperately tried to escape the avalanche of shards that rained down on them. Soon the cream marble floor glistened with bloodied glass fragments.

Totsakan marched into the store, with his powerful arms sweeping aside any pieces of glass that still hung in the gaping hole he had created. He stood for a moment and surveyed his handiwork as wounded customers scrambled to get out of the way, begging for mercy with bloodied hands. He saw a boy about the same age as Rawin sitting hunched on the floor in fear, stuttering into an iPhone. He could see it was similar to the one Rawin had in his cave moments before he escaped on a motorcycle.

'Give me that!' he ordered, snatching the phone from the boy. Totsakan inspected the device and then held it to his ear as if he expected something to happen. 'Are these things magic?' he asked the terrified boy. The child was shaking so much his words were hardly audible. '*I* think so,' he said. Then he added, 'But my mother says they are evil.'

Totsakan grunted. Then he threw the phone through the massive hole in the glass façade. Looking around he noticed that there were display cases containing lots of similar phones. He ripped the cabinets open and threw the phones across the store in a rage. Then he stamped on others, shattering them.

The boy jumped up and began to run out of the store, deeper into the mall. 'Come back!' shouted Totsakan, who set off after him. The boy was fast but Totsakan managed to stay close behind him by climbing over counters and displays of merchandise and knocking down others. The boy hurtled up the nearest escalator. Totsakan followed, striding up a dozen steps at a time, smashing anything that got in his way. They travelled up several floors, terrifying shoppers who fled hysterically in every direction. Many fell over the sides of the escalators, plunging to the atrium below.

When the boy reached the third floor of the mall, he darted through the back exit to the Charoen Nakhon Skytrain station. Totsakan followed. He saw the boy hurdle the entrance gates and then scamper up one more flight of stairs. Totsakan did the same. As the boy reached the top floor he hurled himself through the closing doors of a train that was standing at the platform. Totsakan charged up to the train but the doors clicked shut and the train pulled away just as he reached it. He stopped and watched the boy staring in fear through the window of the train door. He hesitated. Then he noticed on the side of the train carriage a picture of a beautiful woman in traditional attire surrounded by flames. In one corner of the picture a princely male figure was looking at the woman. Totsakan had only a brief second to look at it properly as the train began to pick up speed.

'Sida!' he mouthed. The writing above the picture said:

'The Fire Ordeal of Sida' and below it 'Sala Chalermkrung Royal Theatre Monday to Sunday 2pm and 8pm. Tickets at www.salachalermkrung.com'.

Totsakan stood confused on the station as the train sped out of sight. Then he clambered down the concrete pillars that held up the monorail until he reached the road below. He began to run beneath the Skytrain bridge, looking up to keep an eye on the train's progress.

It was then that the tuk-tuk carrying the children sped along the same road close behind Totsakan.

'There he is,' declared Rawin. 'Keep going,' he told the driver.

Just then Totsakan's arm got caught up in a tangle of overhead cables strung between poles at an intersection. As he continued to run, he dragged them into the road, bringing more down with them. He fell as his body became entangled in a spaghetti of wires. He collapsed into the road, sending two cars swerving to avoid him and spinning into a group of motorcycle taxi drivers waiting for fares at the side of the street. One wire that had been severed in the collapse sent sparks jumping in all directions. Flames leapt up the wires. Totsakan stood up and struggled to release himself from the mesh of cables, shaking and tugging in all directions and bellowing with anger until at last he was able to strip them off his body and carry on chasing the Skytrain. He left behind a labyrinth of cables and burning wires, damaged cars and screaming pedestrians, which the tuk-tuk carrying the four children screeched into, swerving and dodging its way through the chaos and out the other side, only just managing to do so unscathed.

'Phew!' Rawin said, almost in jest. No one else said anything. The tuk-tuk driver showed no emotion.

A few minutes later the Skytrain reached Krung Thonburi station. Totsakan ran up the steps leading to the station platforms above.

'Quick, stop here!' Rawin said.

The tuk-tuk driver pulled up at the side of the road and the children leapt out. Catt stopped briefly and turned back. 'Five hundred baht, right?' she said to the driver.

'Go,' replied the driver coolly, nodding his head

upwards at the station above, 'go.'

Catt gave him a big smile and a thank-you nod and ran after the others.

All four hurdled the ticket gates and galloped up the stairs. When they reached the platform the monorail train was standing empty. Totsakan was nowhere to be seen. They looked up and down the platform but he wasn't there.

'What the…' Sayola said. 'How did he just disappear?'

'Wait,' Rawin said. 'This is the end of the Gold Line. Everyone has to change trains here.'

'Change to what?' asked Meeya.

'To the other line. The Silom Line. It goes into the centre of the city.' He looked around him and saw the signs. 'Quick, this way.'

They ran frantically back down one flight of stairs and along the passageways that led to the Silom Line, keeping an eye out for Totsakan. But he had vanished. They had to vault over another set of ticket barriers and then stopped where one lot of stairs went up to the platform for trains to National Stadium – the city centre – and another out to the suburbs. They heard a train pull into the platform on the National Stadium side.

'Come on,' Rawin shouted. He sprinted up the stairs, followed closely by the others. As they reached the platform they heard the alarm ringing – the train doors were about to close. They looked frantically up and down the platform.

'There!' Catt shouted, pointing into the car just ahead of them. Just visible through the last window was Totsakan in human form, sitting respectfully on the carriage seats alongside unsuspecting passengers.

# CHAPTER
# FORTY-FIVE

'**G**et in!' Rawin shouted, pushing the others through the doors of the carriage behind the one they had seen Totsakan in as the safety barrier closed behind them. Sayola managed to hold on to the mat that hid his spear and Catt's sword as they tumbled into the carriage.

As soon as they had settled down they looked into the carriage ahead of them.

'It's him,' Catt whispered. 'Definitely.'

'He's dressed in his demon gear,' Meeya commented. 'Doesn't that freak people out?'

'No,' Rawin explained, 'This is Bangkok. People do weird things. No one cares.'

'So now what?' Sayola asked.

'Let's just keep an eye on him for now,' Catt suggested. 'At least at the moment he looks pretty calm for once.'

'What made him chase these train things, for goodness' sake?' Sayola asked. 'And where does he think he's going now?'

'Beats me,' Rawin said. 'Make sure he doesn't see us.'

Soon the train crossed the river and arrived at the next station, Saphan Taksin. The children watched the demon carefully, but he made no move when the doors opened.

Soon they were on their way again.

'This is worrying,' Catt said. 'He must have something in his mind, some reason he followed the other train and also why he got on this one.'

When they arrived at the next station, Surasak, a train coming from the other side pulled up at the opposite platform at the same time. Totsakan turned and watched it as it came to a stop parallel with their train. He began to look agitated, turning his head apparently trying to see something. He stood up and pressed his fingers and face against the window.

'Look!' Rawin whispered. 'That's it.' He pointed to an advertising poster on the side of the train opposite: 'The Fire Ordeal of Sida'.

'I know what,' Catt exclaimed. She sprang out of her seat and rushed out of the door, stood for a second outside and then hurled herself back in just as the doors were closing. 'There's one of those posters on the side of the carriage Totsakan is in. He must have decided this has something to do with Sida.'

'Which of course it does,' Rawin said logically.

'Except not the real Sida,' Catt added.

'Yes, but who is the real Sida?' Rawin asked rhetorically.

'Oh, don't,' Catt groaned. 'This is giving me a headache.'

'But what's the fire thing about?' asked Sayola.

'It's from the Ramakien story after Prince Ram and Sida are reunited. Prince Ram thinks that maybe Sida was unfaithful to him when she was Totsakan's captive. He accuses her, so she says, "Test me by making me walk on fire. If the fire doesn't burn me to death," she says, "that would prove I was faithful".'

'Seriously?' Meeya commented.

'Yes, it was common in ancient times all over the world to believe that if someone was innocent of something of which they were accused, they would survive a deadly ordeal, like drowning or, in this case, fire. This is one of the scenes that the Khon masked dancers perform in the Royal Theatre. The male dancer in the poster is Prince Ram.'

'No wonder Totsakan is troubled by it,' Sayola remarked.

'Meeya, what are you doing?' Rawin asked. He had been watching the girl.

Meeya was staring intensely at Totsakan through the doors that separated the two carriages.

'I think she's trying to get into his head,' whispered Sayola, holding up a hand to signal that the other two should not interrupt.

The train snaked its way on to the next stop. Rawin, Catt and Sayola watched anxiously as Meeya continued to focus her eyes on Totsakan.

'He's not letting me in,' complained Meeya eventually. 'My thoughts keep bouncing back at me.'

'What were you trying to get him to think?' asked Sayola.

'I wanted to make him feel sorry for those people he was hurting so that he would stop.'

'But?'

'He's not thinking about them.'

'What's he thinking about?'

'Two things. Sida and...' Meeya stopped and looked uncomfortable. Sayola stopped questioning his sister.

'Well, what's the other thing?' Rawin asked.

Meeya looked at the other three and then cast her eyes downward.

'Come on,' said Catt, a little irritated. 'What's the other thing he's thinking about?'

'You.'

'Me?'

'Yes, you.'

'Do you know what he's thinking, not just what he's thinking about?' Rawin asked.

'No. There's too much going on in his mind. It's like a forcefield I cannot penetrate.'

'So he's thinking about Sida and Catt,' Rawin went on, 'but we don't know what exactly he is thinking about them?'

'I think he's obsessed.'

'With both?'

'Yes. His thoughts are completely filled with them. There seems to be nothing else going on in his mind.'

'So he sees a picture of Sida on the side of the train and

decides to get in,' Rawin reasoned. 'That's because his mind is totally focused on her.'

'And Catt?' asked Sayola.

Meeya breathed in deeply and shut her eyes. Then she looked at the others again. 'I think he just wants to kill her.'

Rawin and Sayola looked at Catt nervously. But she didn't flinch. 'Well, nothing new about that,' she commented coldly.

Rawin grimaced.

'Come on, Rawin, you know it has to happen. Him or me. It's written.'

By now the train had made two more stops above Bangkok's busiest business and shopping areas. Totsakan was sitting down again and acting quite normally, just like any other passenger. After one more stop that overlooked the city's horse racing track, the train rattled straight towards Rajaprasong, Bangkok's busiest central intersection. As it slowed and began curving round towards the next station, Siam, some of the passengers turned to the window and put their hands together in the Thai gesture of respect. Below the train in a small enclosure traditionally dressed women performed a ritual dance to the sound of classical musical instruments. Tourists and other onlookers stood around and waved incense sticks. Totsakan looked down to see what his fellow passengers were showing respect to. Immediately he stood up and again held his hands to the window, desperately trying to see more as the train wound its way past the scene.

'What's that about?' asked Sayola.

'That's the Erawan shrine,' Rawin explained. 'If you're miserable for some reason you can ask the god of creation to free you of your troubles. Then you donate money to the dancers to thank him.'

'So why is Totsakan doing that?' Meeya asked.

The children looked back to the train carriage ahead of them and saw Totsakan banging on the doors, shouting angrily. The other passengers ran terrified to the other end just as Totsakan bellowed loudly, transforming himself back to demon. He grew too big to fit in the Skytrain carriage, so he smashed the roof open and began kicking in the doors. Alarms started sounding up and down the train, which came to a shuddering stop on the elevated rail high above the Rajaprasong intersection. Below, cars, buses and motorcycles inched their way through the city centre's never-ending traffic gridlock.

'Oh my God,' exclaimed Meeya, 'I know what he's doing. He thinks one of those dancers might be Sida.'

Totsakan smashed open the door of the carriage and climbed out on to the concrete overpass. He walked fearlessly along the side of the stationary train looking down at the Erawan shrine, where the dancing and music had stopped. Most of the people at the shrine and on the sidewalks around the intersection were staring in disbelief at the sight of the giant demon on the concrete bridge above them. Totsakan stood with his hands on his hips, head turned slightly up and to one side as he looked down his nose at the scene below him. Only the children, who were now peering through the windows of their train carriage, could see the gash in the side of his green and gold patterned tunic where Sayola's spear had entered. It was still darkened by the blood that had continued to seep from the wound.

Just then shots were fired from the roof of the Erawan Hotel opposite where the train was stranded. A contingent of policemen had rushed over from the Royal Thai Police Headquarters, just half a city block away, having received reports of a commotion on the Skytrain. The police had already been on the alert since their first encounter with the demon outside the Grand Palace a few hours earlier. Bullets sprayed around Totsakan, some hitting him. He howled with pain. He climbed over the top of the train to the other side to escape the gunfire and began roaring with pent-up anger. From there he caught sight of the children who were trapped inside when the train had come to a halt earlier. He clawed at the windows. 'You will die, all of you!' He bent and took hold of the carriage under the chassis, above the wheels and began lifting and shaking it.

'Sayola, quick, your spear,' Rawin shouted.

Sayola unrolled the mat and passed Catt's sword to her. He began smashing his weapon against the window on the opposite side from Totsakan. The other passengers started screaming and hiding their faces in terror. Catt used her sword to help Sayola smash the window.

'Out, out, everybody,' Rawin shouted as the window gave way. Totsakan was still rocking the carriage. It seemed to get higher off its wheels every time he raised it, groaning with the effort. The children hurriedly guided the passengers to the window and helped them jump free on to the concrete bridge. One by one the passengers ran terrified along the side of the train towards Siam station, away from Totsakan. When they were all out, the children followed, first Meeya, then Rawin, then Sayola. As Catt prepared to climb out, sword in hand, Totsakan gave the carriage one more heave. Its weight shifted enough for it to begin tipping over. Catt fell back to the floor of the carriage.

'Quick, Catt, quick,' Rawin screamed.

But it was too late. The carriage lurched over the side of the concrete bridge but did not fall because it was still linked to the train's other carriages, one in front and two behind. The walls of the bridge began to crack and then shatter as the weight of the carriage bore down on them. Totsakan didn't stop. He saw Catt struggling to get through the window and shouted, 'I told you you would die, witch.' Then he pushed on the carriage. It inched down further and began to drag the other carriages with it until there was now enough weight over the side of the bridge to pull the rest of the train down. The screaming of passengers was so loud and distressing that some of those below who heard it began to cry.

Catt managed to scramble out of the window and jump free just as the four carriages plunged to the busy street below. As she stumbled to regain her balance on the bridge she dropped her sword, which slipped over the edge and followed the train down. In a flash Totsakan grabbed her. 'Come here,' he said triumphantly holding her by the throat on the bridge above the intersection.

'Now you will die.'

# CHAPTER
# FORTY-SIX

Rawin, who was watching from a little way down the track, sprinted to within a few yards of Totsakan and Catt. 'Wait-wait-wait,' he shouted desperately. The police had stopped firing, worried they might hit Catt. 'Totsakan, Sir, you think one of those dancers is Sida, right? That's not true. But I know where she is. I can take you to her.'

Totsakan looked intrigued at Rawin. 'Why would I believe your lies again, boy?' Catt struggled, but Totsakan's hold was too strong.

'No, no, Sir, I am not lying. It's the truth, I swear. Look.' Rawin held his uncle's phone with the screen towards Totsakan. He had found a video of the Ramakien Khon dance that Totsakan had seen on the poster. It showed Sida dancing.

'I am tired of your magic tricks. When I am finished with this arrogant girl, I will kill you too, you deceitful little squirt.'

'No, no. It's not magic. You know I can't do what you call magic without the small child. JaoJuk's not here, look. I can only show you what is real. See for yourself.' He took two steps closer, still holding the phone out.

Totsakan hesitated and looked at the phone. 'Bring it closer,' he demanded.

Rawin took a few more steps until he was within reaching distance.

'No, Rawin,' Catt gasped, 'don't come any closer.'

'You shut up,' Totsakan snapped.

'No, Catt, you know that I know where Sida is. Tell him.' He turned the screen towards her.

Sayola sighed with a shudder. 'This is terrible,' he said to Meeya who, like him, was watching fearfully. 'He could easily just swat Rawin off the bridge.'

Totsakan showed more interest in what was on the phone. 'Why would you want to take me to Sida?'

'So that you don't hurt Catt.'

'Ha! How very touching.'

The girl understood what Rawin was doing, so she played along. 'No, Rawin, don't tell him.'

'I said shut up.'

'No, seriously, Sir. You let her go and I will take you to Sida. I know exactly where she is. Look.' He turned the screen towards Totsakan again. The demon watched briefly. He seemed to soften slightly.

'Why is she dancing? She never danced before.'

'You never let her. She's free now.'

Totsakan became thoughtful. Catt struggled again.

'Keep still, you,' the demon demanded.

'I know where she is dancing, right now,' Rawin said. 'But we will have to hurry, otherwise she might disappear.'

Totsakan looked worried. 'Is she far away?'

'No, we can get there in about twenty minutes. You will have to make yourself human again. You can't go looking like that.'

Sayola took Meeya into his arms while they both watched anxiously. 'He's starting to believe Rawin.'

'There is no greater fool than a man in love,' Meeya sighed cynically.

Totsakan stared threateningly at Rawin. 'OK, I will let your little girlfriend go, but you will be my prisoner until I have Sida again.'

'That's acceptable to me, Sir. And, by the way, she's not

my girlfriend.'

'Then why do you care about her so much?'

'I just do.'

'Enough to risk your own life? Because I am telling you, boy, if you are lying to me I will crush you to death and come back for her.'

'We need to go, Sir.'

'Come here.'

Rawin moved right up to Totsakan, who shoved Catt away and gripped Rawin by the throat.

'Go, go,' Rawin said to Catt, choking from Totsakan's grip. She looked achingly at him as she walked despondently away to join Sayola and Meeya, turning back every few steps to look at Rawin.

'This way,' said Rawin with difficulty. He started walking. Totsakan was still holding him by the throat. The others stepped aside to allow them to pass on the bridge as they headed towards Siam station.

'As soon as they are out of sight, we follow,' Catt whispered.

When Totsakan and Rawin reached the platform at Siam station, the demon turned back to human form. The station was empty of passengers and Skytrain staff, but by now several policemen had assembled with guns. But they stayed back as Totsakan continued to hold Rawin threateningly. They ran down the steps of the station until they reached the road. Because Totsakan was now human, no one took any notice when they climbed into a taxi together. The traffic was dense, but a brief gap opened up when an ambulance, siren blaring, sped down Rama 1 Road. The taxi slipped in behind the ambulance, heading for the theatre.

Catt led Sayola and Meeya in the other direction, jumping across from the Silom Line to the Sukumvit line where the two Skytrain routes ran side by side. They raced along the track until they reached Chidlom Station nearby. Then they hurtled down the stairs and into the chaos that was unfolding below. Ambulance and other emergency workers combed through the crowds of weeping and bleeding pedestrians and passengers from the train that had fallen from above. Catt ran to the spot below the bridge where she had dropped her sword. They searched amid the tangled wreckage and broken glass from both the train and vehicles that had been crushed on the road under the weight of the four carriages. The crying and wailing of the injured, the shouting of rescue workers and the constant blaring of ambulance and police sirens stunned their senses, but Catt knew that the emergency services would do their job well and she needed her sword if she was going to rescue Rawin. It was Meeya who found it and as soon as Catt had scooped it up, they ran across the street and further north on Ratchadamri Road. Catt knew that what they needed now was certain to be found there. Sayola and Meeya had to do everything in their power to keep up with Catt, who ran in the middle of the road to get away from the teeming mass of pedestrians who were rushing in panic in all directions. The traffic was at a standstill, so the middle of the road was the best option. All they had to do was dodge in between and around stationary vehicles. It was only a matter of minutes before they reached their destination – the motorcycle taxi rank outside the Big C supermarket.

'Meeya, that one. Sayola, that one,' Catt shouted, pointing to two motorcycles as she approached a third. She spoke to all three riders at the same time, saying the other two should follow hers to the Royal Theatre on Charoen Krung Road. Many lives – maybe the lives of the entire city – depended on them, she explained. They mounted and sped off into the traffic, which was snarled in every direction. It soon became apparent that they would never be able to get out of the Rajaprasong area, so the three drivers conferred with one another before revving their bikes and riding up the steep steps from the road on to the elevated pedestrian Skywalk. All the way past Siam Square to the circular walk at Pathumwan Intersection just before the National Stadium, they rode at speeds that could barely be imagined. Pedestrians scrambled out of the way as the three bikes wove and dodged and braked and accelerated in and out and round every person and every obstacle they encountered on the Skywalk.

Then they bounced back down the stairs until they reached the pavement below, swung into Rama 1 Road and from there were able to twist in and out, through small gaps between vehicles. They kept going under the tollway until they reached the canal, shot left and mounted the wide pavement, swerving, veering and lurching their way to Chinatown. There they made their way through the twists and turns of the bustling neighbourhood, finally crossing another canal and arriving at the theatre a minute or two later.

The Sala Chalermkrung Royal Theatre occupies a corner site in the old quarter of Bangkok, widening out from its narrow entrance. Statues of mythical figures guard its doors. Rawin made for the ticket cubicle as quickly as possible. Totsakan kept his arm around Rawin's neck, which to anyone who might have seen them looked no more alarming than a father or an uncle showing affection to a young boy he had brought to the show. Rawin bought two tickets and hurried them into the auditorium where the matinee performance was under way: 'In here. Quiet,' he said. Totsakan stayed close, arm around the boy's shoulders. 'We have to sit here for a while,' Rawin whispered, gesturing at two vacant seats close to where they had entered. The auditorium was nearly full. On the stage four female dancers showed admiring deference to a fifth one in the centre, who was radiantly lit and dressed in an immaculate golden silk sarong.

Totsakan shuffled in his seat, staring intensely at the principal dancer. Her movements were more elegant and alluring than anything he had ever seen. The dance was the final scene of that part of the story in which Sida has returned to Ayutthaya, but Totsakan could not have known that. All he could see was the woman he had long desired to make his own.

Then the curtain began to come down as the scene ended. Totsakan began to shift around uneasily as the audience began applauding. He turned to Rawin and barked out: 'What the hell's going on?' He got up, let go of Rawin and ran to the front of the theatre and stood looking at the curtain. Then he let out a loud groan as his body expanded and he was transformed back to his demon form. He raised his arms, gripped the curtain in both hands and yanked it down. The curtain rail came loose and crashed on to the stage. The audience began screaming and running for the exits. Totsakan stepped over the fallen curtain and started approaching the dancer. From sheer terror her legs collapsed under her and she fell to the floor, covering her face. Everyone else ran screaming off the stage as Totsakan towered over her.

'Look up at me, Sida!' he bellowed. 'Look up.' As she did so, he lent forward and grabbed her by the shoulders, lifting her like a rag doll and staring into her face. He knew at once that this was not Sida. He threw his head back and roared with anger. Then he turned and looked for Rawin. 'I will kill you for this.' He began to shake the dancer violently when a whistling sound filled the auditorium followed by a dull thud as a spear entered Totsakan's neck. The demon groaned in agony and dropped the dancer, who lay paralysed with fear on the stage floor. Sayola stood watching from the middle aisle of the auditorium from where he had launched his lethal weapon. Then sprinting down the aisle so fast that she appeared to be no more than a flash of theatrical light, Catt launched herself on to the stage as Totsakan staggered angrily around with his arms over the back of his shoulders tugging at the spear in an attempt to remove it.

'I told you this day would come,' she said coolly. Then she came round in front of him and held her sword high up, reflecting the stage spotlights into his eyes. As she did so, Meeya rushed to the dancer, who remained slumped at Totsakan's feet, and stared into her eyes. It took only a few seconds before the dancer jumped up and ran for her life.

'I love her mind,' said Catt as she continued to direct the reflected light from her sword into Totsakan's aching eyes. Sayola came and stood with her. The demon ranted and raged, trying to cover his eyes with one hand and reach the spear with the other. He looked around desperately trying to see Rawin, who stood at the back of the auditorium watching his plan play out. Totsakan turned to Catt: 'I'll kill you first. Then I'll kill your boyfriend.'

'He's not my boyfriend,' Catt said sharply.

'So who is he, then?'

'The bravest person I've ever met.'

'Haaaaaa,' Totsakan cried in a mixture of agony and desperation as he clawed behind his neck at the spear and kept his eyes shut. It was then that she moved. No amount of practice could have brought her to the point of such perfection in what was to follow. Something else was driving her, from deep inside. It took only three steps before she was airborne, hanging in the air at the height of the giant demon's chest, almost as if gravity itself had been suspended. And then she spun her body until she faced him, guiding her sword with impeccable precision, plunging it into his heart. She landed with both feet on his chest and in a flash pulled her sword out and somersaulted backwards, landing on both feet, her knees bent in readiness. But there was no need to be ready. Totsakan clutched his chest and staggered to the edge of the stage and fell to his knees. He looked out over the auditorium and saw Rawin standing at the back.

'So, there you are.' His voice, though faltering, boomed through the theatre, like that of the greatest actors. 'You must be proud of what you have done. I knew you were smart. I should have known you would do something like this. I should never have trusted anyone. Not those who humiliated me for thousands of years. Not the gods who gave me powers that they knew would destroy me in the end. Not my brothers. Not my niece. And especially not you.' Then he turned to Catt. 'Or you. Though I have to say you kept your promise. You said you would get me in the end. Well done.'

Then he roared: 'But you will not have the pleasure of seeing me die. Never!'

He seemed to find new strength, in spite of his catastrophic injuries. He reached behind him and pulled Sayola's spear from his neck and then he puffed himself up to his full height and stepped off the stage, heading for the exit. Catt watched him uneasily but did not move. Rawin backed off as Totsakan staggered down the aisle and out the building. Concerned about what he would do next, they ran after him. When they got into the street, they saw him lurching along Charoen Krung Road. His gigantic size and strength allowed him to move faster than any ordinary being might have done with such injuries. The children had to run to keep up with him.

Catt jogged closer to Rawin and asked: 'How did you know we would come?'

'I didn't.'

Totsakan crossed through Saranrom Park and back on to the street that took him within minutes to the east side of the Temple of the Emerald Buddha. He kicked down a door that said 'No Entry' in the high wall surrounding the temple and staggered into the courtyard. The children chased after him. They saw him stumble and grope his way along the walls that housed the murals of the Ramakien story. Then he fell to the floor. The children ran as fast as they could. But when they reached the point where they were sure he had fallen, he was not there.

'Quick, down that way,' Catt said as she ran across the temple courtyard. But she soon stopped, sure that he could not have gone anywhere without them seeing him.

'Here,' Rawin shouted. 'Here. Blood.' He pointed. Catt joined him. They looked around them, puzzled.

'Where are Sayola and Meeya?' asked Catt.

They looked around them again, but there was no sign of the twins.

'No Totsakan. No Sayola. No Meeya,' said Rawin suspiciously. He looked at the paintings on the wall near the patch of blood. 'Wait,' he said. 'Could it be…?' He began inspecting the murals more closely. 'What's this one about?'

'Just a minute,' Catt said, and ran across the courtyard.

She returned accompanied by a learned looking man who had a photo ID card hanging from his neck that said 'Official Guide'. 'This one. What's this painting about?'

The man looked pleased at having two attentive children who seemed genuinely interested in the paintings. 'Well,' he began, 'do you know the story of the Ramakien?' He looked eagerly at the children.

'Some of it,' Catt said.

'Most of it, but I'm not sure what happens in the end,' added Rawin.

'Well,' said the guide. 'You know how after the many battles between Prince Ram and Totsakan, the evil demon is finally defeated.'

'Yes,' Rawin said.

'Well, this picture – it's number 135 – shows his cremation. It is presided over by Totsakan's brother, the fortune teller Pipek.'

'So,' Rawin began slowly, 'so, according to this painting, Totsakan is dead.'

'That's correct,' said the man. 'Yes, he is cremated. See there.' He pointed at the funeral pyre in the painting.

Rawin and Catt studied the mural closely.

'And those two children standing watching at the edge of the forest?' asked Catt. 'They look so alike.'

'Erm, I haven't noticed them before,' the guide replied. 'There are nearly two hundred separate paintings in the temple and it's not possible to be acquainted with every detail.'

The children looked at each other for a second and smiled.

'Never mind,' Catt said to the guide. 'Thank you.' She turned back to Rawin. 'Come on now, we need to get home. Your mother must be worried about you.'

www.blkdogpublishing.com